Poisoner's Vengeance

TALIA GREER

SKULL & VIOLET BOOKS

For all the weird angry girls who go a bit feral when they don't get what they want

Content Notes

This story contains elements that might not be suitable for all readers, including violence and sexual content. Please visit my website for the full, detailed list of content warnings. If you feel a warning is missing, please reach out!

WINTHORPE & COLETTE

HELENE

ST. MARIGOT

ST. ELIZABETH

CALIVIGNY

MORIAH

CODRINGTON SEA

KENDALE

MANZANILLA

BOISEBELLES

SULVA

THE ISLANDS

Chapter One

"Modern-day Order acolytes 'Ground' themselves by immersing the tops of their feet in dirt from the gardens they tend. The Grounding is an effort to connect with the Revenant Mother. Some of the most devout believe the Grounding transfers the Mother's fabled poison immunity to Her followers."
—Excerpt from An Exploration of the Order of the Revenant Mother and Other Island Religions

M other Vanessa stood too close to the prayer candles for comfort.

My eyes darted between the billowing sleeves of her dirt-colored robe and the black, white, and gray candles stretched tall and thin along the top of the lectern. Behind the lectern hung a mass of deep gray curtains. I couldn't help but wonder what sort of disaster would ensue if those curtains, or Mother Vanessa's sleeves, caught fire. In my mind I saw the whole thing going up in one great pillar of flame and smoke, obscuring the glass depiction of the Revenant Mother that looked down over us all.

Mother Vanessa raised her voice to begin the first of our morning prayers.

"From earth we are born, and to earth we return," she intoned.

I mouthed along without really thinking. I'd said countless morning prayers in my lifetime. My focus wandered, shifting from Mother Vanessa and the prayers as natural as breathing on my lips, and settling once more on the candles. My anxious moods didn't normally lend themselves to arbitrary catastrophic imaginings, but I hadn't slept well the night before. I felt especially unsettled. And watching the candles so close to Mother Vanessa's sleeves was only twisting my stomach.

I pulled my gaze toward the too-familiar setting that rose up behind her. Glass stained black and white, shining windowpanes climbed from floor to chapel ceiling, puzzle pieces that fit together to form the Mother in Her traditional depiction: arms folded directly before Her as if leaning forward. Eyes staring into the soul, head-on. Around this glass artistry hung another set of curtains, their gray luscious like ominous storm clouds. For a moment I wanted to close them, suddenly uncomfortable with the Mother's all-knowing gaze.

I closed my eyes. Opened them again. The wave of discomfort still hadn't passed. I tried to reassure myself with details I knew all too well—the long rectangular room, lined with wooden pews that were stained a deep black; the floor of storm gray hexagonal stone at my feet; the smell of cinnamon chewing gum from the novice seated next to me. None of it worked. My skin felt three sizes too small for my body.

I'd been told before that I noticed too much—so much that I'd trained myself to often pretend I hadn't noticed something, just to make others more comfortable. Sometimes I wished I could flip a switch in my head and be less observant. Less sensitive to my environment. It surely would've proven useful now, when all my senses felt tuned too sharply for comfort.

"And at last we pray for joy," continued Mother Vanessa. She'd moved smoothly along through the morning prayers, and now she let her voice boom loud throughout the chapel for the final lines. "For devotion, and steadiness in our task." She paused and lifted her head to address us all.

"To heal the sick, and sicken the wicked," we all dutifully recited.

A moment's pause, and Mother Vanessa spoke again. "Ground yourselves."

One hundred pious young ladies shifted in our seats in one great rustling of fabric. We slipped off our shoes. Along the floor, near where one's feet rested while sitting in the pew, was a trough just narrow enough to fit the toes and pad of the foot. Inside this small space lay dirt, freshly harvested from the gardens and spread here by the aspirants weekly. To ground ourselves meant to dip our feet into this sacred soil, to connect with the Mother.

This week's dirt was moist and warm between my toes.

Excitement flickered up my spine. My favorite part of morning prayers came right after the Grounding.

The Mother's Aria was a haunting melody that told her story through song, and I had long been the top choice of singer. It was one of few times I felt useful. Admired. Human.

As the Grounding prayer came to a close, I followed my custom of slipping my shoes back on a few seconds early, and prepared to rise. Now Mother Vanessa would call me forward to the lectern, and—

"I'd like to deviate from our usual proceedings today," Mother Vanessa said. I froze, halfway out of my seat. "The newest novice to join our cloister has surpassed even my wildest expectations. As you may have heard, Novice Clee's own abbey was destroyed in a tragic fire two weeks ago. Since she has joined us, I've been impressed by her piety and her kindness. This morning, in the hopes of making her feel a little more welcome, I'd like to invite Novice Clee to join me on the dais to perform the Mother's Aria for us."

Stunned, I sat down hard. A stir traveled through the room. Mother Vanessa never changed the proceedings in this manner. Even the most well-behaved among us couldn't resist a quick word of surprise to their neighbor. Meanwhile, I was reeling.

The Mother's Aria was *mine*. My song to sing. And Mother Vanessa had handed it over to the newcomer with hardly any fanfare.

I couldn't for the life of me puzzle out what I'd done to deserve this.

The room watched with bated breath as Narissa Clee stood from a row near the front and joined Mother Vanessa at the lectern as instructed. She wore the same soil-colored robes as the rest of us—a symbolic tie to the Mother's resurrection from the earth. Her matching headscarf was pinned just so. Not a stray hair in sight. I knew beneath it, she had a head full of loose, honey-gold curls that fell like sunlight along her skin. Most people, myself included, who were native to our dual-island nation had skin and hair as dark as burnt tree bark. Narissa was a foreigner—from St. Elizabeth or some other island run by the pink-skinned warmongers who'd tried to conquer *our* island and failed—and so she had light hair, loose curls, and skin the color of golden clay. I couldn't help feeling a hot, miserable stab of envy looking at her. Narissa Clee could, without a doubt, put a hand through her curls and meet little to no resistance. My hand would get stuck among my thick coils one inch in.

Then she opened her mouth, and began to sing the song that belonged to me. Her voice only made me envy her more. It was high and clear like a bell, so sweet and pretty I wanted to slap her for it. Our harpist, Grace, who normally accompanied the Mother's Aria, stumbled over her notes in pure shock.

The Aria poured out in Narissa's perfect voice. It told of the Mother's origins as a benevolent healer, a life of service cut short by betrayal. The demon She had befriended to help Her investigate medicinal remedies had not been the ally She'd sought. It told of Her death by poisoning, at the hands of the demon She'd trusted, and Her rebirth among the dirt and weeds. There was a terrible irony in it all—Narissa singing of the betrayal that had been the Mother's ultimate downfall, while she betrayed me herself with her very presence at the lectern during *my* song.

It shouldn't have mattered. I'd be leaving soon, anyway, with my award and my freedom in hand. But I couldn't seem to shake the feeling of being wronged.

I gritted my teeth and stewed through the rest of the song, and the rest of morning prayers.

When the hour of worship drew to a close, and the first rays of sunrise shone yellow and white through the windows, most of the others stood. After prayers came breakfast, and no one wanted to be late for that. But I reached for the prayer book next to me instead. As the others collected their things and filtered out of the chapel, they gathered in twos and threes to chatter among themselves. Narissa's name seemed to be on everyone's lips. A few novices actually lined up to catch Narissa on her way out, waylaying her with praise for her faithful singing.

"You were brilliant," came one voice near where I sat. Every muscle in my body tensed in fury as Narissa approached with an admirer in tow. "Your voice is beautiful. Where did you learn to sing?"

I didn't hear Narissa's reply. I couldn't even remember what her voice sounded like. All I knew was an anger so intense and all-consuming that I would doom myself to a week of punishment if I didn't leave the chapel, now.

I stood and rushed from the pew, spinning on my heels toward the door, but I wasn't fast enough.

"Annette? Will you wait a moment?"

I turned, rigid, to find Narissa watching me with wide, doe-like eyes and a guilty pinch set between her eyebrows. She was nearly an entire head shorter than me. Without trying to, I looked down at her. For once I did not temper my gaze to minimize her discomfort.

"I—I'm sorry," she stammered. "I've been watching you sing the Aria for days. I never intended to take this from you." She wrung her hands. "It's just that, well, I mentioned to Mother Vanessa that I sang in my old abbey, before—" She winced. "Before. And I think she got it in her head I might like to continue here. I'm sorry. I didn't mean to step on your toes or anything. I'll speak to her about next time. I wouldn't want to take this from you entirely."

An apology was the last thing I'd expected. I opened my mouth, closed it. Narissa was kind, quiet, and unassuming. If what she was saying was true, she'd done nothing wrong. But it didn't stop me from hating her. I didn't want her damned apology. In fact, it only infuriated me more.

I wanted nothing to do with her, now or ever.

No words came to mind. Typical. I couldn't easily translate my rage into words the way some people seemed so easily able to. While I was struggling to think of a response, Narissa watched me, her face falling.

"Sorry," she said again. "I'll just—I'll leave you alone."

She'd taken my silence as proof of something I hadn't intended. I wanted to tell her how much she'd upset me. But I couldn't shape the sounds to coherence. Not on such short notice.

Narissa made to move past me. No one else was looking. In a split second, without really thinking about it, I stuck out my shoe and snagged the edge of her robe that trailed along the floor, making her stumble. She fell to her knees, then her face, with a startled gasp. A moment of silence and one wet choking noise later, she looked up at me from her hands and knees with blood pouring from her nose.

I felt a mixture of worry for her, and shame for what I'd done, but above all a small, sick sense of justice.

I bent to help her in the ensuing commotion and offered up one of my own handkerchiefs in assistance.

Finally, words came. "You poor thing," I murmured, holding the cloth to her bleeding nose. We locked eyes. I don't know what she saw, but she dropped her gaze quickly as if it stung to look at me, and I knew then that I'd gotten my message across.

Take what's mine again, and see what happens.

Now the attention was on me, for coming to her aid. I soaked it up like a plant drinking sunshine. I shooed the others off, took Narissa firmly by the arm, and escorted her upstairs to the infirmary. I didn't look at her again.

By the time I arrived at breakfast, the food had gone cold, but I didn't mind.

I derived a lot of pleasure and comfort from the abbey's little validations. The sudden and inexplicable withdrawal of this one had given me whiplash. But I'd made myself heard, in a way, even if I was the only one who knew how Narissa had truly fallen.

I didn't feel any better about it all. But surely, I'd made Narissa feel worse, and that was all that really mattered.

Chapter Two

"*The term 'acolyte' refers to any general member of the Order, of any rank. A 'novice' is a nun in training, usually between the ages of twenty and twenty-five, who has not yet taken their vows. Once an Order acolyte becomes avowed, they earn the right to be called Sister.*"
—Your Guide to Religious Life Within the Order, created and issued by Moriah Abbey

I wasn't proud of it, but I thought about Narissa, and what I had done, for the rest of the day. I turned the subject over and over again in my mind whenever I had an idle moment.

It seemed bottled, menacingly warm and burning, inside my chest, the way things that bothered me often did. It wasn't so much that she had embarrassed me by stealing my song, or that I felt guilty for purposely tripping her and making her bleed—it was that she had bothered to exist in the first place. Changes, and especially big, unusual ones—like a new novice suddenly joining us without first formally completing her aspirancy and postulancy—never sat well with me.

I needed time to prepare myself against the possibility of the change and its eventual existence. Narissa's sudden appearance just weeks ago was a jolt to my own carefully constructed mental concept of the abbey. Was it really any surprise that I resented her for it?

Fingers tightening around the bronzed bottom of my candlestick, I tried to shake the irritable, uneasy mood. It was late, past midnight. All the other acolytes slumbered peacefully in their beds. Their snores trailed through our thin bedroom doors and drew long, crackling sounds across the otherwise quiet night. When I couldn't sleep, I often took to wandering, allowing the visual consistency of the abbey's many interior walls and hallways to act as a lullaby of my own. Soon I found a rhythm with my walking, and my mind quieted, melting back into itself like a spent wave collapsing against the shore.

At night, when all the others were asleep, I felt the most comfortable. The most *free*. No one lingered to send puzzled or disdainful looks my way, or to whisper about me to their friends while they thought me too self-absorbed to hear. Waking life was an exercise in the constant torture of being perceived—and knowing, somehow, that nothing I did ever matched up the way it should.

I wandered the second floor halls until my candle had burnt another quarter inch down, until I began to feel warm beneath my nightgown. As I pointed myself back toward my bedroom, I crossed the portion of the second floor hallway that looked over a railing upon the austere entrance hall below. It should have been a dull tableau in shades of gray, with bluish-white moonlight streaking in through the windows that framed our towering front doors. Instead, my gaze caught on a flash of dingy brown. Frowning, squinting in the dark, I paused and edged closer to the railing.

In the middle of the hall stood one of the Sisters. She faced the doors, bolt upright, still wearing her day robes and scarf, so I couldn't tell who it was. The set of her shoulders put me on edge. For a long moment, the Sister was motionless. Then, she gave several small twitching motions. Her arms jolted erratically at her sides. That must have been the flash of brown I'd seen—this sleepwalking Sister, far from the comfort of her bed.

I gripped my candle tighter in suddenly sweating fingers and called out quietly, "Sister?"

She whipped her head up toward me in one quick, unnatural jerk. I stumbled back.

It was Mother Vanessa. But our abbess did not sleepwalk, at least not to my knowledge. Her eyes were blank and lifeless, alighting only in my general direction and not on my face. Without thinking, I stepped back once more, feeling suddenly as if I should put space between us.

Mother Vanessa continued to stare.

Then came a quiet voice from behind me. "Annette?"

Surging rage at the interruption crashed against all my uneasiness, and I whirled to find Narissa, of all people, behind me. Wide-eyed, skin pale as milk above the collar of our ivory abbey-issued nightgowns, she blinked at me several times.

"Why are you here?" I asked. I knew my face had screwed itself up into an unkind expression by the way she hesitated.

"Out for a midnight stroll. Same as you."

I was only out walking at this time of night because I had reason to be. Daytime was far from friendly to me. Narissa, on the other hand, had been beloved by nearly every acolyte within these walls from the moment she arrived. What right did she have to intrude upon my sanctuary?

What reason did she have to seek solace in yet another thing that had, for so long, been only mine?

I looked at her, disbelieving, a moment longer. There was no polite avenue to articulate my annoyance. I certainly held no actual claim on midnight strolls. It was more the principle of the thing, and the fact that *she* was the one doing it.

Narissa's thin curls were pulled into a wispy bun at the nape of her neck. She scratched absentmindedly at the spot just below her bun, looking delightedly uncomfortable.

"Listen, Annette, I know you don't like me, but—"

There came a high and pained wheeze from below. Narissa abruptly cut off whatever impassioned plea she'd been about to make, and both of us looked down to see Mother Vanessa moving once more. She was no longer twitching, or staring, but she now paced the entrance hall in aimless circles, muttering to herself.

It was deeply unusual behavior, even for a sleepwalker. Several of the younger girls would often wander from their beds, but I had never seen any of them act like this.

"What's wrong with her?" Narissa flicked her eyes over to me. "Is she injured?"

An unkind retort leapt to the tip of my tongue—the only thing I seemed able to summon on command—but I forced it down as my curiosity won out. Without answering Narissa, I pressed on down the stairs, Narissa's bare footsteps following me the whole way down and landing on the ground floor a moment after I did.

"Mother Vanessa?" I called out.

All I wanted was for Narissa to leave me be. I would wake Mother Vanessa, we could all return to our rooms, and I would be spared suffering any more of Narissa's presence.

But Mother Vanessa did not respond. Eyes blank as before, she looked to us, and it was then I saw a splattering of dark spots along her collar. My eyes trailed upward to the side of her neck, where several fresh and wet scratch wounds glittered in the thin moonlight.

"Mother!" Narissa cried, charging toward her.

I stood motionless, still trying to process her wound. My heart clanged as bold and panicked in my chest as a bell hung off-kilter. Why had she scratched herself?

What sort of itch necessitated a scratch that deep?

"Mother Vanessa. It's me, Narissa. . ." She carried on speaking to Mother Vanessa in low, soothing tones, like trying to calm a panicked animal. It seemed to make no difference. While Mother Vanessa allowed Narissa to grasp her hand, she was no more aware of us than she had been before. I couldn't be sure, but I doubted that she was sleepwalking. And yet, neither was she awake, nor fully present.

A shiver ran up my spine. My candle's flame flickered with the movement.

"Annette, we must do something!" Narissa cried. "She's clearly very disturbed, perhaps she had a terrible nightmare—"

"Yes, that sounds plausible," I snapped, alarm ratcheting higher. "A terrible nightmare that nearly made her claw her neck clean off. Happens all the time."

Narissa flinched. So often was my truest, most natural self hidden behind a mask of my own making that I forgot the pleasure of dropping the disguise, even if that meant weathering others' discomfort.

"Well, if you're not going to do anything, I will," she said, voice like a whip.

Narissa squared her shoulders and took off at a sprint down the hall to the left, to the first floor hallway where the rest of the Sisters slept. I felt sufficiently chastised, but a part of me didn't care. I couldn't quite muster up Narissa's level of concern—the level that spilled over into needing to involve another Sister, who was bound to bustle in with a litany of questions and admonishments regarding rules that made little sense to me. Here, Mother Vanessa was the utmost authority. She was the abbess. She could care for herself. I couldn't deny that the scratches on her neck perturbed me, but I also did not feel it was my right to question her behavior.

And if I was being honest, a larger, meaner part of me still hadn't forgiven Narissa for stealing my spotlight, and did not want to give her the satisfaction of being right.

Suddenly, Mother Vanessa broke into big, heaving gasps, like grotesque sobs without the crying. She crumpled to her knees, then the floor, wailing and whining. All rational thought flew out of my head, and I followed her, crouching nearby.

"Mother?"

At this angle, thin moonlight illuminated twin tracks of tears down her brown cheeks. One arm twitched in my direction as if to touch me, then changed course at the last moment. She sank her fingernails into the skin of her opposite wrist and began to claw at an unseen, almighty itch.

I understood all at once how the scratches on her neck might have come to be.

"Mother?" I repeated, reaching for her. The frantic clawing of nails on skin produced a dry, frenzied rasping noise that made me want to cringe.

"Help me," whispered Mother Vanessa. "Help me, please."

My entire body had broken out in goosebumps. Mother Vanessa's sleeves had fallen back with her movements, and beneath the bare skin, I caught what looked like the undulations of hundreds of small, worm-like creatures. Her skin rippled and churned before my eyes. I stared back in a blank sort of horror.

On her left wrist was a tarnished golden bracelet I'd never seen before.

A chorus of shouts came from my left. Narissa and several Sisters spilled into the entrance hall. Soon, the five of us were all crouched beside our fallen abbess, nightgowns pooling on the ground. Sisters Edna and Colette spoke quickly amongst themselves, gesturing to us novices. I heard them all as if from very far away. The bracelet loomed large in my vision, in my mind, bringing with it a quiet terror I didn't quite know how to name. I tried to untangle my tongue to point it out—if anything could be the cause of Mother Vanessa's collapse, this was it—but, as usual, the words stuck in my throat.

The Sisters helped Mother Vanessa to standing and half carried, half dragged her back toward the Sisters' quarters. Narissa followed them closely behind, with only one final, reproachful glance back at me. In moments, they had all left me alone in the entrance hall, which seemed suddenly so much quieter and colder than before, in a sinister way I felt in my bones.

By then, all I wanted was my bed. I fled upstairs and locked myself into my tiny, rectangular room. My candle had snuffed itself out during my flight. I set the holder on my night table and crawled beneath the covers. For long moments, I lay there, until my heart calmed and my panic leeched away into the repetition of Narissa's words: *If you're not going to do anything, I will.*

I knew now, in retrospect, that there had been an expected manner in which to act in that situation, and that I hadn't performed accordingly. So often, I realized this after the fact, when my help was no longer any good to anyone. I hadn't expected Mother Vanessa to try and harm herself *again*. I should've acted more quickly, along with Narissa.

We were set to take our vows in mere hours. Would this reflect badly on me? Would the Mother glance down from above and deem me unworthy, even as I stood in Her holy garden and pledged myself and my life to Her service? The mere thought was enough to turn my stomach.

I had to speak to someone about what I'd seen. The bracelet—Narissa hadn't noticed it. I felt obligated to report all that I'd seen in case it could help the abbess, even if I wasn't believed.

In the morning, I would speak with Sister Colette. I would simply not be able to live with myself otherwise.

Chapter Three

"Relics are objects of reverence. They can take the form of a body part from a deceased holy person or their belongings, and are often believed to imbue the relic-holder with power. Relics can hail from both maternal or demonic origins—meaning from the Revenant Mother or from the demon Aran. The full extent of their usage is yet unknown."
—Excerpt from An Exploration of the Order of the Revenant Mother and Other Island Religions

"*G*arden *Above*, Novice Boodram," said Sister Colette upon finding me seated outside her office early the next morning. "It is *half past seven*."

I scrambled to my feet. "Yes, Sister, I apologize."

Sister Colette offered me a weary look, then swept into the next room and gestured for me to follow. The space was about the size of two broom closets shoved together. It housed two narrow, rickety desks and their chairs and one low, long bookshelf that ran along the far wall below the only window. Pastel pink sunlight glowed through the frame. I squinted. Beyond the abbey, the land dropped away into a verdant green valley, extending all the way to the roiling aqua inkspill of the ocean.

I hovered patiently near the doorway as Sister Colette sank heavily into her desk chair. Only now did I notice the fatigue pulling at her eyelids. She had even yet to don her day scarf. Graying coils hung long and loose around her shoulders. When she noticed my prolonged stare, her forehead pinched with a frown, and she quickly slid the scarf over her head. She wrapped the excess around her head once, twice.

I had barely slept, but my mind roared instantly to full alertness. Had Sister Colette been back to sleep after seeing to Mother Vanessa last night? Or had she lain awake for hours, like me, with worry gnawing at her chest?

"Speak, child. What ails you?"

I bristled. At twenty-five, nearing the end of my five-year novice period, I was an adult preparing to take my lifetime vows. I was hardly a child. But I couldn't help that so many of the Sisters viewed me so. No matter how mature I objectively became, in many of the Sisters' eyes, I would forever be the unruly ten-year-old who'd been deposited screaming on the abbey's doorstep, infantile and inconsolable.

Blinking away my irritation, I stepped closer to her desk. "I need to tell you something. About last night. When I saw Mother Vanessa, she—"

She waved a hand. "The abbess is doing well now. You can expect to see her later at the Ceremonial Profession."

"She's alright?"

"Yes, dear. Why ever wouldn't she be?"

I stared at Sister Colette for a long moment, unsure if she meant to tease. We had both seen Mother Vanessa's perturbing behavior mere hours ago. Was I supposed to pretend it hadn't happened? That I remained unconcerned?

As I began to frown, Sister Colette pressed on. "She had an unusual nighttime disturbance. But I assure you, all is well."

At this, she offered me a small smile. My frown deepened. I might not have been the most adept reader of social cues, but smiles and all their various permutations were something I'd learned to interpret. Genuine ones lit up the person's entire face, brightening their eyes and animating their brows. Other smiles appeared kind, but beyond the surface screamed *leave me alone, you're annoying.* Sister Colette's smile was something different. Whatever her true feelings were, she had packed them away neatly behind this smile meant to disarm. For some reason, she wasn't keen to discuss this.

I would have to tread carefully.

"Sister, I regret the way I acted. Novice Clee encouraged me to go for help much sooner, but I hesitated, unsure what to do. I admit I feel somewhat responsible for any suffering the abbess might've endured."

Now the Sister laughed. "Don't be silly! None of that was your fault."

"I understand that, but I still felt the need to say something. I also noticed the abbess wearing an unusual bracelet I'd not seen before. I wondered—"

"If she had suffered an adverse reaction to the metal?" Sister Colette shook her head. "I'm sure she appreciates the concern, but it's nothing to worry about." Now her voice softened. "I know how sharp your focus is, Annette. It's truly admirable. But I believe in this case, you're reading something from nothing. We all have various indulgences we allow ourselves after hours—like uncovering our hair, for example, or wearing jewelry among other avowed friends. You likely just witnessed the abbess enjoying the sparkle of an item not often worn." She chuckled. "A bracelet is hardly cause for concern."

My mind reeled. I'd been unconcerned with any reactions to the metal. What most intrigued me, *worried* me, was where the bracelet might have come from. Normal jewelry like what Sister Colette described was an inert object. It wouldn't cause the twitching, the blank stare, or—I shuddered—the writhing movements I'd seen beneath Mother Vanessa's skin. It wouldn't have caused her to itch so fiercely she made a wound. And what else could I attribute the behavior to, other than a bracelet that had appeared on her arm out of nowhere?

"Sister," I said slowly. "With the utmost respect. . ." I trailed off, unsure how to proceed. My thoughts had taken off like a flock of birds in flight, and now I couldn't pin any of them down.

I felt in my bones that something was wrong, and I couldn't figure out why Sister Colette wasn't more worried. But I had no proof, no way of convincing her that didn't rely on my own biased recollection and weak adamance.

Sister Colette turned to her desk as if she hadn't heard me. She began to sort through the small pile of correspondence that had accumulated since yesterday afternoon. Delivering all mail upon arrival was tasked to the youngest acolytes, the mere aspirants who lived at the abbey on a trial basis to gauge their appeal in religious life. Judging from the Sister's quick eye roll as she glanced at one letter, someone had messed up this delivery.

"I have much to do before the Profession at noon," said Sister Colette a moment later. "You'd best run along and prepare. I hear someone will be receiving a special award at the ceremony, hmm?" She said this last part with a wink in my direction. It was meant to be friendly, though it didn't put me at ease. I could hardly focus on the ceremony, and the award that would come with it—a culmination of my life's work at the abbey—when something undoubtedly strange had befallen the abbess last night, and I was the only one who seemed truly concerned.

While I struggled to gather myself, Sister Colette cast her eyes over to me one final time.

"Is there anything else?" she asked, in a tone that told me, *you're dismissed.*

I swallowed. There was so much more I wanted to say. I felt it all withering to ash on my tongue. Crestfallen, and frustrated with my own shortcomings, I shook my head.

"No, Sister. There's nothing else."

Chapter Four

"The five-year novice period is one of intense study, prayer, and formation. At the end of this period, vows are taken during the Ceremonial Profession—one of the Order's highest holy days. These vows are meant to be a lifetime commitment. The word of the Ceremonial Profession is considered Order law."

—Your Guide to Religious Life Within the Order, created and issued by Moriah Abbey

M oriah Abbey, and the largest sect of the Order of the Revenant Mother that lived within its walls, blinked slowly to life around me as I left Sister Colette's office. Out of habit, I ducked inside the refectory, though I wasn't really hungry. I grabbed one serving each of our usual breakfast—saltfish on roti, and boiled cassava with butter—and ate it quickly, the normally vibrant food sludging down my throat like clay. Though I could do little about the situation now, I had yet to shake my uneasiness with Sister Colette. Food finished, I traipsed along the familiar path back to my room.

On the weekends, we did not assemble for morning prayers, and so most acolytes seized the opportunity for extra sleep, praying privately in their rooms before strolling leisurely down to the refectory for breakfast around eight o'clock. They clumped together for the short walk in loose groups that never included me. I skirted between them, the obstacles, moving past the classrooms where we studied both scripture and science. Passing the laboratory, I caught the scent of musty, bitter liquid, open flames, and burnt cauldron bottoms. I wrinkled my nose, but it comforted me all the same. I felt for all the world like today was a regular day. Like I would wake up tomorrow and simply resume the soothing routine of my lessons without interruption.

This, however, was no ordinary weekend.

The Ceremonial Profession would commence at noon. The Mother was set to receive an all-new flock of loyal servants, myself among them. And tomorrow, with my newly awarded title in hand, I would leave the abbey, travel the Islands, and begin my new life.

All of us Year-Five novices had been given the morning off from our usual daily duties in order to prepare. Years of intense study and prayer had culminated in this moment—avowing ourselves to the Mother's service as fully professed members of the community. In a few short hours, I would no longer be Novice Boodram, but instead Sister Annette. For the first time since arriving at the abbey fifteen years ago, I had no poison brewing lesson to rush off to, no row of toxic plants to tend in the garden. I almost didn't know what to do with myself. But the abbey had raised us well, ingrained in all of us precise methods to occupy an idle mind.

I returned to my room and cleaned. I gathered my meager things, packed my bags. I allowed myself a long, luxurious, tepid-water bath behind one of the curtained stalls in our washroom. My hair was a mess, so I coated it in a thick conditioning mask after washing, then took my time wrangling my tight, coarse coils into thumb-sized twists that dangled delightfully from my scalp like snakes. Sometimes, when the other acolytes were particularly insufferable, I took great pleasure in pretending the snakes were real and that I could will them to bite people on my command. Had that been reality, I'm certain no one would have ever dared look at me the wrong way again.

All the while, Sister Colette's dismissal hovered in the back of my mind like an ingredient added too late, not quite combined with the rest.

Clean and polished, I dressed in a fresh pair of brown robes before heading to the gardens.

Heat suffused me in its suffocating grasp as I stepped outside. The abbey's stone walls kept the interior at a comfortable temperature, but outside, I could not ignore the persistent moist, muggy air, nor the oppressive warmth. I'd been born here on Moriah, had lived here my whole life, and yet my body had never quite seemed to adjust to the climate the way other islanders did. In this, like so many other things out of my control, I felt set apart. Other.

I frowned and walked on. This set of gardens was lush and green, and mostly nontoxic. Vibrant snake plants, pigeon pea, orchids, and wild poinsettia swayed gently in the warm breeze. Lining the garden walkway were stone benches, most of which were occupied by the other Year-Fives. Some had their noses in prayer books; others had their eyes squeezed tightly shut, lips mouthing along to one prayer or another. I couldn't understand the impulse toward last-minute practice. The Ceremonial Profession wasn't difficult. We all knew the vows already. We had merely to formally recite them. I'd never had reason to doubt my faith, and I wasn't about to start now. The Mother would see me through, I knew it.

In the far corner of the garden stood a white-wood gazebo surrounded by temporary outdoor pews. A Sister I didn't often see, who taught the younger girls—the postulants—waited there to receive those of us who arrived early.

"Novice Boodram." I bowed my head in greeting to the Sister. "Welcome to the Ceremonial Profession. Please take a seat."

"Thank you, Sister."

By the time the bell tower rang at noon, each seat was occupied, and the nervous energy of the Year-Fives became something like gauze in the air, a heat-haze glimpsed from a distance.

The proceedings began shortly, with little fanfare.

Sisters trailed toward us in a pristine line down the garden path. Each and every one turned out for the Profession, one of our highest holy days. The beautiful symmetry of the Sisters' identical robes calmed me in a deep way I could never explain. Despite the heat, and the fact that I was already sweating beneath my robes, I felt a small chill. Joy bubbled and burst in my chest.

One ceremony. One award. A lifetime of freedom.

My destiny, my future, was so close I could almost reach out and touch it with my fingertips.

Once all the Sisters had arrived, they formed a neat line on either side of the gazebo. One familiar face stepped confidently onto the gazebo's raised platform.

Mother Vanessa.

"In reminiscence of the Mother's afterlife—Her beautiful, endless, sweet-smelling garden—we gather here in these North Gardens today for the year's Ceremonial Profession." She spoke clearly, confidently. Like she hadn't been writhing on the entrance hall floor and clawing at her skin mere hours ago. "Today, we welcome our novices at the end of their fifth year of reception, recognize them formally as devoted servants in the eyes of the Mother, and avow them to their life's purpose."

I could not stop staring at Mother Vanessa. She seemed to have made a miraculous recovery. That, or perhaps her incident last night had been less severe than it appeared. I squinted, studied her more closely, and that was when the truth laid itself bare. Despite the strength in her booming voice, the abbess looked shakier than usual. Ill, in a vague, nondescript way. Her scarf covered her neck and the scratches I knew were there. Were they healing? Had she, once carried out of sight, enacted similar damage upon her wrist?

The sound of wheels on stone broke into my thoughts. Sister Edna came around the corner pushing a large wheelbarrow heaped with soil and rolled it to a stop just short of the gazebo. She emptied the soil along the front of the gazebo platform, right below Mother Vanessa's feet. As she carted the wheelbarrow away and out of sight, Mother Vanessa continued.

"Please join me in our opening hymn, the Mother's Aria."

We raised our heads skyward. The Aria poured forth from numerous lips as one, our assembled voices crisp and clear against the sway of garden plants. I felt rapturous. Though I would no longer be singing the Aria at morning prayers, I still felt a tug in my heart at the familiar melody. It felt so special sung like this as part of the ceremony, divorced from the mundane nature of morning prayers. It belonged to me in a way no one could ever take away.

Not even Narissa, who, for some unknown reason, was staring at me.

Her gaze prickled the back of my neck from several rows back and to my left. I knew it was her from a quick glance over using my peripherals. Not wanting her presence to take away from this holy ceremony, I did my best to ignore her. What did it matter if she stared at me? Soon, the abbey would no longer be my home. I was leaving, and in doing so I would free myself from the petty squabbles that came along with living in a building full of other women.

The Aria drew to a close. Mother Vanessa then launched into prayer.

"Novices," she intoned once the prayers had finished, "I will now invite you forward for your Profession."

Mother Vanessa seated herself upon the edge of the gazebo. Removing her sandals, she dug her feet into the soil Sister Edna had dumped. Another Sister sat at her side to assist.

"Approach," said Mother Vanessa, gesturing to the nearest novice.

There were eight rows of pews in all. I sat at the left end of the third row and patiently awaited my turn. One by one, each of us approached the gazebo, knelt, head bowed, before Mother Vanessa, and sank our hands into the dirt. She placed a hand on our heads to murmur a quiet prayer in which we were expected to participate, then posed to us the most important question of our lives. Upon answering, the other Sister handed Mother Vanessa a silver pin, which she then attached to the upper right corner of our robes while imparting her final words.

This portion of the ceremony seemed to fly by. When my turn arrived, I went to Mother Vanessa, knelt on the scratchy garden rock, and thrust my hands into the soil. It was like a Grounding, but different. Instead of soil kept cool by the chapel's thick walls, this soil was sun-warmed and thick in my hands. It felt heavier, somehow, like the import of the ceremony had affected its mass.

Mother Vanessa set a warm hand on my head, and together, we prayed.

"Novice Boodram." Mother Vanessa's voice shook slightly, just enough to spear a thin crack of worry in my heart, and it took everything in me to keep my eyes averted to the dirt as expected. This close to her, I heard the exhaustion rasping her voice. But she continued as if nothing was amiss. "Having completed your fifth year of formal reception, what is your wish?"

The words poured forth effortlessly. Fifteen years of my life had led up to this.

"Abbess, today I wish to dedicate myself to the Revenant Mother. I ask your permission to join in the holy community of the Order, to forever enact Her glory and Her word, and to give my life in service to Her Order."

"I humbly offer my blessing. May the Mother welcome you warmly into Her Order, and may you step forward into Her glory."

Mother Vanessa accepted a silver pin from the Sister to her right. I caught a glimpse of it, bright and shining in her brown hands, as she positioned it to attach to my robes. The pin was rounded and offered a minuscule depiction of the manchineel tree, its branches wide-reaching and heavy with fruit. These trees grew in clusters along the Islands' beaches and mangroves and boasted deceptively tempting greenish-yellow fruit. I had always known it as the Tree of Death, as its fruit and most other components were highly poisonous. To find such a tree on the pins of fully professed nuns of the Order was no surprise; I had simply never seen the pins up close.

The shoulder of my robes pulled taut, Mother Vanessa introduced the pin to the fabric. She misjudged the distance. I bit back a hiss of pain as the sharp end poked my shoulder, but the abbess heard, shaking her head slightly and tutting. I took this as an apology. She seemed to fumble with my pin for a moment longer than necessary, or perhaps it was the trembling I suddenly noticed in her fingers slowing her down. I chanced a look up at her face while she was distracted. Fresh sweat beaded along her brow and upper lip, while the rest of her face already shone damp, giving her an almost feverish appearance. The heat had me sweating, too, but something about Mother Vanessa still didn't feel quite right, and I couldn't put my finger on what it might have been.

She clasped the pin, and I dropped my eyes.

With her hand on my shoulder, she intoned, "To heal the sick—"

"—and sicken the wicked," I finished.

"Rise, Sister Annette. Rise and take your place as one of the Mother's Holy Order."

I rose as instructed and shook the excess dirt from my hands. To anyone else, they were utterly ordinary words, but as I returned to my seat on wobbling legs, I felt transformed. Transcendent. This was the only place I had ever belonged, and now I was official.

The heat on my skin no longer felt oppressive and suffocating, but instead gentle, as if the Mother Herself had cupped my face in Her hands and kissed my forehead. Chills of emotion raced along my limbs. Nearly moved to tears, I sat.

The remainder of the ceremony passed without incident. Once we had all completed our Profession, Mother Vanessa offered us a brilliant smile.

"Welcome, my dear Sisters, to the Order of the Revenant Mother."

The other Sisters each broke into grins, too, tossing aside their usual solemnity. All of us Novices-turned-Sisters breathed a collective sigh of relief. Then came the applause, a smattering at first, then, as more of us joined in, a soaring crescendo that grew to a roar. For once, I didn't mind the noise, didn't feel an instinctual urge to cover my ears against the onslaught of sound.

I closed my eyes and felt the warmth of the sun, the Mother, and my community, and when I opened them again, the colors surrounding me had never seemed so bright.

Sister Edna took to the platform next. "Please be seated." She waited. "My most heartfelt congratulations to all of you on your Profession. I welcome you to the Order and look forward to serving in the Mother's glory alongside you all. Next, we will commence our awards ceremony."

The tense atmosphere that had blanketed us during the Profession had slipped away, replaced now with something lighter, more jovial. Now that we had all been successfully avowed, the awards were less a source of stress and more a cause for celebration. There were only three: Distinguished Service, Top of Class, and Chief Poisoness.

And the latter award was mine by rights.

As Chief Poisoness, the highest ranking bestowed on any newly avowed Year-Five who specialized in the brewing or cultivation of poisons, I would be free to leave the abbey. I would have my pick of high-paying poisoness jobs anywhere among the Islands. It meant that I could leave Moriah and explore the world beyond the limits of the abbey's gray walls. It meant stability and security to me—two things the women in my family had never had. Unlike my mother and older sister, whose lives had been destroyed by their dependence on the men who had failed them, I was determined to support myself through life, to be fully financially self-sufficient and dependent on no one. The Chief Poisoness title would be irrefutable proof of my success.

It seemed I had an affinity for the brewing of poisons unmatched by any of the others. Over the years, I'd made the abbey countless amounts of money with my brews. I'd served the Mother and the Order well with my talents. Now I relaxed in my seat and trained my attention on Sister Edna, ready to receive my long-awaited reward.

Sister Edna consulted the thin sheaf of papers held in her wrinkled fingers. "First, our award for Distinguished Service to the Order. This award goes to the Year-Five whose work on fundraising, community ties, and general philanthropic efforts has stood out more than any other. The recipient of this award will be sent away on a special envoy to Helene to further the Order's philanthropic aims." She paused, directing a warm smile toward her right. "Sister Victoria, please rise and accept this award."

Applause rippled throughout the crowd. Sister Victoria, a quiet-yet-popular woman with a high, lilting laugh and plenty of friends, quickly approached the gazebo. Sister Edna placed into her hands a deep brown folder, open to reveal the formal wording of the award written in script on thick, cream-colored paper. Smiling down at the award, Sister Victoria remained standing before the gazebo, looking radiant.

"Next, we turn to the award for Top of Class. This honor is bestowed upon the Year-Five with the highest marks across all coursework for the duration of her novice-hood. The recipient of this award has received a coveted invitation to work in the Order's central scriptorium in the capital." Port of Usmela, the capital city on Manzanilla, housed the Order's largest repository of scripture and history. Any scripture specialist would've been honored to work there. "Sister Lorna, please rise and accept this award."

I knew little of Sister Lorna, save for the fact that she was originally from Boisebelles and spoke with a thick nasal accent. As she went to join Sister Edna, I caught the glimmer of tears in her eyes, and felt an unexpected rush of fondness. Perhaps it was the ceremony of it all, the ritual pulling at something among my normally dormant heartstrings. Not usually the sentimental type, I found it ironic that my emotions toward the abbey would finally kick in right as I stood on the precipice of leaving it forever.

Sister Lorna's applause faded politely away as she took her spot next to Sister Victoria. The two of them embraced each other from the side.

"And finally," said Sister Edna, "we come to the award of Chief Poisoness." A hush fell over the assembled crowd, and all of a sudden I felt my heartbeat rapid and insistent like a rabbit's, thrumming against my ribs. "This award goes to our most talented poison brewer or gardener. The recipient of this award will be given leave to travel the Islands with her training and work wherever she pleases." Numerous pairs of eyes fell on me. It was no secret that I was the abbey's most accomplished poisoness. I prepared myself to rise, started thinking about how I might most appropriately arrange my facial expression—

"Sister Narissa, please rise and accept this award."

I felt like my chest had imploded. The pain was sharp and acute and shocking.

Sister *Narissa?*

There came a split second of shocked silence. Applause stuttered, then continued, only now the sound felt like an attack on my senses. I watched in horrified slow-motion as Narissa rose with a deep uncertainty about her figure, glanced back at me with an incomprehensible look on her face, then slowly made her way to the gazebo to join the others.

An elbow lodged itself in my side. "What's happening?" hissed the Sister next to me. I recognized her, but couldn't recall her name. The world as I knew it was slipping away into bleak blobs of grayness. "Shouldn't that award be yours?"

All around me, I was vaguely aware of nods and whispers, perplexed looks. This gave me some small measure of comfort. At least I hadn't been the only one who believed the award was meant to be mine.

Sister Edna continued speaking. She beamed down at Victoria, Lorna, and Narissa as she did. I could no longer hear the words. My heart had ceased its earlier excited beating and now pulsed sickly, my chest heavy with a pitiful sense of dread and disbelief. I pictured my heart shriveling up into a blackened husk of what it was meant to be. It fell down through the space of my rib cage, dropping out of sight, and then my ribs went along with it, breaking in half in a gentle clanking of bones and tumbling down into the dark.

My vision blurred. I was crying. I couldn't remember the last time I had cried.

My entire adolescent life had been leading toward this, and now—what?

At ten, my parents had abandoned me to the abbey's care. I was told I was a difficult child, who had been expelled from school for messing about with plants out of mere curiosity and accidentally sickening another classmate whose family was well-connected. I never intended to harm, never intended to offend, but it seemed as though my very existence was enough to incite anger in others, and nothing I did could change that.

I remembered little of my first few years at the abbey, traumatized and miserable as I was. But what loomed large in my memory was Mother Vanessa, who'd seen my interest in plants as something to be nurtured instead of destroyed, and opened up a world of poisonous possibilities for me beneath the Order's auspices. She had cajoled me into obedience with her kindness. Because of her, I believed that if I followed the rules, I'd be rewarded. The Chief Poisoness title was meant to be my reward. Mother Vanessa had told me so herself, all but confirmed this mere months ago.

But Mother Vanessa was no longer acting quite like the abbess I knew.

How much of her comforting words had been a lie—nonsense, soothing susurrations meant to reassure a troubled child? To offer that child hope where none truly existed?

My throat tasted sour all of a sudden. Mother Vanessa's carefully constructed image of the abbey as a paragon of meritocracy crumbled to dirt before my eyes. I looked skyward, seeking out the Mother's warmth, but clouds had crawled across the sun, and instead of the closeness I'd sensed earlier, I now felt nothing.

I had no backup plan. No one had ever told me I needed one. Without this award, I would remain an ordinary Sister, compelled to live out my days inside the abbey. Trapped, forever, in the same place that had long been my prison.

The Mother could not possibly condone this much suffering.

Once more, applause swelled, and the ceremony concluded with one final prayer. I sat motionless in my seat—a stubborn, useless pebble stuck in the middle of a buoyant stream of joy. All around me, the other newly avowed Sisters rose and found their friends, eagerly anticipating the special luncheon that would follow.

Over the top of the shifting brown robes, I caught Sister Colette's gaze. Her brow was furrowed in concern. The barest hint of an idea bloomed in me, desperate and weak.

Sister Colette hadn't listened to me before. But now, in the wake of what surely had to be a cruel mistake, I was sure she would.

Chapter Five

"As the highest-ranking nun in each Order abbey, the Abbess is expected to be a strong and reasonable leader. She must be knowledgeable yet humble; firm yet kind. She must not be prone to favoritism or irritation. She must resolve conflicts with poise."

—Excerpt from An Exploration of the Order of the Revenant Mother and Other Island Religions

"Sister Colette!"

I caught up with her just inside the hallway leading to the gardens. As the others returned to the abbey's interior in an unending stream of brown robes and gleeful chatter, I stepped to the side. Down by my hips, beneath my robes, my hands were clenched into fists, and I couldn't seem to let them go.

"Sister Annette." Sister Colette seemed distracted, but her eyes eventually landed on me. "Congratulations on your Profession."

I stared at her. I was meant to thank her, but politeness stood at the bottom of my priority list at the moment. "What happened to my award?"

Sister Colette hesitated. Beckoning me closer, she dropped her voice. "I'm so sorry—I'm not sure."

Still, I stared. Her words weren't making sense. She was assistant to the abbess. How could she not be sure what had happened?

"But—" I shook my head. My voice inched higher, shriller, as panic mounted. "You said this morning I would receive it. That's what you were hinting at, right?"

"Yes," she confirmed, nodding, and my face fell. She reached out to lay a hand on my shoulder. "Even *I* was sure it would be yours. I haven't the slightest idea what changed."

Her touch should have been a comfort. Yet all I wanted was to fling her hand away, and violently.

If I was meant to win the award, why had it gone to Narissa? What sort of horrible mistake had occurred?

"Did—did I do something?" I cast my mind around frantically. The loss of the award felt like a fresh wound amid my brain matter. I was built to seek meaning. I needed order, structure, expectations, and outcomes clearly aligned. If I was being denied my award, surely there was a concrete reason. I looked up at Sister Colette in a fresh wave of alarm. "Is this because I hesitated to get Mother Vanessa help last night?"

My voice cracked. I was near to tears again, and that simply would not do. I reined my scattered emotions in with a tight fist.

"Dear, of course not," said Sister Colette softly. She blinked rapidly several times, and it was only now, after finally parsing her expression, that I realized what I hadn't before: she, too, was confused. At least now I felt somewhat validated in my outrage. "I wish I had an answer for you. I know how troubling this must be." Her gaze shifted to something behind me. "Might I suggest you speak with Mother Vanessa?"

I turned, followed her gaze. As the stream of newly avowed Sisters tapered off in the direction of the refectory for the celebration luncheon, Mother Vanessa brought up the rear. But instead of following them, she veered to the right, moving quickly but calmly in the direction of her office.

"Perhaps she can shed some light on this unexpected situation," offered Sister Colette.

I was already moving. Mother Vanessa would speak to me. I was going to demand an explanation, and I would not leave her office until I had an answer.

Sister Colette said something else I didn't catch as I hurried to catch up with Mother Vanessa. It didn't matter. Each of the Sisters possessed a mental flipbook of meaningless platitudes they enjoyed bringing out in an attempt to soothe away bad things, and I was far from interested. I cared only for answers.

Despite how ill she'd looked during the Profession, Mother Vanessa moved swiftly, and I lost sight of her for several moments. By the time I reached her office, she was lowering herself into her seat with a heavy sigh. I stepped inside and shut the door behind me.

I felt wild, untamed in my anger. I wondered if she could sense it.

Silence reigned for a stretch. Then, weary: "Yes, Annette?"

"Why did Narissa receive my award?" I blurted out.

Another sigh. She looked awful, pale and feverish. Mother Vanessa shut her eyes, elbows on the desk, and rested her head on her hands.

I didn't care. Inside, I was a restless jumble of panicked energy without a proper outlet. One way or another, that energy would have to emerge.

"Are you going to answer me?" My voice escalated in volume, quivering with righteousness. I wasn't by nature a loud person, but given enough reason, I could bellow as loud as the crankiest of the older Sisters. And this tired, cowering routine Mother Vanessa was offering me was *not* going to be sufficient. "I spoke to Sister Colette. She's just as confused as I am. I was under the impression that the Chief Poisoness title was mine."

"Yes, I know," Mother Vanessa ground out.

"Then what?" I demanded. "What happened?"

I knew, on some distant level, that I was being rude. That under no circumstances was I allowed to speak to the abbess this way, with such disrespect. But I was hurting and angry, unsettled and confused, and with the life I'd long imagined falling apart around me, I cared little who else might be struck by the debris.

"Annette, *please*, let us discuss this later. I have a terrible headache—"

"You promised me!" The shout tore from my throat, leaving me shaking. "You took me under your wing and made me believe I could have this elaborate fairytale of a life, and finally, when the time comes, you give my title to *Narissa*?"

Mother Vanessa stood, her fatigue falling away all at once like shedding a cloak. It was as if a switch had flipped, and the abbess who'd moments ago been begging to discuss this another time now advanced on me with fury lining her face.

"Do not presume to speak to me this way, *child*!" she snapped, and I flinched. "I will offer you no explanation. There isn't one. And you have no right to march into my office and demand I explain myself." Her voice had changed, growing meaner, raspier.

It was time to apologize. Prostrate myself and drop the subject. But, frowning, I felt my rage become something uglier. And instead of backing down like I was meant to, drew myself up to my full height and stared her down.

I spat the words out like nails from my lips. "Mother, I am merely asking for what I am owed. I've done everything you asked—aced every exam, written every paper, memorized every bit of scripture, grown and brewed every poison—"

"You are owed *nothing!*" Spittle flew from Mother Vanessa's lips as she roared, and despite my heady indignance, I stepped back. Mother Vanessa could be cruel, but it was done in a kind, firm way, meant to build us up rather than tear us down. I saw no trace of that version of Mother Vanessa here. She came closer, going on, "The world is wicked and harsh, Annette. I've done my best to protect you from that, but now it's time for you to face reality. I promised you nothing and nothing is exactly what you'll get."

She accentuated this with a shove against my shoulders, and I stumbled back, reeling. My idiotic pulse hammered along in my throat and my breath came fast in my chest. I didn't understand. How could she say these things to me? She had indeed all but promised me this award. Had done so for years. She knew well what it meant to me. Now in a sudden stab of catastrophic paranoia, I wondered if I'd wildly misinterpreted this thing, like so many other things. Was she right? Had I merely deluded myself into believing I deserved the Chief Poisoness title?

Mother Vanessa stood before me now, chest heaving. She looked like a stranger.

"But—" I struggled for meaning, grasping wildly at anything resembling it. "But you said—you *said*—"

"I said nothing." She had mostly reined in her anger, now, coaxed it quiet and well-behaved. Looking down at me, as if I were a smear of fertilizer on her shoe and not the woman she'd raised in the Mother's image for the past fifteen years, she added, "Be grateful for what you've been given, Sister Annette. You're an avowed Sister of the Order. Is that not enough?"

No. No, it wasn't. My face crumpled, and I couldn't hold the tears back any longer. "Please, Abbess, I don't understand."

Her eyelids slipped closed. For one brief, miraculous moment, I thought I had finally gotten through. I believed, foolishly, that now she would tell me what I had been missing, why she'd so capriciously denied me the only thing I'd ever truly wanted.

Instead I felt her palm connect with the side of my face.

Pain bloomed along my cheek. I threw my hands up to defend myself on instinct, but still, she hit me three more times, each slap seemingly more forceful. The final one caught my bottom lip between my teeth. I tasted blood on my tongue.

We stood staring at each other. I was shaking. My cheeks burned from the force with which she'd hit me. I was whimpering, cowering, like a kicked dog in a dirty street gutter.

My whole life, I had looked up to Mother Vanessa. I had idolized her for years. That she had so rapidly and completely shattered that image shook me to my core. I scrambled back further away from her, toward the door. Tears would come worse than they already were, and I didn't want to give her the satisfaction of witnessing that.

Mother Vanessa's eyes widened all at once. "Annette," she gasped. "I am so sorry—"

But I didn't believe her. When she reached for me, I did the only thing that made sense—I shoved her with all my strength. Mother Vanessa toppled onto her rear. The front of her desk broke the worst of her fall.

The quiet horror of what I had just done swelled up between us.

I expected retaliation. I expected punishment. I did not, in *any* way, expect Mother Vanessa to look up at me and *smile*.

Something broke in me, then. And instead of checking on the abbess, or apologizing, or any of the myriad things I should have done—I fled.

Chapter Six

"When the Mother returned from the earth, reborn of dirt and weeds and poisonous plants, those who had rallied around Her in life now flocked to Her again in death and rebirth. They ate the plants from around Her resurrection site and were rewarded with visions of Her, and spurts of strange abilities suspected to hail from demonkind. The Mother granted these original followers immunity to the very poisons that had both killed and saved Her—proof that everything exists on the knife's edge of balance. Rather than shy away from this balance, Her followers chose to embrace it. Thus a new mantra was born: 'To heal the sick, and sicken the wicked,' and with it the Order came to be."
—The Gospel of the Order, Book 1, Testament 1

My tiny third floor room had never felt more like a prison.

Inside, I locked the door and collapsed into a seat on the edge of my bed. I was hyperventilating, my lip was bleeding, and every inch of my body shook, covered in clammy sweat. Rules, structure, and justice were the pillars on which I'd built my life here at the abbey. There was none of that now, and I felt hopelessly adrift, like I'd been tossed out to sea during the worst storm of the season.

Never in my fifteen years of knowing her had my respect for Mother Vanessa wavered. But her sudden disregard of the responsibilities of her own authority had shaken me, as had her beating. The world was tilted on its axis, and I was clueless as to which side I could grab to right myself.

The room spun. I tried to stifle a sob with my hand pressed to my mouth, but all that brought me was a fresh wave of pain in my lip, and a smear of blood on my hand whose texture made me want to crawl out of my skin.

Mistake or not, Mother Vanessa was not going to give me the award. I knew that now. I wasn't sure what had changed, but the Mother Vanessa I thought I had known no longer existed. And if she wouldn't help me, none of the other Sisters would. I was on my own.

Utter hopelessness pressed down on me. Perhaps I should simply grab my bags and leave—

I whirled to seize my bags, then froze.

Without the abbey, I had nothing. No family, no home, no money. And without the Chief Poisoness title and the job it conferred, I had no means of making a living on my own outside the abbey. Leaving these walls would mean taking my chances on the streets.

I was trapped.

Half hoping I would suffocate, I buried my head in my pillow and screamed. I pounded the mattress with my fists until they ached.

I let my body writhe and contort with the ebbs and flows of my anger. Snatching off the vow pin I'd just been gifted, I tossed it across the room, then followed suit and tossed my bag, too, for good measure, and took great pleasure in the clothing and prayer books spilling untidily from the bag's open mouth.

It wasn't *fair*. I simply needed things to be *fair*. Otherwise, what was the point?

I couldn't remember the last time I'd melted down like this. It had been years since I'd truly cared about anything this much. I was accustomed to saving up my big emotions and acknowledging them only in private. But never before had I felt this out of control. Desperation clawed at me the way Mother Vanessa had clawed at her skin the previous night. I had half a mind to try and claw out my own heart if only that would tame the pain.

Soon, I exhausted myself, and tumbled into an angry, restless sleep. I dreamed of worms beneath brown skin, of a golden-haired Sister stealing my voice and my life, of the chapel floor crumbling, opening wide to swallow me whole. When I woke, afternoon sun was bleeding into early evening light. I felt calmer, exhausted, but no less devastated.

I sat up. The first thing I saw was the cut glass figurine of the Revenant Mother on my night table. It had somehow survived my whirlwind of destruction, and now caught the sunset's last rays of creamy golden light within its crystal clear kaleidoscope.

It hit me all at once.

Like the Mother Herself, I had been betrayed by someone I trusted, and though the abbess hadn't killed me outright, I felt close enough to death for the parallel to ring true. The Mother had returned, had risen from the dirt with leaves and poison at Her fingertips, and leaned into the darkness borne of Her betrayal to move on with Her life with a renewed strength.

There was no reason I couldn't do the same.

The light shifted, falling away from the Mother's figurine. Still I felt that holy presence. A sense of conviction.

I wiped the dried blood from my lips and stood.

The vows I had taken earlier were for life. I had no desire to turn my back on the Mother, and no plans to. I meant to honor my commitment to the faith that had raised me. It was that faith, *not* Mother Vanessa, that had made me who I was, and that loyalty was what I would cling to during these dark times. I needed the Chief Poisoness award in order to continue along the next step of my life, and if dirt-damned Mother Vanessa wouldn't give it to me, I would find another way to take what was mine.

Pacing along the meager length of my room, my mind raced, thoughts crashing and tumbling together, though I felt a sudden and utter calm like the eye of a storm.

In a few weeks, we would reach the end of the calendar year. The first of the new year would mark the abbey's recertification period. Every three years, the Prioress, the holy-ordained right hand of the Mother and the highest-ranking Sister, would visit all Order abbeys across the Islands for an in-depth inspection and renewed blessing. Moriah Abbey had never, to my knowledge, failed a recertification. But I knew that a failed recertification would throw the abbey's legitimacy into question. It meant all of the recently avowed Sisters would be forced to retake their vows under a different, certified authority. If I could find a way to ensure the abbey failed its recertification, I would be given another chance at my vows, and another chance to wrestle my award back from Narissa's grasp.

It was not a kind train of thought. In fact, I should've immediately gone downstairs to the chapel to pray and repent for my vengeful mind.

But I didn't.

With the recertification visit on the horizon, the Sisters would be beside themselves with preparations. I'd been through a recertification before, knew what to expect. Knew, fortunately, that it was the most hectic season, during which I doubted anyone would pay close attention to me.

I turned to face my figurine of the Mother. It had gone gray now, cast against the night sky as the last fingers of sunset disappeared from high up on the horizon. Another acolyte might have taken this as a sign of Her displeasure, but I *knew* my Mother. She understood. She forgave. I could only hope that, in time, She would come to see the necessity of my actions, and that if She did not intend for me to serve Her in this way, She would intervene.

The Mother was not necessarily a benevolent god. And I felt no particular obligation to be Her benevolent servant.

I knelt. Touched the figurine. The glass was cool beneath my fingertips.

"Mother, forgive me," I murmured. "I feel it only prudent to warn you that I intend to step sideways out of the warmth of your glory."

Chapter Seven

"A proper Order acolyte would do well to avoid things such as eavesdropping, gossip, and poking around where they do not belong. They should take care to respect the integrity of the Order above all else. An acolyte's decisions should always be made with the glory of the Mother in mind."
—Your Guide to Religious Life Within the Order, created and issued by Moriah Abbey

The preparations for the abbey's recertification began in earnest the next morning.

Following morning prayers and breakfast, we gathered in the chapel for a special assembly. Sister Colette presided over the proceedings, and Mother Vanessa was nowhere to be seen. That was perfectly all right with me. I still felt the ghost of her blows on my cheek. Beyond a bit of puffy skin and tenderness, she'd left no marks on me. I hadn't told anyone, and didn't plan to, seeing no point, but I certainly didn't want to be around her if I could avoid it.

Again, I had slept little. I'd laid awake for hours, staring at the ceiling and occasionally crying. I had unpacked my bags. Pretended, through elite mental contortions designed to protect myself, that I'd never truly packed them in the first place. If I somehow managed to convince myself I hadn't just been on the cusp of the rest of my life, only for it all to be snatched away, perhaps it would hurt less. Instead I found myself sitting bitter and restless in my usual seat in the chapel. I felt for all the world like some sort of miserable leftover.

But I wasn't the only one who seemed out of place. For reasons unknown to me, despite winning the award I'd long believed was mine, Narissa had decided to defer her departure until after the recertification. I wanted to throw something at the back of her head.

Instead I trained my eyes on Sister Colette and tried not to look as wretched as I felt.

"Three weeks," Sister Colette said. She rapped her knuckles atop the lectern for emphasis. "That's all that remains before the arrival of our Prioress. We'll be expected to greet her with a pristine abbey and a beautiful dinner. During her stay, she'll be conducting an in-depth inspection of our facilities, and renewing our official Order blessing for another three-year period." Now the Sister paused, looking sternly at us. "I understand that many of you have just been formally avowed and are still very much in the mood to celebrate, but I am expecting all of you to be on your best behavior going forward. Is that understood?"

The entire chapel murmured, "Yes, Sister Colette."

"Very good. Mother help us all," she said with the faintest hint of exasperation. She shuffled the papers in her hands. "As you can imagine, much needs to be done between now and the Prioress's visit. We'll need to scrub the building top to bottom, inside and out. Our gardens must be immaculate. Our classrooms and materials must be well-organized. If the Prioress deigns to rest her hand upon any desk inside this abbey, I expect that hand to come away clean. No dust, no grime. To that end, we'll be splitting you all into working groups to tackle the recertification preparations of specific areas."

Sister Colette went on to describe the possible groups, but I had already mostly stopped listening, already started wondering how I might use the preparations to my advantage. The fabric of my robe twisted in my hands as I thought. No one could suspect what I'd be doing, which meant I'd need relative solitude—so, a group with as few people as possible—and a reasonable amount of autonomy.

"—in addition to reorganizing, restocking, and conducting inventory of the refectory and the kitchens, we'll also need one or two of you to work on cleaning up the archives—"

My attention returned all at once like the snap of an elastic band.

The archives. I'd been down there once, as a child, in one of our first introductory lessons about Moriah Abbey and its history. Each abbey contained one central archive of official records and historical materials pertaining to the Order. It housed everything from membership and financial records to meeting documentation and photographs.

In other words, it sounded like an excellent place I could start looking for a way to ensure the abbey failed its recertification.

I thrust my hand into the air. Several of the others around me startled at my sudden movement and turned to look.

Sister Colette broke off. "Yes, Sister Annette?"

"Sister, I'd like to volunteer to take on the organization of the archives."

"Oh." I could tell from her voice that I'd surprised her, though I wasn't sure why. "That's. . .excellent, dear. However, I should warn you that this will be a massive undertaking. No one's been tasked with overseeing the archives full-time since Sister Leonora passed."

I knew that. It didn't matter. A year ago, Sister Leonora, who'd looked over the archives for nearly thirty years, had died of old age and passed into the Mother's Garden. I imagined that keeping the archives tidy hadn't been much of a priority since, and now, with the recertification looming, it was suddenly at the top of the list.

I nodded. "I trust that Sister Leonora—may the Mother's dirt hold her soul gently—implemented systems I'll be able to interpret."

"You're certain?" Sister Colette studied me. I had the sense that she was asking me one question, while really wondering another. "The archives are quite untidy. I think perhaps it would be best I pair you with at least one other Sister, to make the work go faster—"

"No, Sister. Please," I insisted. There was no way for her to know what had passed between me and Mother Vanessa. But Sister Colette was canny. She knew I was upset and on edge after being denied my award, and I suspected she worried about the pressure of all this preventing me from completing the task. But if she stuck me with another Sister, I could never do what I needed to do. Firmly, as politely as I could, I added, "I can do it on my own."

She regarded me for one long stretch, then nodded slowly. It seemed likely that her pity for me was the deciding factor. "Very well. You're tasked with bringing the archives back to their former glory over the next three weeks."

Relief crashed through me as I sat back in my seat. Around me, I heard a few hastily disguised chuckles and whispers. I didn't even bother straining my ears for the details—I could guess. My interests and preferences had never matched up with what the others liked. They found it odd that I would willingly volunteer to spend weeks alone looking through old books and papers instead of working with a group elsewhere, chatting the hours away in the bright sunshine, perhaps. But I no longer saw sense in worrying over their opinions of me.

I would descend into the archives, find what I needed, reclaim my award, and then I'd be gone.

I loved books. I loved being alone.

How awful could the archives be?

When the assembly finished, all tasks and groups assigned, I slipped away, worried Sister Colette might corner me and try to talk me out of this. Now fully avowed, I had no lessons to attend. I was free to spend my life in prayer, study, brewing, teaching, or quiet contemplation as I saw fit.

And no matter how difficult, I intended to thoroughly investigate the archives.

Moriah Abbey housed its archives in a sub-level basement room off the main entrance hall. I took the short flight of stone steps quickly down and pushed open the door.

"Oh," I said, with no small measure of disgust, and all of my fragile anticipation shattered like porcelain on stone.

The archives were housed in one sprawling room that seemed to stretch nearly along the length of an entire wing. A chill had set upon my skin as soon as I'd opened the door. One level below ground level, it was even cooler here than elsewhere in the abbey. The large room was stuffed full of tables of various sizes, the occasional desk, unruly stacks of books, and overflowing filing cabinets and bookshelves lining most of the walls. One window high up the wall in the far-left corner let in a tiny wink of light. From the ceiling hung a dusty chandelier, its candles melted halfway to nonexistence. Old, yellowed stacks of parchment covered nearly every surface, some loose, some tucked into folders and books. The air smelled cramped and musty and full of dust and old paper. Around a darkened corner, I glimpsed two closed doors.

Wrinkling my nose, a series of quite unkind thoughts about Sister Leonora came to mind, but I quickly shoved them away.

With a sigh, I retreated to the entrance hall and lit two spare candles from the mantel there. I set them both inside the first candlesticks I saw within the archival room, then left one on the central table and used the other to light all remaining candles in the room, including the chandelier, which I reached by standing on the table. This brought just enough light to the space that I thought reading might be possible. Then, in the better light, I took another look.

Everything was caked with dust. Cobwebs were laced between the arms of the chandelier and stretched along the room's upper corners. Had *no one* tended to this room since Sister Leonora's passing?

"How vile," I muttered. It wasn't what the cobwebs represented—I didn't mind spiders—but I took personal offense at the level of dirt and disrepair that had been allowed to accumulate here in the course of a year. I'd hoped to walk in and begin my search immediately, but I knew now I'd have to achieve a basic level of cleanliness before I could proceed.

Like Sister Colette had said, this would be no easy task.

To start with, I shoved some papers aside at random. Dust bellowed up and into my nose. I sneezed for what felt like an eternity. Once I'd recovered, eyes watering, I looked in a slow circle around the room. Overwhelm, and despair, threatened to creep in.

I was only one person. How was I meant to sort through the entire archives by myself in a mere handful of weeks?

Just as quickly as the doubt arrived, I steeled myself against it. My award, and my future, depended on my success here in this room. If there was anything that could help me sabotage the abbey's recertification, or point me to something that could, the odds were it was in this room.

I set my shoulders and got to work.

The entire first day, I spent cleaning. I spent hours sweeping. I wiped down the tables as best as I could around their towering contents. I lugged bucket after bucket of water downstairs, scrubbed at the floors and walls on my hands and knees, and dusted until I felt like I'd never stop sneezing. I discarded all the old candles, replacing them with new ones. There was more to be done—namely, investigating and cleaning the rooms around the corner—but for now, I felt good about moving forward.

So the next morning, I returned to the papers.

Within the hour, I'd made progress in an initial inventory. I'd divided the room into quadrants and labeled each with a rough idea of its subject matter and time period, taken from a glance at the materials and a snap decision on my part. With this rudimentary organizational framework set, I retreated to the far corner again, beneath the window, for a second and more detailed pass.

The first thing my fingers touched was an old, lumpy paper envelope about twice the size of a prayer book. Its edges were crumpled and torn from being shoved into the small space between the table corner and the wall. A spider in webbing clung to the envelope; I blew it off and it tumbled away into the dark. There was no label, no markings. I felt it with my hands. The only thing I could imagine was that perhaps it was full of rocks, and if that was the case, I was going to be very, very annoyed with the late Sister Leonora for wasting my time.

I lifted the flap and dumped the envelope's contents out onto the table.

Three velvet pouches of prayer beads. A handful of sacred herbs inside a smaller envelope, old enough to be on the verge of disintegration. Dirt gone old and stale that smelled just like the abbey's gardens. And an old ring box made of warped and worn wood.

I frowned. What had been the point in keeping any of this? Was I doomed to keep stumbling upon things like this, that would be of no use to me?

Making a noise in my throat, I made to collect the items and return them to the envelope. My hand brushed the ring box and—

Split-second flashes of a red sky. A pillar of black smoke. One high, keening scream.

I snatched my hand away, startled. Suddenly, I felt my pulse in my throat. I stared at the ring box, and it regarded me in return. Giving myself a little shake, I reached for it again, sure I was just imagining things—

Images flashed before my eyes again, though quieter, this time. Less urgent.

A garden burning gold. Ink-black clawed hands scrabbling at stone. The spill of fresh blood, oozing across flesh.

I no longer felt as if the box had burned me and needed to be dropped. Instead, I felt an odd compulsion to open it, and I did.

Inside, nestled among emerald velvet bedding, sat a silver ring, its center an ornate oval. Set within the oval was an utterly clear, colorless diamond no bigger than my pinky nail. As I turned the box this way and that, the stone caught the candlelight in a million different ways, each of them opalescent.

I had never seen anything so beautiful.

The ring seemed to emit its own music, a high-pitched, tinny noise I heard deep in my head and felt at the back of my throat. Despite the low lighting, it sparkled. It seemed to have its own pull, singing to me with untold power. The tinny ringing noise dialed up in intensity. Now I felt it in my chest, my fingertips, my gut, felt it tickling inside the crown of my head—

My finger seemed to touch the ring of its own accord, and once I did, the ringing ceased.

I swallowed. Now that I suspected what this was, I couldn't put it down. My first day in the archives, and I held in my hand what I suspected to be a rare maternal relic: an object reminiscent of the Mother, imbued with any range of power. Some were formed from Her body parts, but those hadn't been seen in thousands of years. Others, blessed belongings, were easier to come across.

That would explain the visions. The strange, indescribable pull I felt tugging me toward the ring. It was said that the Mother had left behind bits and pieces of Herself in such objects, intended to bestow holy power upon only the most devout of Her followers in a time of need. Some believed that the use of relics would enable communication with a shard of the Mother's spirit, that one could consult said spirit for guidance.

I couldn't believe my luck. I reached for the ring, tugging it from its velvet casing, and held it in my fingers. My breath came in quick little huffs that would've embarrassed me had I not been alone. I had come here looking for anything that could give me the upper hand in my quest. If this was indeed a relic, who knew what power it held? There was no telling what secrets or knowledge the spirit inside might be able to impart. At the very least, it could point me in the right direction amongst this sea of endless paperwork.

But relics were not meant to be worn. They were meant to be kept, and studied, and looked upon with reverence, for just as the Mother had maternal relics, so did the demonic counterpart who had betrayed Her.

This ring had clearly been in the abbey for years. Nothing entered or left these archives without Sister Leonora's knowledge, and if Sister Colette was to be believed, no one had been down here since Leonora's passing. I saw no reason for the abbey to be in the possession of a dangerous demonic relic. I knew, desperately, in my wild and faithful heart, that this was a maternal relic, not a demonic one.

And if by some chance it wasn't. . .well. That was a risk I was prepared to take.

My whole life, I'd followed the rules to the letter, and look where that had gotten me. For once, I was willing to shrug off my meek and obedient tendencies if it meant a chance at grasping for something greater.

The ring was cool and smooth as I slid it onto my finger.

At first, I felt nothing. I wasn't sure what I expected. As the seconds passed, I stared at the ring in frustrated expectation, wondering if I'd mistaken it for mere jewelry—

Then came a rush of pure agony inside my head. My vision blurred, and I dropped to my hands and knees with a cry.

There was a feeling like the scrabbling of claws along the space between my brain and my skull.

The world swung sideways, my cheek hit cool stone, and then I knew no more.

Chapter Eight

"It was demonkind who aided the Revenant Mother in Her efforts, and demonkind who ushered in Her downfall. The demon can present as kind, helpful, and selfless, with an impressive knowledge of botany and phytotoxicology, but remember this: a demon's knowledge is its only value. They are deceptive and conniving. They should never be trusted."
—The Gospel of the Order, Book 2, Testament 12

A strange, muted humming inside me woke me an indeterminate amount of time later. I was dizzy and vaguely nauseous. Searing pain radiated throughout my head. Slowly, I pushed myself up to my elbows.

The candles I'd lit previously had burned low. I glanced at the archival room's tiny window. The angle of the sun had shifted. Judging from the light, it seemed to be late afternoon.

How long had I been unconscious?

Groaning, I sat up. It was then that I caught another glimpse of the ring, and remembered what I had done. Even in the room's dim light, the ring sparkled as I considered it. Where was the promised spirit? It was meant to speak to me. Had I done something wrong, and that was why I had such a terrible headache?

Hello.

The voice came from *inside* me. Like someone had pressed their lips against the inside of my ears, and I heard the sound only in an odd reverse on its way out. But it startled me beyond all belief, and I scrabbled back up against the nearest table all the same. My eyes darted back and forth across the legs of the tables before me as if I could pick out someone there, hidden and speaking to me with unusual power.

I APOLOGIZE. I DID NOT INTEND TO ALARM YOU.

The voice was raspy, not unlike the sound of Mother Vanessa's nails scratching her skin. It made the insides of my ears itch.

"Who are you?" I asked, and my voice trembled.

YOU WOKE ME FROM THE RING, WHERE I HAVE RESIDED FOR MANY YEARS.

So the risk I had taken had paid off. This was indeed a relic, with a shard of spirit inside that now spoke to me. I could hardly believe my luck. Unsettling, yes, but I had hoped for this.

DOES THIS SURPRISE YOU?

"Yes. I didn't—I wasn't sure if this would work." I felt insane, speaking aloud to no one, and hearing a response inside my head.

Now my mind was spinning again, sorting through the possibilities. The relic seemed hesitant, and very polite. Its voice struck me as neither particularly male nor female, nor anywhere in between. I sensed no ill intent from it, only a *presence*, as if something great and vast now sat within me. How was I meant to know if this was truly a maternal relic? "Is it really as all the texts say?" I hurried on excitedly. "Are you truly a shard of maternal spirit?"

The relic considered my question for a long moment.

Yes, it said eventually. Yes, I suppose you could say that.

That was all I needed.

"And may I ask your name?"

Another considering pause. You may call me Jay, if you'd like. Otherwise, simply '"relic" will do.

"J, like the letter?" How odd.

Yes.

This, I shrugged off. I had no right or reason to question a spirit's preferred name. For all I was concerned, the spirit could have called itself Holy Chicken, and I would've treated it with the same reverence. I didn't quite feel comfortable addressing it so casually, but at least I knew some form of address if needed.

It spoke again. And your name? If you don't mind me asking.

"Annette," I told it. "Sister Annette." The longer we spoke, the less my head seemed to ache. My ears no longer itched with phantom discomfort. I imagined I was adjusting to the relic's presence somewhat.

Ah, a nun. A brief, amused pause. Pleasure to meet you, Sister Annette, and thank you for using the ring. I felt the relic's presence move, shuffling around my body. My eyes grew heavy as it moved there, used me to see what it could not. The archives, hmm. Its gaze swept the room, dragging mine along with it. As it came to the closed doors around the corner, it lingered slightly, then quickly veered away. What is your purpose here?

"I—" How could I explain? My situation was complicated, and not exactly sanctioned. Another possibility struck me. Could the relic read my thoughts? Know my truest desires?

Would it be able to tell if I lied about why I had really used the ring?

Before I could answer, a faint cough came from one of the closed doors in the corner. I froze, and so did the spirit inside me, both of us turning toward the noise.

"What was that?" I wasn't sure why I was asking the relic as if it knew, but I was unused to having company. It felt nice to direct my thoughts to someone in particular.

I felt its regard sharpening inside me with a brief wobble of vertigo.

IS SOMEONE ELSE HERE?

Then came another voice: weak, brittle, and barely audible: "Hello?"

This second voice was undeniably corporeal. What if someone else was here, and had seen me don the ring and revive the relic? What I'd done was expressly forbidden. It could get me in loads of trouble before I even had a chance to attempt my plan. Somewhat unsteadily, I got to my feet, grabbed a candle, and went toward the voice.

I saw only the two doors from before. Upon closer inspection, the doors had small openings about two-thirds of the way down, each covered with a sliding wooden latch. The openings were large enough to admit envelopes or small packages, or perhaps a tray of food. As I grew closer, my candlelight fell upon the upper half of the doors, which boasted semicircular openings barred in iron—consecrated iron, if my glance at the symbols etched into the bars was correct.

Another cough, and a slight clearing of the throat.

I held my candle up to the bars. Within was a tiny rectangular room—a cell. Frowning, I moved closer.

Skeletal fingers curled around the bars. Then, slowly, a man's face came into view, skin pulled tight around emaciated features. His skin was brown, though much lighter than mine, the undertones leaning more reddish-orange. His eyes were the deepest black I'd ever seen. A swath of greasy chestnut hair covered his head and half of one eye.

I felt the sudden urge to recoil from him, though my curiosity, and my concern over what he might have seen, won out.

"Who are you?" I demanded.

It seemed to cost him greatly to speak. His voice rattled up out of a throat gone dry with disuse.

"My name is Rigo," he said. "Please, I need your help."

I brought the candle even closer, though something told me to keep my distance. Inside me, the relic *did* recoil, and scurried away to rest in a far corner of my mind. That, too, was odd, but not as odd as this impossible man locked behind a door in the archives. With the candlelight as my guide, I studied him. I saw the orange flame reflected in his eyes—deep, still pools of liquid black, with no colored iris in sight—

I stumbled back with a gasp. "You're a demon."

My heart thumped so loud I feared it would drown out everything else.

He said nothing, just pressed his lips into a firm line, which told me I was right. That explained my initial reaction to him. Order acolytes were taught to be skeptical and wary of demons, as it had been demonkind who had betrayed the Mother. Despite their innate knowledge of medicine and poisons, and the many demonic scholarly texts we consulted as part of our schooling, they were not our allies. We were meant to regard them as enemies.

And yet there was a demon imprisoned beneath the abbey. One I might never have known about had I not volunteered to organize the archives.

How long had he been here? *Why* was he here? How had I failed to notice him when I'd first entered the archival room? Had he been watching me this whole time?

"Please," he begged again, more desperate now. "I've been here for—I've no idea how long. I need food, water. Please help me."

He talked like his tongue was sandpaper and his mouth otherwise completely devoid of moisture. Which, I supposed, it was. Our teachings taught us that demons could go many months, or even years, without sustenance, as they did not require it to live. But its absence weakened them. They were humanoid creatures from Below, a mirror world, who tended their upside-down earth in much the same way as we tended our gardens Above. As I continued to study him, I noted that his skin wavered somewhere between transparent and opaque. He seemed half a spirit himself.

Bars of consecrated steel on the door, an entire abbey of consecrated stone above. No wonder he looked so terrible.

Against my better judgment, I met the demon's eyes once more.

"Please," he whispered.

He sounded pathetic, begging me like that, and I hated to see any creature in pain. But he was a demon. I couldn't decide if he deserved my sympathy. And before I could dive any further into that train of thought, the dinner bell reverberated overhead, startling me. Mother's wounds, I'd missed lunch. I couldn't afford to miss another meal—my absence might be noticed, and then would come questions about what had kept me so occupied in the archives all day, and I couldn't have that.

I gathered up my robes so I wouldn't trip, then turned from the demon without a final glance.

"I'll come back," I told him. It was all I could bring myself to offer at present.

I rushed to dinner and ate quickly. The ring felt too hot and obvious on my finger, so I kept that hand tucked beneath the table, paranoid all the while that someone could sense the oddities that had befallen me. But no one spoke to me as usual.

After, many of the others would retire to the parlor for an hour or so to pass the time with reading, needlepoint, painting, or prayer. I usually joined them for the sake of keeping up appearances and read a book quietly in the corner. But as I approached the parlor threshold, I began to feel suddenly ill. Warm and feverish, and so, so fatigued, like I'd come down with a bout of influenza over dinner. I leaned against the wall.

I'M SORRY, came the relic's voice out of nowhere. THIS IS LIKELY MY FAULT.

Shocked, the words fell out of me far too loud. "Where were you?"

A few heads turned toward me from the parlor. I quickly retreated around the corner.

The relic had been absent since I'd discovered the demon. And we'd been in the middle of a conversation. How rude.

I'VE BEEN HERE ALL ALONG. That didn't answer my question, but I felt too poorly to push it. ANYWAY, IT'S LIKELY MY PRESENCE THAT IS CAUSING YOUR BODY TO FEEL RUN DOWN AS YOU ADJUST. I SUGGEST YOU GO AND REST.

That was news to me. I'd never heard of relics making their wielders feel ill. Shouldn't a maternal relic have rendered me healthier, in representation of the Mother's glory? But then again, there was much I hadn't heard of relics to begin with. The relic—Jay, I told myself—had a point. I dragged myself along up to my room, feeling worse as I went, and by the time I arrived and collapsed into my bed without even washing my face, I was glad I'd listened to it. I pulled on one of my thick blankets, suddenly chilled, and curled up atop the sheets. Moaning with body aches that came and went, I lay there for a while, wishing I'd thought to at least grab a pitcher of water.

Then the relic spoke to me once more.

PARDON THE INTRUSION, BUT I COULDN'T RESIST—I'VE SORTED THROUGH YOUR THOUGHTS, SISTER, AND BEHELD YOUR EMOTIONS. I'M FEELING A GREAT DEAL OF RAGE AND MISERY, UNLIKE ANYTHING I'VE FELT FROM A HUMAN BEFORE. It paused, as if choosing its words carefully. I was beginning to realize I knew very little about relics, much less than I'd thought. WOULD YOU LIKE TO DISCUSS IT?

How oddly touching. Why would a relic care about a lonely nun's small problems?

I wasn't sure how I felt about that, so I said, "So you can read my mind."

If it *could* read my mind, then perhaps I didn't need to speak aloud to it at all.

NOT EXACTLY. IT'S. . .MORE OF A GENERAL SENSE I FEEL. THE MORE PRECISE THE SENTIMENT, THE CLEARER IT COMES ACROSS. AND YOU ARE TELEGRAPHING YOUR STRUGGLE TO ME LOUD AND CLEAR.

That was ironic. A spirit from a ring I'd found in the archives was temporarily sharing my body, and somehow it had taken my measure better in hours than any of the other Sisters who'd surrounded me for years.

"I suppose it can't hurt," I murmured. "Can I just. . .think at you, and you'll hear? Or do I need to speak aloud?"

WHICHEVER BRINGS YOU THE MOST COMFORT.

So I spoke to it. As if one would speak to a friend. At times I used my voice, and when that grew too uncomfortable, I simply retreated into the comforting haven of my thoughts, explaining the rest that way. I told it about Narissa, and how she'd stolen first my song at morning prayers, then my award. I told it of how I'd pleaded with Sister Colette and Mother Vanessa for answers. About how Mother Vanessa had responded, with cruel words and even crueler hands. Finally, I told it of my plan, which it seemed to appreciate with carefully banked interest.

And the relic listened thoughtfully in a way no one had ever deigned to do before. Others tended to treat me as if I were something strange to be tolerated. But the relic seemed genuinely interested in my plight. I found it surprisingly—shockingly—easy to talk to. Easier, even, than talking to my fellow Sisters.

When I'd finished, I felt strangely close to tears. I didn't often share so much, not with anyone. It felt *good*. The relic and I sat in comfortable silence.

Then: IF YOU'D LIKE, I BELIEVE I CAN HELP YOU.

I stilled. "What do you mean?"

You mentioned you're looking for something that will make the abbey fail its recertification. I'm not sure what that could be, but I do know that I've been imprisoned in that ring for countless years. I'm somewhat familiar with the abbey itself. With my help, perhaps you could more quickly find what you seek.

Interesting. I hadn't considered that. A great spirit shard borne of the Mother would surely know more than I ever could. The sooner I could unfurl my sabotage, the better. I had far too much at stake to leave this until the last minute.

"What would I owe you in return, relic?"

Jay, it reminded me.

"Jay."

Nothing major, Jay said quickly. Only permission to remain in your body indefinitely. I cannot simply share your flesh sack forever without your permission. The longer I remain in your body without official invitation, the worse the physical consequences will be for the both of us.

The phrase "flesh sack" made me shudder, but that wasn't my focus. It truly wanted nothing from me in return? But of course, a maternal relic would have the Mother's generosity and altruism. It made perfect sense for it to demand nothing of me.

Yet, I hesitated. It all seemed too easy. I had hoped, however selfishly, that the spirit inside the ring might sympathize with my situation and validate my vengeful aims. Jay had done not only that, but they'd offered to help. I was so accustomed to things never going my way—to always being the brunt of the joke—that it was hard for me to accept this relic's kindness.

But I would be a fool to pass up this opportunity. Any risk posed by trusting the relic and formally granting it permission to stay in my body would be worth the reward. It was offering me the upper hand in my quest for revenge and asking very little in return. I was not stupid enough to refuse that.

"Okay," I said, yawning, as the long day with its many shocks and revelations caught up to me all at once. "I accept your offer of help. I invite you to share in my body, and give you my permission to remain until I so choose."

The relic's excitement skittered through me like baby spider legs along my spine. OH, WONDERFUL. ALL YOU NEED TO DO NOW IS SLEEP. YOU'LL FEEL BETTER IN THE MORNING.

"Good." I snuggled into my pillow, my eyes falling shut.

AND SISTER?

"Yes?"

SLEEP WELL. FOR WE HAVE MUCH WORK TO DO.

Chapter Nine

"An avowed Sister's commitment to the Mother should be of the utmost importance. While Sisters need not remain celibate, they should take care not to allow outside relationships to compromise their religious duties. Whether or not a Sister's dalliances interfere is for her Abbess to decide."
—Your Guide to Religious Life Within the Order, created and issued by Moriah Abbey

The moment I opened my eyes the next morning, the relic spoke to me.

AT LAST! it cried, startling me as my brain worked toward wakefulness. YOU SLEEP LIKE A ROCK. I'VE BEEN TRYING TO TALK TO YOU FOR HALF AN HOUR.

For a moment, utter confusion swept over me. I wasn't prepared for the voice in my head, and didn't at first remember what I'd done. Then it all came rushing back: the archives, the relic and the spirit inside, and the strange demon imprisoned below.

"Oh. Uh. Sorry?" I sat up, wiping my eyes. The relic had been right—I *did* feel better, no longer ill, with just a touch of fatigue lingering.

LISTEN, I'VE BEEN THINKING, AND I THINK YOU SHOULD INFORM ONE OF YOUR SUPERIORS ABOUT THIS— Here the relic paused, then continued with a huff of disgust, —THIS RIGO. THIS DEMON.

I made a face. "Why?"

I owed the demon nothing. I did not even intend to give him the satisfaction of referring to him mentally by name.

HE DIDN'T LOOK WELL. ENEMY OR NOT, I AM CONCERNED FOR HIS SAFETY. I CANNOT IN GOOD CONSCIENCE LEAVE HIM TO DIE. AND, IF HE SICKENS FURTHER, THAT COULD REFLECT POORLY ON US.

That was a possibility. Something else occurred to me, then. "Why did you hide?"

WHAT DO YOU MEAN?

"When I first discovered the demon. I felt you, tucking yourself away into a corner or something. Do you know something about him? Something I should also know?"

I had the sense of the relic drawing itself up to its full, ghostly height. Inside me, its presence rippled with indignation, like an affronted bird ruffling its feathers.

IT IS OF NO CONCERN TO YOU. I SIMPLY DID NOT WANT THE DEMON TO SENSE MY PRESENCE.

Frowning, I asked, "Why not?"

I'M NOT SURE, it said, and paused. Then it added, THE SAME WAY YOU, TOO, INITIALLY RECOILED UPON THE SIGHT OF HIM. HIS VERY PRESENCE OFFENDS THAT WHICH IS HOLY WITHIN US.

That explained how *wrong* I'd felt, wrong to my bones, while looking into the demon's eyes. I nodded.

"He repulsed me, too."

YES, AND GIVEN HOW LONG IT APPEARS HE'S BEEN THERE, I SUSPECT HE'S BEEN FORGOTTEN. IF YOU BRING IT TO THE ATTENTION OF THE OTHER SISTERS, IT COULD BE THAT THEY WILL MOVE HIM ELSEWHERE TO A MORE SECURE LOCATION. SOMEONE'S OFFICE, PERHAPS. THEN, YOU AND I CAN SEARCH THE ARCHIVES IN PEACE.

I hadn't considered that. Might the demon prove a troublesome distraction from my task? That was something I couldn't abide.

At breakfast, I inhaled one serving of roti with saltfish, then went to the table where our instructing and administrative Sisters sat. Sister Colette was just approaching with a bowl of porridge in her hands.

"Sister?"

"Yes, Annette, what is it?"

I hesitated. How was I supposed to tell her there was a long-forgotten demon prisoner in the basement without sounding out of my mind? In the end I just forged ahead, hoping for the best.

"Sister, when I completed my initial inventory of the archives yesterday, I discovered something odd. There is a. . .prisoner, there." I dropped my voice. "A demon."

Sister Colette's eyeballs nearly bulged out of her head.

"Merciful Mother. A demon?" I nodded. A bewildered expression covered her face, then resolved into resignation. "Bleeding wounds. A demon. Yes, you're correct."

It was the closest I had ever come to hearing one of the Sisters curse. Inside my head, the relic cackled with joy.

"You know the demon I am referring to, then?"

"Unfortunately," responded Sister Colette, sighing. She lowered her voice even further. "I'm not proud of this, but I forgot about him, and I'm sure I'm not the only one." She studied me for a brief moment. "You're already down there organizing—would you mind taking charge of his care?"

"Uh—" That wasn't what I'd intended. The relic had said she would move the demon elsewhere!

Sister Colette hurried on. "We simply need someone to keep an eye on him until I can figure out how best to proceed. You'll need to feed him. I suspect he's in a weakened state already, if Leonora was the last to tend to him. Speak to Sister Denise in the kitchens about a daily tray of food." She shuddered. "He may be our enemy and a prisoner, but we will not treat him poorly, is that understood?"

"Yes, Sister."

"Furthermore, no one else is to know of this. Speak of it to no one else. I will inform others as necessary."

With that, she bustled away out of the room, porridge bowl still in hand.

THAT WAS. . .ODD, the relic offered.

"Odd, indeed." Why couldn't anyone else know about the demon prisoner? Was the fact that he'd been forgotten some sort of embarrassment?

I SUPPOSE IT'S NOT THE END OF THE WORLD, THOUGH THAT WAS NOT THE OUTCOME I'D HOPED FOR. WE'LL BE ABLE TO KEEP AN EYE ON HIM THIS WAY. A pause. DEMONS ARE HIGHLY UNTRUSTWORTHY, YOU KNOW.

"Yes, I'm aware."

A gaggle of young novices passed by me. One of them, upon seeing me talking—seemingly to no one—widened her eyes and hurried her gait to keep up with the others. The group of them descended into whispers and badly-concealed curious glances in my direction.

Sister?

"Yes, Jay?" It still felt odd to call the relic something so human, but I was trying to accustom myself to it.

It may be wise not to attempt to speak to me out loud when others are around. I fear those girls think you're talking to yourself. Given your task, it may be unwise to draw unwanted attention.

I rolled my eyes. "You're probably right," I said. "But they all already think I'm weird beyond belief anyway."

I set off down the hallway outside the refectory, which opened up into the kitchens. Sister Denise was a hulking, broad-shouldered woman, built like a bear, who presided over the kitchens with a fearful kind of efficiency. As soon as I stepped inside, her eagle eyes sought me out as an unexpected element that did not belong within her system.

"Sister Annette," she said sharply, storming over to me. "You have no kitchen shifts today. Or ever. What brings you here?"

I relayed to her what Sister Colette had told me, and watched, with no small pleasure, as she cycled through the same shifting array of expressions. When she'd recovered, she simply nodded and snapped her fingers at one of the kitchen novices. Within moments, a tray of food had been placed into my hands, and Sister Denise had all but shoved me out of her space.

Feeling grumpy at the unwanted task, I shuffled reluctantly down to the archives in the basement. Setting the tray on the table, I went through the same routine of lighting enough candles to read by, then took the tray and approached the corner door where I'd previously spoken to the demon.

I cleared my throat, but he was already waiting at the door.

"I heard you come in," said the demon in response to my puzzled look. "You came back."

"I said I would, didn't I?" I moved the latch for the opening aside and slid the tray through. Sister Denise had given him a bowl of porridge topped with peaches, and a tall container full of water that *just* fit through the opening when turned on its side. "Here, I've been instructed to give you food."

The demon's eyes went wide and disbelieving. He didn't take the tray immediately, seemingly unconvinced I truly intended to give it to him. But when I shook it expectantly in my impatience, he took it, and retreated back into the shadows of the cell. There he fell upon the food like a man starved. I had never seen anyone eat so fast, or with so much gusto. It was like watching an animal devour a carcass. With the food gone, he turned to the water, which he started on in slow, thoughtful gulps.

I quickly grew uncomfortable watching him feast like some sort of creature, so I decided to return to my archival work, trying to ignore the slurping sounds the demon made as he drank.

THIS IS EXCELLENT, said the relic, appreciatively assessing yesterday's work along with me, through my eyes. THIS CLASSIFICATION SYSTEM YOU'VE IMPLEMENTED IS QUITE NEAT. IT SHOULD MAKE IT MUCH EASIER TO SORT THROUGH ALL OF THESE DOCUMENTS.

The relic's praise felt to me like stepping into a shaft of warm sunlight on an otherwise cool day. It was nice to be recognized for this—the unique gifts no one else seemed to care about. Once, I'd blown up at another novice for disturbing my carefully arranged seed-sorting system. I couldn't help it. My mind preferred the world organized in tidy, clean rows. And I hated having that messed up.

You seem surprised.

"I've. . .been teased before, for my affinity for systems."

The relic seemed to puzzle over this in silence.

"Nun?" The demon's voice came from the corner, instantly raising my hackles.

"What?" I called. "And the proper term is *Sister*."

"I apologize, *Sister*." Was I hearing a sarcastic smile in his voice, or imagining it? "I merely meant to thank you for your kindness. The food and water is much appreciated." There was a small clatter as, I imagined, he shoved the tray back outside the door.

"You're welcome," I mumbled, and turned to the nearest table. I meant to simply pick up where I had left off yesterday, but—

"What is your name?"

No, I would not deign to speak to the demon beyond what was necessary. I ignored him, reaching instead for the envelope in which I'd discovered the ring. Since the relic had so far proved helpful, I wondered if tracking down the envelope's origins might provide further discoveries. Perhaps there was more to learn from whoever had sent the envelope, more that could help me.

"Are you ignoring me?" asked the demon.

I shut my eyes in irritation. Opened them again with renewed focus, and reacquainted myself with the contents of the envelope. I made to turn it over to look at the address—

I know this may seem odd, but. . .maybe you should talk to him. The demon, I mean.

"What? Why?" I believed the relic on principle, trusted it not to lead me astray. But I could not see how the demon was relevant.

Now the demon sounded amused. "I haven't said anything. Are you talking to yourself, Sister?"

"Be *silent*," I hissed at the demon. I tossed away the envelope in frustration. To the relic, inside my mind, I said, "**What use could he possibly serve?**"

IF WE ARE TO BE IN CHARGE OF HIS CARE, IT WILL BE BETTER TO EARN HIS TRUST, EVEN SOMEWHAT, THAN TO NOT. WOULD YOU RATHER HAVE A COOPERATIVE DEMON, OR AN UNRULY ONE?

I pinched the bridge of my nose, sighed. Nothing irritated me more than having my focus broken or being distracted from my original objective. I didn't want to help the dirt-damned demon, and I resented the idea of helping it in the first place. Demons were less than. He wasn't worth my time. On top of that, he'd done something awful enough to get himself locked up here, and was likely dangerous.

I was here with a purpose, and every second I spent talking to the stupid demon was a second wasted in the dwindling hours before the recertification.

But as annoying as it was, the relic had a point.

I stormed over to the demon's cell. "What do you want?"

His face appeared behind the bars. In the dim light, he smiled, showing rows of perfect teeth. He still looked unwell, but the food and water had brought a bit of life back to his skin tone, made him a little less transparent. He was handsome, I would grant him that.

"What do I want? Merely to know the name of the one who took pity on me. Fed me. It's possible I would've died had you not intervened."

"Wouldn't that have been a shame," I muttered.

SISTER, said the relic, in gentle admonishment.

As the relic spoke, the demon stilled. His pupil-less black eyes seemed to cut right to my soul with a sharp, piercing regard.

"What is that?" he asked.

"What is *what*?" Could he sense the relic? Impossible.

The demon's gaze skittered quickly over me, head to toe. He zeroed in on the silver ring glittering on my finger, and had the nerve to smirk. "Where did you get that?"

"I. . .found it here, in the archives."

"And has it spoken to you?" I stared blankly at him, reeling from his correct guess. "So it's no mere jewelry. You've got a relic, then. That's what you were talking to earlier. That's the strange energy I sense about you."

Frowning, I looked down my nose at him. How had he known? Mother have mercy, I was going to have to learn more about demons, and quickly.

DEMONS CAN BE PARTICULARLY ATTUNED TO HUMAN ENERGIES. SINCE I RESIDE WITHIN YOU, IT'S POSSIBLE YOUR HUMAN ENERGY LOOKS OR FEELS DIffERENT TO HIM, the relic chimed in. WE WOULDN'T HAVE BEEN ABLE TO HIDE IT FOREVER.

I considered this. "And if I do have a relic? What business is it of yours?"

The demon's smile widened, becoming more spindly. Less humanoid, and more like too-long fingers reaching through the dark.

"Nothing, nun. Nothing." He slunk back into the shadows. "It's not my business at all."

The relic said nothing. Bewildered, I stormed away. I didn't have time for this. The demon was interested in my relic, though I wasn't sure why, and it didn't matter much anyway, because the ring was on my finger and the demon was behind bars. Demons had silver tongues and wanted nothing more than for you to act against your own best interest. He was trying to trick me into something, or *would*, I was sure of it.

No matter what the relic said, I would not speak to the demon again. I would harden my heart. And carry on as if he did not exist.

Chapter Ten

"*What Order-controlled texts tend to ignore is that, within their own faith, there is a long and established history of Order acolytes collaborating with demons for various purposes. Regardless of whether the outcomes are positive or negative, it seems that the Order wishes to maintain their distance from demonkind, and does not freely circulate this information among its own.*"
—Perspectives on the Below: A Scholarly Approach to the Demon Mirror World and Its Inhabitants

Over the next few days, the demon made repeated attempts to talk to me. And I expended considerable effort toward ignoring him completely.

Without my lessons providing the usual rhythm to my days, and being as naturally driven as I was to seek out some sort of stasis, I quickly slipped into a new routine. I spent virtually all my time inside the archival room. I emerged only for regular meals and sleep, and even then only when my body threatened to give out from fatigue. All the while, the relic kept me quiet company inside my mind. It pointed me toward this document or that record, and occasionally offered advice as to what could be set aside and what warranted further investigation. So far, it was proving so helpful that I doubted I would come to regret my decision.

But the relic wasn't perfect. It would not, for instance, relent on its insistence that I befriend the demon.

SISTER— it started again, early one afternoon.

"No, relic." I had taken to calling it relic, instead of its true name, whenever it annoyed me. "I will not."

I already knew what it would ask. We had been circling this same argument for days.

I ONLY WISH TO IMPLORE YOU ONCE AGAIN TO—

"Absolutely not," I interrupted again, my voice low—I didn't want the demon to hear us if I could avoid it.

IF YOU WISH TO GAIN THE DEMON'S TRUST, YOU MUST INTERACT WITH HIM BEYOND SIMPLY DELIVERING HIS TRAY OF FOOD AND DRINK!

"I do not wish to gain the demon's trust!" I snapped.

The relic fell silent. A candle crackled gently at my side. Then came a low, amused chuckle from the direction of the demon's cell.

"Perfect," I muttered. "Now he knows we're talking about him."

Ignoring my outburst, the relic kept on. I DO NOT MEAN TO ANGER YOU. BUT YOU MUST UNDERSTAND: I AM BUT PART OF THE MOTHER. MY NATURE IS TO BELIEVE DEEPLY IN THE INHERENT GOODNESS OF ALL CREATURES, EVEN THOSE WHO WISH TO DO US HARM. I TRULY BELIEVE THAT SHOWING THIS DEMON KINDNESS WILL WORK IN OUR FAVOR.

I scowled, wishing the relic could see my expression. I understood well that the spirit inside represented a shard of the Mother, that it acted within Her holy authority. Any advice it distributed was not to be taken lightly. But had the spirit forgotten our beliefs? Existing demons were all descended from the original demon, Aran, who had *betrayed* the Mother. I would pity the basement demon's plight. But I would go no further.

"You know as well as I do that demons were the Mother's downfall," I hissed. "And you're saying I should trust him?"

No, replied the relic calmly. I AM SAYING THAT YOU SHOULD SHOW HIM MERCY. AT THE VERY LEAST, YOU'RE THE ONLY PERSON HE'S TALKED TO FOR YEARS. WHO KNOWS HOW LONG HE'S BEEN DOWN HERE? HE NEEDS MORE THAN FOOD AND DRINK—HE NEEDS CONNECTION, INTERACTIONS WITH OTHER BEINGS. HOW WOULD YOU FEEL IF YOU WERE IN HIS POSITION?

Rage and indignance bubbled up in me, mixed with a swiftly rising flicker of shame, and simmered down.

I had no interest in showing the demon mercy—I was already feeding it! Was that not enough?

But, as much as I hated to admit it, I was very familiar with the ache of loneliness. I knew how it felt to constantly be misunderstood and left out, through no fault of your own, despite making an effort to be like the others who surrounded you. It wasn't a feeling I would wish on anyone. Not even the demon, no matter how much I distrusted him.

Instead of answering the relic, and admitting that it had made its point all too well, I fell silent. I turned my attention to scanning through a leaflet of old birth and death records and tried to ignore the relic's smug presence reclining in a corner of my mind. Just because it had gotten through to me didn't mean I had to do as it asked.

When I returned to my archival work after lunch, there was a telltale scrabbling from behind the demon's cell door. His face appeared behind the bars as I approached. He often slept straight through the morning after I'd brought him his rations. I wasn't sure if he was nocturnal, needed more sleep due to being in his weakened state, or if he normally required more sleep than a human. For all I knew, demons were like cats, and I could expect him to sleep for up to sixteen hours a day.

"Sister." He cleared his throat and pushed hair out of his eyes. His voice sounded stronger, steadier with each passing day. "I wish to speak with you."

"Well, aren't I blessed," I muttered.

Inside my head, the relic gave a short, disbelieving snort. You KNOW, it observed. FOR SOMEONE WHO COMES ACROSS PRICKLIER THAN A PORCUPINE, YOU SURE THINK A LOT ABOUT WHY OTHERS DON'T LIKE YOU. DO YOU REALLY CONSIDER IT THAT MUCH OF A MYSTERY?

Gritting my teeth at both the relic and the demon, I paused before the demon's cell.

"Well?" I prompted, eyebrows raised. The relic had convinced me to speak to the demon. It hadn't dictated how nice I needed to be to him.

The demon approached the bars until his whole face loomed out of the shadows. He had a startling, mesmerizing presence that both unsettled and intrigued me.

Which was why I was so resolved to keep my distance.

His ultra-black eyes found mine and pinned me with his gaze, much like a dead butterfly caught as a specimen. "I'm aware you don't like me—"

"Correct. I do not."

He carried on, unperturbed. "—and I know your relic has been trying to convince you to speak to me."

I kept my face neutral, disinterested. I would neither confirm nor deny the presence of the relic.

"But I wish you to know that I'm not utterly useless." Here he paused, as if gathering his thoughts, and I realized this was the longest stretch I'd heard him speak. He spoke my language, Moriahan, fluently, but he had a slight accent—Sulvan, maybe—that came and went like the tides. "I'm a gifted observer, Sister. I notice things, things that others don't, and when I need to, I trade in information."

Now I studied him more sharply. A slight smile quirked his mouth, as if he knew he'd gotten my attention.

"You might have been intent on ignoring me these past few days, but *I've* been observing *you*." That caught me unaware. He'd been watching me? "You're diligent, deliberate, and methodical. Intuitive, though you hesitate to show it, and I can't figure out why. You've made more progress organizing the dreaded archival room in a week than that Leonora woman did for years. You see an inefficient system and improve upon it, effortlessly. I'm guessing you volunteered for this task—because you enjoy solitude, and the presence of other humans irritates you on some level. Down here, it's quiet, and you can avoid the incessant chatter of the other nuns. And as much as I annoy you, you prefer my presence, and the relic's, to that of your fellow Sisters."

I stared at him. Even the relic was left stunned speechless. A chill traveled along my arms, pebbling the skin. The texture of my own gooseflesh against the fabric of my robes was strangely pleasurable.

I had always been told I was an enigma. Something impenetrable. Because I did not freely volunteer information about myself the way others did, I was seen as haughty, standoffish, and uninterested in belonging. The truth was sometimes I wanted to belong so badly I could hardly stand it. I just didn't know how to ask, and no one seemed interested in navigating the mazelike corridors of my mind.

That the demon had picked up on all of these things about me over the course of mere days, without even speaking to me, was deeply unsettling. I felt almost as if I stood naked before him.

"I'm right, aren't I?" he asked, that stupid smirk only growing as my silence stretched on.

I cleared my throat. "Regardless of whether or not you're right, why should I care about what you think of me?"

I'd moved closer without realizing it, drawn by curiosity. The demon curled his fingers around the bars at the top of the door and brought his face closer to them.

"You shouldn't. I merely believed you might find it interesting."

I frowned. "Then why bother telling me all of that?"

"Mostly so I could see the look on your face when you realize you're not as opaque as you believe yourself to be."

"And now you think you know me?" I scoffed. The utter gall of this demon, it was unbelievable. "You watch me for a few days and think you're an expert on my behavior?"

"Like I said, Sister, I'm an observer. You're down here for a reason, and it's not just the solitude, though that's a bonus. You wouldn't be attacking this organizational challenge with that level of fervor if this was a casual assignment."

ON SECOND THOUGHT, the relic said, choosing now to chime in again, PERHAPS IT WAS A BAD IDEA TO SPEAK TO HIM. HE'S A BIT CREEPY.

Sighing, I waved off its warning. It was too late to backtrack now. The demon knew he'd gotten my attention, and I'd have a harder time ignoring him from now on. Finally, tired of this game, I blurted out, "Fine. You're right. I'm not down here just for leisure."

The demon's regard sharpened on me. "Then why are you here?"

I hesitated. Then, and I'm still not entirely sure why, the whole miserable story came pouring out, much like when I'd told the relic not long ago. It had been so long since anyone had genuinely seemed interested in speaking to me that all it took was a simple ask for me to let down my guard. Despite my better instincts, I told the demon all about being denied my award, and why I was down here, looking for something that might help me get it back. By the time I'd finished, his brow had furrowed, his eerie black eyes glazing over in thought.

"So, you're out for revenge," he summarized. "Against your own holy Sisters. The abbey. All of it."

That was the simplest way to put it.

"Yes."

"And you intend to accomplish that. . .how?" He sounded skeptical, which I hardly appreciated.

"Don't mock me, demon," I said, narrowing my eyes at him. "*You're* the prisoner here. And I'll remind you that I'm in charge of your care."

He held up his hands in a placating gesture. "I apologize. I wasn't trying to mock you. I'm genuinely curious."

"And how am I to know you're not lying? Trying to manipulate me?" As usual, once I'd opened up to him, regret chased in to drown whatever catharsis I'd achieved.

When he didn't offer me an immediate response, I turned on my heel and made to return to all my papers.

"Wait! Sister. Please, wait." He sounded desperate, and I'd only heard that tone from him once before, when he'd begged me for food and drink.

I knew well what it was to be desperate.

"What?" I snapped. "Last chance, demon. Out with it."

He had already persuaded me to break my vow of silence toward him. I thought I'd erected a sturdy wall, but in mere days, he'd proven how quickly and easily he could weasel past my defenses. Untrustworthy or not, those same qualities could be useful, in the right settings. And I needed all the advantage I could get. *Any* observations on the abbey he could offer me were not something I could turn away.

"I can help you," he said. "Help you find what you need." A pause. "You sure seem like you need it."

That wasn't what I'd expected. I thought he just wanted to talk more. He wanted to *help* me? How? And for what in return? What more could *his* help offer me? I had already secured the relic's assistance.

I should have rebuked his offer outright.

I should have left. I should have walked away and returned to my inventory, returned to ignoring him. I had no business accepting help from a demon, or even entertaining the idea.

Instead I paused and said over my shoulder, "I'm listening. Tell me more."

The demon forged ahead into the opening I'd given him.

"You wear the relic because of its knowledge and power, correct? I can offer you similar knowledge. I've been imprisoned here a long time, seen many Sisters come and go and stumble around through this untidy room. If you let me, I can assist you, just like the relic—by aiding your search for some way to discredit the abbey."

Frowning, I considered this. He'd been here long enough to grow weak, to be forgotten about once Sister Leonora passed. I had never actually heard of the abbey holding anyone prisoner before, which meant that his original crime must have been great. His long imprisonment struck me as both intriguing and suspicious.

"What exactly did you do to end up locked away in here?" I asked. "The abbey doesn't keep prisoners, not to my knowledge."

The demon hesitated. "It was. . .a misunderstanding. Wrong place, wrong time. But I could not prove my innocence, so I allowed myself to be imprisoned."

That wasn't the whole story, though I supposed it was better than nothing. "And how long have you been here?"

"Years, Sister," he replied wearily, again after another pause. His gaze swept me head to toe. "Nearly as long as you've been alive, I imagine."

"Hmm. Let's say I do allow you to assist me. What would you expect from me in return?"

What could a demon possibly want from me? I'd been disgraced by my award going to Narissa. Everyone pitied me more than they admired me. I felt like some sad sort of charity case only allowed to remain here because I was unusual, had a special set of skills, and had nowhere else to go.

"I want the relic," he admitted, prompting the relic to startle inside me and focus its attention. "When you awakened the relic, you awakened me as well. I believe the sudden burst of the relic's power was something my weakened body drew from as soon as it was sensed."

Interesting. "And you want the relic because. . . ?"

For this, at least, he had the decency to look ashamed. "I believe it will restore me to full power. Allow me to escape, and move on with my life."

I snorted. "You must be joking," I retorted. "You think I'll willingly agree to an arrangement that ends with you escaping? Do you think I'm stupid? I alone volunteered for this task. If you suddenly disappear, all signs will point to me. I've already fallen from favor enough as it is."

"I understand that, but at my full power, I'm capable of so much more. It would be easy to escape and make it look like an accident. Tell them I hypnotized you, or whatever terrible, evil thing it is that you all believe we do. The other nuns will believe you." He said this with a hint of scorn I didn't appreciate.

"And how do you expect me to explain away your sudden return to full power?"

"If you give me the relic in exchange for my assistance, once you've accomplished your task, and then both the relic and I go missing, it'll be all too easy to read between the lines."

I had already opened my mouth to protest again. Now I paused, realizing he was right. The other Sisters and acolytes might have disliked me for vague social reasons, but they had no reason to doubt my faith. If I indeed claimed the demon had manipulated me in some way to make his escape as he suggested, I knew they would believe it.

I returned my gaze to the demon to find him watching me closely. He had an uncanny, penetrating way of looking at me that made me feel like my innermost fears, desires, and worries were simply writ large across my face.

"Talk it over with your relic," he said. "I'm sure it will have advice of its own."

I shot him a look of warning that I hoped communicated *do not try anything, demon* and went around the corner to converse with the relic in peace.

THAT CONNIVING LITTLE CRETIN, it broke in immediately. HOW DARE HE MAKE TO BARGAIN FOR MY POSSESSION AS IF I WERE JUST SOME OBJECT—

"Relic." I carefully refrained from confirming that it was, indeed, just some object, as I suspected that would only incense it further. I added, **"It matters little to me whether or not you care for the demon's character. What do you make of this offer?"**

The relic gave a grand, dramatic sigh. I had a sense of it pacing back and forth as its ghostly presence inspected the demon's offer from every angle.

I DOUBT THERE IS ANYTHING THIS DEMON CAN DO THAT I CANNOT, said the relic. AT LEAST IN TERMS OF WHAT WILL ACTUALLY MAKE A DIFFERENCE IN YOUR QUEST. HE MAY HAVE SOME IMPRESSIVE MAGIC, BUT UNLESS HE CAN SPIT ON A STACK OF PAPER AND INSTANTLY IDENTIFY SOMETHING OF VALUE TO YOU, I'M NOT SURE HOW USEFUL HE'LL BE.

This did not surprise me. The relic's usefulness, at least, was a guarantee. The demon's would surely prove to be a dangerous gamble.

However, the relic continued, HE'S AN ANNOYING LITTLE CREATURE, DON'T YOU THINK? IF WE REFUSE HIS OFFER, HE MAY MAKE OUR TASK HERE DIFFICULT. LIKE I SAID BEFORE, THERE ARE BENEFITS TO KEEPING HIM HAPPY AND OCCUPIED, EVEN IF IT'S ONLY AN ACT ON YOUR END.

My jaw dropped open. "**Are you suggesting—**"

SISTER, HE IS A DEMON. HE IS WORTHY OF OUR MERCY, BUT NOT OUR TRUST. FEIGN AGREEMENT TO HIS REQUEST. KEEP HIM OCCUPIED. MAINTAIN THE ILLUSION OF COMPLICITY, AND USE HIS ASSISTANCE TO YOUR ADVANTAGE. HE DOES NOT NEED TO KNOW THAT YOU HAVE NO INTENTION OF HANDING ME OVER AS REWARD WHEN ALL IS SAID AND DONE.

A mixture of horror and disgust rose in me, but it was short-lived, soon replaced with a growing respect toward the relic. It was not in my nature to be deceitful toward anyone, demon or not. But I had already wasted time playing by the rules as prescribed, and still, I'd lost. I was no longer willing to be sweet, obedient, obliging Annette, when all it had gotten me was three slaps in the face and the denial of the award that would've changed my whole life.

And if there was anyone I could lie to while feeling little remorse, it was this demon.

I returned to the demon's cell. He had glanced up expectantly at my approach, and now watched me with the wary eye of a beast who could not tell if it would soon be whipped or cradled.

"You make a good case, demon." I stood before his door with my arms crossed. To create the illusion that his argument had swayed me, I chose my words carefully. "The relic can only do so much. If I'm to bring this miserable place to its knees, I need all the help I can get. Adding your efforts to the relic's could help me reach that goal more quickly."

He grinned, slow and syrupy. "So you accept?"

I nodded. "I accept." Suddenly, an idea struck me. Internally, I recoiled from it, but the relic praised my train of thought, so I pushed on. "As a show of good faith, I'd like to seal the deal the human way. With a handshake."

The demon's smile wavered. "A handshake?"

Good. I'd unnerved him. "Yes. Is there a problem?"

"No, I'm just surprised. I've never met a nun who would lower herself to the level of touching one of my kind."

Shrugging, I said, "I'm not your average nun."

I stuck my hand up, in the direction of the bars. The tips of the demon's fingers, spindly and skeletal, were just narrow enough to fit through.

A brief grasping of fingers, his skin warm on mine, his grip surprisingly sturdy despite his obvious physical weakness. Though I had never touched a demon before, and did not plan to again, I couldn't help noticing how *normal* this felt. The demon lore had me convinced touching him would make me sprout boils, or grow thorns from my ears, or any number of other unpleasantries. He was evil, sure, and my spiritual enemy, but touching him felt no different than clasping my own hands.

I didn't know what to make of that.

With the handshake complete, I made to pull away.

"One more thing," he said quickly. His fingers tightened on mine. My pulse gave a nervous flutter. He could not harm me through the bars, I reminded myself. "You must call me Rigo."

I scowled. "Why?"

"Because I don't like being referred to as 'demon' any more than you like being referred to as 'nun.'"

My frustration bubbled over, and I could've screamed. I kept a lid on it instead, despite a feeling like the frantic buzzing of bees beneath my skin. I hated to admit, even to myself, that he had a point.

"Fine. *Rigo*," I spat, "I accept your offer of assistance with my task. Once you've performed to my liking, I will relinquish this relic to you. Satisfied?"

The demon—*Rigo*—smiled. I snatched my fingers back, and shot him another scowl over my shoulder for good measure, before walking away.

Chapter Eleven

"While not much is known about the interactions between relics and relic-holders, due to the rarity of relics in general, it is generally believed that a relic of demonic origin is more powerful. Maternal relics have reportedly granted their holders increased good fortune and mild immunity when it comes to handling poisons. Demonic relics reportedly tend to take great pleasure in causing the misfortune of others, and can impart disturbing visions."

—Excerpt from An Exploration of the Order of the Revenant Mother and Other Island Religions

"A week?" cried the Year-Three novice next to me. "But that's hardly enough time!"

The full impact of Sister Colette's statement rippled through the assembled acolytes in the chapel. I'd been scanning the area behind the lectern, looking for Mother Vanessa, so it took my still-awakening brain a moment to fully process what she'd said.

A voice near the front chimed in over the din, "And you're certain? This isn't some sort of ruse to encourage us to work faster, is it?" That triggered a brief peal of laughter, though most of us quickly returned to worried murmuring.

"Oh, enough," said Sister Colette wearily. "Mother have mercy. I told you, we received correspondence from Prioress Rosalind herself—look—" She brandished a sheet of parchment, then cleared her throat. "'As we return from Order business in Winthorpe & Colette, the captain reports that the southeasterly winds are in our favor. I intend to arrive, along with my Holy Retinue, a week earlier than expected.'" Now she glared down at us all from the lectern. "There is no ruse here. And frankly, I'm quite offended you think I would stoop that low."

The worried murmurs descended into chastised grumbling.

"Calm yourselves," continued Sister Colette. "We are the Mother's mighty Order. This abbey has survived many a recertification before. We *will* persevere."

She went on to solicit a progress report from each assigned working group. I noticed Narissa seated a few rows in front of me, her head turned to the side as she spoke with another acolyte. She'd been assigned to work closely with Mother Vanessa as a private assistant of sorts for all the recertification preparations, and as such, I'd barely seen her. Strangely enough, she didn't seem at all worried, which baffled me. Her workload had to have been twice mine—so why wasn't she more concerned by the new timeline?

Frowning, I dropped my gaze to my hands as Sister Colette's words fully sunk in, my processing of them somewhat delayed. All I seemed able to focus on was the phrase *a week earlier than expected.*

We were already short on time to begin with. One week had already passed. And now the timeline had been compressed further? This was impossible. I had only just finished my initial inventory of the archives. I had yet to start truly searching for information that might help me. My breathing went shallow with a feeling like a fist had seized one of my lungs.

SISTER, ventured the relic cautiously. IS EVERYTHING ALL RIGHT?

I shook my head. Surrounded by other people, I couldn't risk speaking to the relic here. And my thoughts had ground momentarily to a panicked halt.

WHAT IS IT? WHAT'S WRONG?

I felt the relic's awareness scan my body, searching for injuries. I didn't know how to explain to it that the problem was all in my mind.

SISTER?

The fist around my lungs closed tighter.

I FEEL EVERYTHING YOU FEEL, REMEMBER? YOU'RE MAKING ME FEEL ABSOLUTELY WRETCHED.

If I couldn't find a way to make the abbey fail its recertification, I would never have my revenge. Narissa would hold my award forever, and I'd never be free of this dirt-damned island. And now, with less time, I would be under even more pressure. I'd been assigned the archives, but there was no telling what other tasks I might be called to help with. All I wanted was to lock myself in the archives until the job was done. But I needed to keep up appearances. How was I going to manage this?

AH. Finally, the relic rifled through my racing thoughts, an odd sort of double-consciousness that made me slightly dizzy. YOU'RE

WORRIED ABOUT THE TIMEFRAME. It paused, considering. THAT CERTAINLY DOES COMPLICATE THINGS.

I nodded. "Just a bit, don't you think?"

The girl next to me froze. Her head turned slowly in my direction. I caught a glimpse of her wide eyes in my peripherals and realized, too late, my mistake.

"Who are you talking to?" she asked nervously.

"No one." But she had heard me speak to someone, and if I wasn't speaking to her or the acolyte on my left, the only logical conclusion was that I was speaking to myself.

To my surprise, she leaned closer to me. "You're a freak, you know that?" The harsh whisper of her words felt like ice across my skin. With a final look back of disgust, she rose and moved to a new seat across the aisle.

Excellent. Now she, along with everyone else, thought I was insane. I couldn't breathe very well, my pulse was racing, and my mind seemed stuck on a loop of *you can't do this you're going to fail why even bother why did you try*—

WELL, THAT WAS AWFULLY RUDE. The relic seemed offended on my behalf. AND WHAT A MISERABLE YOUNG WOMAN. I THOUGHT ALL YOU NUNS WERE SUPPOSED TO BE KIND AND PLEASANT. It focused its gaze on the girl as she settled into her new seat. LET'S MAKE HER THINK TWICE ABOUT MESSING WITH US, HMM?

"How—"

Mentally, the relic shushed me. I turned my attention mostly back to Sister Colette, who was still speaking, and tried to listen and calm myself at once. I watched the girl from the corner of my eye. In moments, she let loose a small yelp and stood to look at her seat. There was a flurry of chatter around her, a startled gasp, and then she took off running from the chapel. When I turned to get a better look at what had upset her so much, I saw a spreading dark stain along the back of her robes.

I faced front, heart now thudding for a different reason entirely. The relic's presence felt smug. Had it really—?

YES, it replied. YES, I DID.

Inside my head, I said, "**You can't just go around** *making people piss themselves—*"

"Sister Annette?" Sister Colette's voice cut in. "How go your organizational efforts in the archives?"

It was my turn. I blanked for a moment. Then: "I'm doing just fine, Sister. I've made a preliminary inventory of the archive's contents as a first step, and intend to proceed more thoroughly this week," I reported in a wooden voice.

Sister Colette nodded. "Very good. Please don't hesitate to ask if you need assistance. Now, what about my group of Year-Ones in the southern gardens?"

As she moved on, my attention swiveled back to the relic. How had it done that? For all my readings and scripture and knowledge, this was an ability I was unaware relics could possess. Especially the maternal relic in this ring I wore, who, ostensibly, would have no reason to harm one of the Mother's devoted servants.

I DIDN'T HARM HER, the relic cut in haughtily. SHE WAS RUDE TO YOU, AND SHE GOT WHAT SHE DESERVED. SHE SUFFERS NO LASTING PHYSICAL AILMENT.

I wasn't sure if its explanation made the situation better or worse. Was that power something I could learn to wield? Were there other abilities I could utilize while I'd temporarily granted the relic access to my body?

If I could learn something like that, perhaps all my stress and struggle with the archives could simply be avoided. Perhaps I could take the award back by force. It was certainly worth exploring, even if only as a backup plan.

"**Relic**," I thought, choosing my words carefully. "**Is that something you could teach me?**"

SISTER, THAT IS ONLY THE BEGINNING. WITH ENOUGH PRACTICE, I CAN TEACH YOU ANYTHING YOUR VENGEFUL LITTLE HEART DESIRES.

A human voice interrupted the beginnings of my response.

"Annette?" There was a Year-Four standing before me at the end of the aisle. The assembly following morning prayers had ended, and I'd barely noticed. Everyone else was filing out of the chapel. "Sister Colette said you might be able to help me with something?"

"Oh. Um. Yes?"

"I've been asked to help Sister Henrietta organize her herb stores, only. . ." The girl hesitated, dropping her eyes to the floor. "I was laid up in bed yesterday with horrible cramps. I'm dreadfully behind. And Sister Henrietta hasn't been the most helpful. . ."

That was a diplomatic way of putting it. Sister Henrietta was nearly as old as Sister Leonora had been, and she'd only gotten crankier with age. She would be a nightmare to assist even without having lost a day of work.

The girl lifted her eyes to me once more. "Sister Colette seemed to think this was something you could help me with quickly. So you could return to your archival work?"

My first instinct was to refuse. It wasn't that I didn't want to help—I simply didn't have the time. I *needed* to get back to the archives. But I felt Sister Colette watching us from the lectern as she prepared to leave, and knew I couldn't refuse.

I was expected to continue being the kind and obliging Annette who always dropped her own tasks to assist others. It was an awful habit I'd developed over the years in a futile attempt to seem more likable. All it had done was lead everyone to believe I was a pushover.

But if I was to pull this off, I needed to keep pretending like nothing was wrong.

So I swallowed all of my raging emotions and followed the girl to Sister Henrietta's herb stores.

It was what I considered quick work in that it wasn't difficult—simply identifying unlabeled jars of herbs, spices, poisons, and dried tinctures in one section of Sister Henrietta's massive personal storage closet—but it ended up taking most of the day. And with Sister Henrietta lurking in her office around the corner, calling out to us every few minutes like some massive, crotchety bird, I didn't want to leave the Year-Four alone with her until I'd at least helped her make up for her missed work. By the time we finished, sun was setting, and dinnertime loomed, the smell of sweet corn soup wafting through the abbey's halls.

I ate quickly and returned to my room, where for the first time all day, I felt able to relax. Sitting on my bed, I let out a long, anguished grunt, and with it all of the day's stifled frustrations.

The relic swooped in almost immediately, having left me in peace for hours.

"Teach me that trick," I demanded, before it could even speak.

SISTER, I'M NOT SURE THAT'S WISE—

"Well, then don't teach me that one. But do teach me *something*," I snapped. "I'm so sick of feeling helpless."

Its presence wavered in confusion. YOU'RE NOT HELPLESS.

"But I—" How could I make it understand? "If I can't find what I'm looking for before the recertification, I'm doomed. This is my only chance, do you understand? If it doesn't work, I need to be prepared with an alternative—"

AND THE ALTERNATIVE IS WHAT? MAKE THE ENTIRE ABBEY PISS THEMSELVES SO YOU CAN STEAL YOUR AWARD PAPERWORK BACK AND RUN AWAY?

"Don't mock me!" I snapped. If the relic was surprised I'd raised my voice at it for the first time, it didn't show. "This isn't a game, relic. This is my life. And it's slipping through my fingers."

ALL RIGHT. The relic seemed cowed, now. Subdued in a way I couldn't pinpoint. Had it not liked me ordering it around? It sounded like its feelings might be hurt. LIE DOWN.

"Why?"

YOU'VE NEVER CHANNELED POWER FROM A RELIC BEFORE, HAVE YOU? HOW AM I TO KNOW HOW IT MIGHT AFFECT YOU?

It was right. I laid down.

WHERE DO YOU FEEL MY PRESENCE? IN YOUR BODY, I MEAN?

I considered this. "In the back of my head. Almost like I'm wearing a heavy cape of some sort. You know, it actually feels quite like how my scarf used to feel before I got used to the weight of it."

TRY TO GRAB THAT VEIL. METAPHORICALLY, IF YOU WILL.

I closed my eyes. I could hear the relic inside my mind clear as day. Trying to grasp at its presence, however, was like trying to keep water in my cupped hands. Each time I reached toward it, my fingers slipped cleanly away. It was as impossible as trying to hold my tongue still.

Frustrated, I blurted out, "Can't you just—gift me the power, or something? This is so difficult."

Unfortunately, no. If you are to wield my power, you must first channel it.

Mentally, I let loose with the nastiest curse I knew.

That was unkind.

"I apologize."

With a deep breath, I tried again. And again, my fingers could not seem to grab hold of the relic's presence inside me.

I'm not sure how long I tried, only that eventually, a throbbing headache sprouted between my eyebrows. I wanted to push harder, and would've, if I hadn't felt like my head was about to explode.

The relic, sensing my rising frustration, attempted to cut in. Sister—it's all right, this is a difficult task—

"No. I can't do it. Forget I asked."

I was done trying. I hated the way I felt when I couldn't pick up on a skill quickly. It brought me back to the very first time I'd started school as a child. I'd tried my hardest to fit in, but I knew there was something wrong with me, something none of the other children had to worry about. It felt like they'd all been given a handbook on life and interacting with others, while I was left alone to fumble around directionless in the dark. When I couldn't strong-arm my way to success with my intellect, I quickly grew hopeless, because my intellect was all I had.

I shouldn't have allowed myself the misplaced optimism of believing I might be able to share in the relic's power. Things like that only proved futile, when it came to me.

It was becoming clear that I couldn't rely on any one thing alone in my quest. There would be no secret weapon to achieve my aims.

I would need to use all the methods and resources at my disposal, or I would fail.

The relic said gently, YOU HAVEN'T FAILED, SISTER, YOU NEED ONLY TRY AGAIN—

But I wasn't listening. My thoughts had turned to the archives and the secret demon prisoner in the basement. That demon had promised me his help, and it was that help I was determined, in my current fragile state, to immediately demand.

Chapter Twelve

"Mother Gloria,
The incident in your North Wing this year is not to be
discussed with anyone. Strike it from record. There will be
no recertification; we will resume in three years during the
next cycle. Care for your acolytes, and shepherd them back
beneath the Mother's embrace.
Burn this letter upon receipt."
—A letter to Mother Gloria, Abbess of Moriah Abbey,
from Prioress Nadine, in the Year 543 of Order Record

"D emon."
No response. I raised my voice.
"Demon, wake up."
After a moment, there was a rustling noise from inside the cell. Soon the demon's eyes, bleary with sleep, appeared behind the barred door. My hastily lit candle cast dancing shadows across his face.

"Nun?" His voice was warm and raspy from sleep, surprisingly pleasant. "I mean—Sister?"

"You said you would help me. I would like to request your help right now."

The demon frowned, stifled a yawn. "I thought we agreed you were going to call me Rigo."

Merciful Mother, give me strength. "You claimed to have knowledge of this place. Do you not?"

"I do," he responded slowly. His eyes narrowed against the darkness. I didn't understand how he could see me at all in the candlelight, but he sure seemed able to, looking me over in that careful, penetrating way of his. "Are you well? You seem. . .agitated."

I *was* agitated, and the fact that he could tell only agitated me more. I fixed him with my meanest stare. "Start talking or there'll be no food or water tomorrow."

Another frown. "Tomorrow?" Only now did he seem to notice the time of day. "Oh. I've been asleep since you were here last." A pause. "It seems there was no food or water today, either."

"I was busy."

"That's all right." One more moment's hesitation, and he relented with a sigh. "Your abbey keeps records of everything, I'm sure you've noticed."

"Yes, I'd say the literal mountains of documentation would confirm that."

The demon's lips twitched as if he were holding back a smile. I got the sense that he found my ire comical. If I could've fit my arm through the bars, I would've punched him in his stupid demon face.

"So," he said, as if it should be obvious. "Start with the recertification records. You said you're trying to ensure the abbey fails its upcoming one. If it's never failed, you might find it helpful to know why."

His suggestion was solid, and it irritated me. Though I'd asked him for help, that didn't mean I was thrilled by the prospect of acting on it. But he was right—I knew what the recertification entailed in theory. I'd never read the reports. And nothing was done on official Order business without a report.

Now he did smile, realizing I'd seen the validity of his suggestion. Worse, though his smile should've unnerved me, it didn't. Warmth flickered briefly in my middle. I ignored it, unprepared to explore what that meant. Rolling my eyes, I turned away, and went to the tables.

As I did, I realized the relic had gone completely silent. I still sensed it—it hadn't left me—but it seemed to be keeping itself at a distance, or. . .was it sleeping?

It was not the first time the relic had scuttled away in the demon's presence. Strange.

So far, I'd organized things roughly according to time period, and within each time period, roughly according to category. For the next few minutes, I bent low over the tables, scanning my own hastily scrawled notation labels in search of anything mentioning recertification. It didn't take long for me to locate a box full of file folders labeled MORIAH ABBEY RECERTIFICATIONS: YEARS 500-560 OF ORDER RECORD that I'd found a while ago and set aside, not fully appreciating its importance. A quick scan of the folder labels revealed that they went back nearly sixty years. Sixty years, twenty-one recertification cycles. All that should've been missing was this year's recertification report, three years later. That was as good a place to start as any.

I sat on the floor before the demon's cell with my box of folders so I could consult him as necessary.

"Did you find anything?" Rigo wondered.

"Lots and lots of recertification records," I said, giving the folders another glance-over. "Wait. . ." I counted the folders, then counted again. "There's supposed to be a recertification every three years. The records go back sixty years, so there should be twenty-one folders. But I only count twenty."

"Hmm. Which year is missing?"

"542."

He was silent for a long moment. "That's strange," he said eventually. "What about the recertification year after the missing one? Might be an explanation there?"

I flipped through the folders as quickly as I dared. My strange mood made me restless, and the news of the Prioress's earlier-than-expected arrival hung heavy in the back of my mind. I had to create momentum in my search, or I would never get anywhere.

The recertification report from Year 545 detailed the usual topics—an introductory section that discussed the history behind the need for recertification in the first place; an overview of the official proceedings; and then, that year's report. Mindful of time, I skimmed around for the most important bits.

"*All was deemed normal during the recertification Year 545. No official complaints or demerits were recorded during the proceedings.*"

How could everything have been deemed normal if there was no report for the year before? It wasn't like the abbey, or the Order in general, not to be thorough. A missing file for one recertification year was strange enough. But to find no possible explanation for why? Nothing that hinted at what might have happened that year?

"Nothing," I reported to the demon. "Which is. . .odd, to say the least."

I kept reading. The report contained nothing else of note. At the end, it said simply, *"In the Year 545 of Order Record, Moriah Abbey has been officially recertified by Prioress Nadine."*

As I was about to move on to another folder, something else caught my eye. An addendum, written in script so small as to be nearly illegible, just above the paper's edge.

"All records regarding the incident in the North Wing have been relocated to—" There was no conclusion. Whatever word made up the end of that sentence had been scribbled over so forcefully and thoroughly it could no longer be read.

What incident in the North Wing?

Someone had tampered with this recertification report. So, why? What had been awful enough that it needed to be scrubbed from the official record?

"Sister?" said the demon, after I'd been quiet for a while.

I read aloud to him the statement that had just captivated me.

"The North Wing?" he repeated. "What do you know about it?"

"Nothing. It was sealed. . .I mean, it's been sealed off since before I began my schooling at the abbey." I thought back to those early and lonely days after my arrival, when Mother Vanessa had taken my hand and given me a tour. "It was badly damaged in a fire. We're told never to venture there, for it's too dangerous."

"And yet this report mentions it."

I murmured my agreement. "And the part pertaining to where those records were moved has been covered."

It seemed we were both thinking the same thing. "Do you have access to this North Wing?" Rigo asked.

"In theory, yes." I knew where it was. Its large, closed door loomed large in my memory. It had always seemed like some great, unapproachable beast along the main stairwell. "But it's forbidden."

The demon scoffed. "Do you want your award? Or do you want to follow the rules some more?" When I hesitated, he continued. "I know it's forbidden. But not all rules are good ones. Has it ever occurred to you that by marking that area as forbidden, they've also telegraphed its importance?"

"You think the records are there?"

"Not necessarily, but they could be. Anything else that's stored there instead of here is absolutely worth your attention. People don't tend to leave proof of their possible misdeeds in plain sight."

For the first time since I'd declared my intentions to my glass figurine of the Mother, I felt a sense of possibility. I was no longer simply fumbling around for an idea I couldn't be sure even existed. The demon, once again, was right. The North Wing could hold the answers I needed, the key to ruining this year's recertification.

Forbidden or not, I needed to get inside. Sooner, rather than later.

Chapter Thirteen

"The Order as a whole frowns upon the use of corporal punishment. It is seen as an antiquated and barbaric form of discipline and has no place within abbey walls. Its usage has been largely phased out, but the matter is ultimately at the discretion of the Sister in the disciplinary role. Acolytes should take care to ensure that their behavior does not cross boundaries that may render this type of punishment necessary."

—Your Guide to Religious Life Within the Order, created and issued by Moriah Abbey

I had never been more terrified, and the abbey had never felt more alive.

The doors of the forbidden North Wing loomed before me. I kept placing my hand on the dust-encrusted handle and removing it, my courage rising and falling like the tides. This was expressly forbidden—I shouldn't have been here.

And yet I could not step away.

My fingers curled around the heavy, ornate key ring in my palm. I'd taken it earlier, slipped it off Sister Colette's sleeping form. With any luck, she'd sleep the night away, slumped over her office desk, and I could return the set of master keys before she ever noticed it was gone.

Before I could think about it too much—again—I stuck the key into the lock and turned. Heavy metal gave with a thick clunk. I removed the key, pushed the door open a crack, and slipped inside. My back pressed against the other side of the door as it shut with a muffled snap. Heart racing in my throat, I paused, sure that at any moment I'd be caught. But as moments passed, and all I detected were small scratching noises, likely from mice, some of the tension fled my muscles.

It was surprisingly easy in theory to break the rules, even after a lifetime spent playing by the book. I'd made it inside. I'd taken that first step. But as I stared into the lush dark on this side of the door, a new obstacle presented itself: I couldn't seem to make myself move.

Gently, the relic broke in. SISTER.

"Yes?" I swallowed.

I AM NOT UNSYMPATHETIC TO YOUR STRUGGLE, BUT I'D LIKE TO REMIND YOU WE DO NOT HAVE UNLIMITED TIME.

"I know." Deep breath. "I'm trying."

There was nothing here apart from mice, I knew that, but I still couldn't shake the feeling of being watched. And it was colder, somehow, on this side of the door, an odd and foreboding chill clinging to my often-overheated skin.

A pause. PERHAPS YOU COULD START BY LIGHTING YOUR CANDLE? SO WE'RE NOT SIMPLY STANDING HERE IN THE DARK?

Nodding, I fumbled in my pocket for my matchbook and candlestick. The flame took instantly, the candle's subtle glow helping me to feel less alone.

REMEMBER WHY YOU ARE HERE. I was touched by the relic's gentleness. I could only imagine the absolute mess it was suffering inside my head. YOU'VE BROKEN THE RULES, YES, BUT FOR GOOD REASON. YOUR PURPOSE IS JUST. SOMETHING HAS BEEN TAKEN FROM YOU, SOMETHING YOU WERE RIGHTFULLY OWED, AND EXPLORING THIS WING IS THE fIRST STEP TOWARD GETTING IT BACK.

Closing my eyes, I let the relic's reminder sink in. It was right—I was struggling to urge myself on because this task went against every facet of my own internal rule system. But I *did* have reason to be here. So far, the "right" rules had only failed me. I needed to take matters into my own hands, no matter what it cost me.

"Okay." I thought briefly of Narissa, her perfect hair and her perfect voice, and of how she'd stolen my chance at a perfect life by accepting my award. That hot flush of injustice rose within me. Eyes open, I set my shoulders and lifted the candle. "Let's go."

For supposedly having been irreparably damaged in a fire long ago, the North Wing struck me as surprisingly whole. From the main door, it stretched north into a long hallway with a common area at the end. Hallways branched off on either side. It was almost a perfect mirror of the wing where I slept now. As I walked the creaking floorboards, my shoes leaving prints along the thick layer of dust, I couldn't help wondering why this area had been sealed off. It was abandoned, and clearly hadn't been cleaned in some time, but it seemed structurally sound to me. Had the damage we'd all been warned about been exaggerated for some reason?

I moved slowly down the hall by the light of my candle. The flame was bright, but ultimately weak against the North Wing's persistent gloom, leaving me feeling quite close to blind and helpless. There was not even any moonlight to assist, as all the windows had been boarded up as well. Soon, I came to the common area, which had an old crumbling fireplace as a centerpiece, and a messy semicircle of ancient furniture facing the hearth.

WHY ON EARTH WOULD ANYONE ON THIS BLASTED ISLAND NEED A FIREPLACE? the relic remarked, almost to itself.

I let out a small, mirthless laugh. On the other side of the couch, something on the ground caught my eye. It looked at first to be a second, thicker layer of dust. Crouching, I brought the candle lower for a better look.

"Relic," I said, as the hair on my neck stood on end.

Its vision focused with mine on the thick and circular scorch mark. The mark looked to be made of two untidy swipes, each forming half a circle. I put a finger to the black smudge, expecting it to rub off on my finger, but whatever had happened here had long passed, and the residue was caked into the ground, almost lovingly. My finger came away clean.

THAT IS...ODD.

"Have you ever seen anything like this?" It looked to me like some minor explosion had taken place, or at the very least, like someone had attempted to draw a circle of fire along the floor.

I DON'T THINK SO. It, too, seemed puzzled, and a bit hurried, like the sight of the marks on the floor disturbed it for some reason. I wasn't sure what to make of that. LET'S KEEP LOOKING. THAT FOLDER YOU FOUND IN THE ARCHIVES MENTIONED SOME RECERTIFICATION

RECORDS WERE RELOCATED HERE—WE SHOULD LOOK FOR AN office, OR DOCUMENT STORAGE OF SOME SORT.

It took me a moment to parse the relic's statement. I stumbled over it, replayed it, and my thoughts stuttered to a stop.

Slowly, I said, "The information I found never said where those records were. The end of the sentence was scribbled over. And you weren't even here, not really, when I was looking through those files with Rigo. You were distant." I evened out my breathing, forcing myself calm. I wasn't sure how the relic would react to being called out, but I couldn't leave this alone. "How did you know the records would be here?"

The relic, too, seemed to stumble. I— A long moment passed in which it said nothing. Brief and panicked desperation sang through our bond, almost too quickly for me to notice. Then it returned to its normal self, attention sharpening within me like a blade. IT WAS YOUR OWN GUESS, WASN'T IT? MAYBE I MISATTRIBUTED THE SOURCE, BUT I'M CERTAIN YOU SPOKE TO ME ABOUT THIS, OR AT LEAST THOUGHT ABOUT IT. Another pause, this one shorter. IT'S LIKELY YOU FORGOT. YOU HAVEN'T BEEN SLEEPING WELL, WHETHER YOU REALIZE IT OR NOT.

My mind raced. I *did* feel tired, and it was true that I often couldn't quite decipher the signals my own body sent me, but that wasn't the point. It had completely ignored my question about its absence in Rigo's proximity, and tried to imply that I'd been wrong about what I'd seen in the files.

I knew I wasn't wrong. I just didn't understand why the relic might want me to believe I was.

Before those thoughts took on too firm of a shape, I quashed them. I needed the relic cooperative and helpful, not suspicious that I was nitpicking its every word. I'd deal with that later.

"Fine," I said, forcing a sigh. "You're probably right. Where do you think I should look? I can't imagine where the records might be. This is very similar to my wing, and there's no office there."

PERHAPS A CLOSET? REPURPOSED? the relic offered after a moment of consideration.

I nodded and stood.

The first hallway beyond the common room was silent and utterly ordinary. Doors lined each side of the hall, thrown open to reveal empty bed frames with sagging mattresses and desks caked with cobwebs and dust. Acolytes' rooms, like mine on the other side of the building. I pressed on, keeping my eyes peeled for a closet. Our wing had a small closet full of spare linens and cleaning supplies, so it was reasonable to assume a similar structure might exist over here.

The end of the hallway came all too soon, and there was no closet in sight. Disappointed, I turned to retrace my steps, and the candlelight flickered across something that finally caught my attention.

One of the rooms to my left had been nearly destroyed, burnt almost utterly black.

I stepped closer with a small gasp. It had to have been an acolyte's room like the others, but any furniture inside had been burnt beyond recognition. Scorch marks, much like what I'd seen in the common area, scrabbled along the walls, floor, and ceiling. Wallpaper had curled backward off the walls as they burned, leaving unnatural, twisted curlicues dangling like broken limbs. The scent of old smoke, along with something else—something acrid and bitter—clung to the inside of my throat.

"How did this happen?" I wondered aloud.

I moved my candle slowly for a better look, over-conscious of the fire risk. But even as I worried, something told me no mere candle had caused this. It was impossible. We all had small water basins in our rooms for quick, private washings-up outside of the bathrooms. Even if a candle had caught fire, there was no reason the acolyte in this room couldn't have quickly put it out.

Which made me wonder if this had been done on purpose.

THIS IS STRANGE, SISTER. THIS ROOM IS BURNED ALMOST BEYOND RECOGNITION, BUT THOSE NEXT TO IT ARE PERFECTLY INTACT. SO IS THE REST OF THE HALLWAY.

"You're right. How is it that this room burned so badly, and everything else emerged unscathed?"

Neither of us had an answer for that, and it left me unsettled.

Leaving the burned room behind, I returned to the common area. The relic expanded its consciousness, searching, leaving me slightly dizzy.

It was then I noticed a grimy set of class photos on the wall that I'd overlooked before. Blurry, sepia-toned, and honestly a bit creepy, I'd seen similar displays throughout the abbey—plain photographs of the abbey's inhabitants throughout the years, clustered by time period and hung on the walls wherever there was space to be found. I inched closer for a better look. Nothing seemed out of the ordinary at first, but as I slid my gaze along the neat rows of framed photos, a glaring omission became obvious.

The class photo for 542 was missing. The same year from which the recertification records were also missing a folder.

Something had happened. I felt it in my bones. But I didn't know *what*, and until I did, I couldn't prove anything.

I needed to find out why the photo and the folder were missing, where they had gone, and why someone here was keeping secrets about that year.

The relic startled suddenly in my mind.

SISTER!

"What?"

HIDE— It hissed. SOMEONE'S COMING.

My skin rippled with a sudden chill. I snuffed out my candle and dove behind the couch, holding my breath. I couldn't hear anything except my own frantic pulse, but I trusted the relic.

For one long stretch of a moment, I hoped it was mistaken.

Then icy fingers clamped around my upper arm in a bruising grip and yanked me to my feet.

Before me stood a hooded figure in Sister's robes, unnaturally still and silent. How had I not heard them approach? Or close the big, heavy doors?

"Annette."

The voice was both familiar and a shock. "Mother Vanessa?"

Without my candle, I could hardly see, but I caught the glimpse of a grimace beneath her hood.

I hadn't seen Mother Vanessa in days. All at once I thought back to that night I'd seen her in the entrance hall behaving oddly. To her obvious struggle during the Ceremonial Profession. I'd assumed she had taken ill and the other Sisters were keeping it quiet until she healed out of privacy. But she stood before me now, seemingly in perfect health.

"What are you doing here?" Mother Vanessa asked.

"I-I could ask you the same, Abbess. I thought you were ill?"

She shook her head—more of a quick jerk than anything.

"No. I am alright." Still she stood there, nearly motionless. She held herself stiffly. "Again, I ask—what are you doing here?"

Now her tone had turned more accusing, and I remembered where I was—in the forbidden North Wing, in the dead of night. I swallowed.

LIE, said the relic.

"I was sleepwalking," I said. I feigned a confused shrug. "I woke up to see you here."

LIE BETTER, said the relic.

"I see." There was something sinister in the way she said it. I felt her studying me, but I still couldn't see her eyes. Why wouldn't she show me her eyes? Why did I get the sense she was half-sleep-walking herself? "You're aware this wing is forbidden?"

"Yes, Abbess, I know—but I was sleepwalking, I—"

Without warning, Mother Vanessa grabbed me again. I cried out at her grip. We were moving forward, her strength shocking and unshakable. I stumbled along to avoid being dragged.

"Abbess—please—you're hurting me!"

She did not listen, and did not stop until we'd exited the North Wing. I tripped over myself and fell in a heap just outside the doors. Mother Vanessa reached inside her robe. On this side of the door, moonlight streamed through the windows, and it was in that light I caught the long, sleek angle of a rattan cane.

I recoiled in pure animal horror. The Sisters hadn't caned any of us in years. I thought it had been done away with. But as Mother Vanessa curled her fingers around the cane's end, I saw, unmistakably, her intent.

"I'll ask you again. Why were you in the North Wing?" She said this softly, with care, like a benediction. "And do not lie to me."

Panic scrabbled along the inside of my chest. Desperate, I cried, "Sleepwalking, I told you—"

The first blow hit my upper arm. It was a deep, stinging pain, sure to bruise. I cried out and fell forward, almost prostrate, as my arm went slack in agony.

"Do—*not*—lie!"

Punctuating her words with swings of the cane, she was merciless. I could not catch my breath in between the bouts of pain. The cane landed repeatedly along my hands, forearms, and shoulders, ruthless in its onslaught. At one point, tears streaming down my face, I became convinced it would never stop. She would carry on until she'd rendered my arms limp sacks full of shattered bone. Then, all at once, it was over.

I was sniffling and whimpering on the floor, curled up on my side, my vision hazy with the aftermath. My entire body shook. Inside my mind, even the relic had fled to some far-off corner and knotted itself up tight against the pain. I felt its horror and rage as a twin pressed against my own.

"Return to your bedroom." Mother Vanessa tucked the cane back into her robes as if stowing away a letter and not something she'd just used to beat me to tears. She wasn't even breathing heavily. "You're to stay there for three days as punishment, leaving only to use the restroom. And do not venture into the North Wing again."

I wanted to throw up, I was in so much pain. I didn't think I could even use my arms. But the idea of remaining around Mother Vanessa after what she'd just done to me was even worse.

Somehow, I pushed myself to my feet and half stumbled, half ran in the direction of my room.

Before going inside, I chanced a glance over my shoulder, back in the abbess's direction. I'm not sure what I was looking for. A hint of remorse, maybe? But she had already gone.

I fled inside and locked my door, collapsing on the bed. My arms ached with the many ghosts of her beatings. I could not move any part of my arms or hands without pain rioting up and down the limb, leaving me weak and panting. The relic flitted around inside me, taking inventory of the damage and murmuring what I imagined were supposed to be comforting words. I wasn't paying attention.

As I lay on my bed trembling, snot dripping sideways from my nose, concern over my own pain bled away into a quiet and sinister sort of certainty.

Somewhere in the North Wing, there was proof of exactly what I sought. Proof of something that the abbey wanted to keep hidden. Something *important*.

Mother Vanessa wouldn't have beat me halfway to unconsciousness if there was nothing in that wing to be found. I'd nearly stumbled onto something, or been close enough to threaten that, and that was why I was punished.

Which meant—as much as it pained me to admit it—that I had to go back.

Chapter Fourteen

"When asked about common disciplinary methods within the Order, one acolyte said, 'Once, I dropped a whole pot of tea on our abbess's lap while serving her table at breakfast. Complete accident, I swear to the Mother. But for my clumsiness, I was punished. Perhaps I should've expected it—our abbess was quite strict. She sentenced me to a week's solitary confinement in my room. I almost lost my mind.'"
—Excerpt from An Exploration of the Order of the Revenant Mother and Other Island Religions

I cried myself to sleep that night, unable to steer my body's focus away from the pain, and woke at dawn to fresh waves of agony that refused to subside. There was nothing I could do but endure it. Even if I attempted to sneak out to the infirmary, I had no doubt Mother Vanessa had warned them against providing me painkillers as part of my punishment.

So I fetched water from the restroom, cold as the taps would go, and lay my forearms inside the basin until some of the residual cane sting had subsided. My arms, when I lifted them from the water and caught a glimpse in the shaft of early morning light, were a mottled mess of bruises beneath even my dark brown skin.

The relic stirred to life inside me, staring down at my injuries with its usual disorienting double vision.

WHAT A WRETCHED WOMAN, it remarked with no small measure of disgust. WHAT AN EVIL OLD BITCH.

I gasped. "Relic!"

Mother Vanessa was our abbess. The relic should've revered her as the rest of us did, no matter her faults, no matter how severely she erred. The Mother forgave. It was not our way to judge like this.

YOU CANNOT SERIOUSLY MEAN TO TELL ME YOU STILL THINK KINDLY OF THAT WOMAN. SHE BEAT YOU UNTIL YOU CRIED, SISTER.

Discomfort wormed inside my belly. "She did, yes. But you can't just—"

CAN'T JUST WHAT? SPEAK THE PLAIN TRUTH? ABBESS OR NOT, YOU DID NOT DESERVE A PUNISHMENT SO SEVERE.

I wasn't sure how to respond to that. The relic went on.

WHAT, YOU'RE TELLING ME YOU NEVER USE FOUL LANGUAGE? NOT EVEN A LITTLE?

I shook my head. Such language wasn't forbidden—the others used it often—but it had never appealed to me. "Sometimes I use 'damn,'" I admitted, "but it's rare."

The relic chortled. GOOD FOR YOU, THEN.

It let the subject drop. With nothing else to do, and three days of punishment confined to my rooms stretching before me, I crawled back into bed.

The fact that I'd lost three days of time in the archives gnawed at me like an invasive worm on a garden plant. But there was nothing I could do. The chances that Mother Vanessa might go looking for me here in my room or in the archives to ensure I was complying were high, and the last thing I needed was additional punishment. Instead, I tried to content myself with mentally reviewing what I'd learned so far.

A younger acolyte came by and brought me food, but the pain in my arms had stolen my hunger. I dozed on and off for the rest of the morning. For some reason, my hazy, undirected thoughts kept tugging me in the direction of the demon prisoner in the basement. At one point, deep in a dream, I saw him clearly in my mind's eye. His night-black eyes peered carefully into my own. Looking at him stoked a strange warmth within me. I reached out as if to touch him and woke with a handful of pillow instead.

I sat up, feeling unsettled. My pulse was racing. Why had I dreamed of the demon? I wanted to shake the mere memory of it off my skin.

Mentally, I poked at the relic for a distraction.

"Relic?"

YES, SISTER?

"Will you try to teach me to channel your power again?" Its hesitation wavered through me. I knew we were both remembering my frustration from last time. "I will try to be more. . .patient this time."

The relic's hesitation shifted over to reluctance. VERY WELL.

Like before, it directed me to lie down. I remembered its instructions from last time, quickly latching onto the directive to keep my mind off the pain, off the lingering confusion of my dream. I breathed in and out and searched for the relic's presence in my body as a tangible thing. This time, I felt the weight of it more easily. I reached out and grasped it.

WELL DONE, SISTER! The relic's excitement felt like the flapping of butterfly wings beneath my skin. NOW LET'S SEE IF YOU CAN CHANNEL MY POWER.

"What sort of power do you have? Beyond making people lose control of their bowels, of course."

Again, it hesitated. I wasn't sure why. It wasn't as if I was going to judge it. I POSSESS A GREAT NUMBER OF DIFFERENT ABILITIES, SISTER. It seemed to be considering which abilities I might find most interesting. I CAN DIRECT YOU IN BREWING ALMOST ANY POISON OR ANTIDOTE YOU WISH. I CAN IDENTIFY ANY PLANT ON SIGHT. I CAN—

"Relic, with all respect, I'd like to learn something immediately useful to me. I can brew poisons and identify plants on my own—it *is* my life's work, after all."

HMM. WHAT ABOUT MOVING THROUGH THE WORLD, UNSEEN?

I raised an eyebrow. "Are you claiming to be able to turn yourself invisible?" It wasn't a relic ability I'd ever heard of before, but then again, this relic seemed far from ordinary.

YES. WOULD YOU LIKE TO TRY THAT?

With a slight smirk, I agreed. There was an almost-comical irony in the relic offering to teach me invisibility—everyone already treated me, pretty much, as if I didn't exist.

GRASP MY PRESENCE, it directed me. AND IMAGINE IT RISING UP OVER YOU AS IF YOU'RE LOWERING YOURSELF INTO A BODY OF WATER.

You'll know its working if you feel a sensation like cool water.

As instructed, I focused, and took hold of the relic's presence once more. I thought of how angry I was with Mother Vanessa for what she'd done to me, how badly I wanted to simply escape. I drew my thirst for vengeance around me like an old cloak. Finally, I thought of Narissa, and it was the possibility of sneaking my award back from right under her nose that at last made everything click.

The relic's presence, its power, dropped to my toes, then rose up. It felt indeed like sinking into cool water. A curious sensation traveled from my toes to my head, oddly soothing on my aching arms.

Sister. The relic had a smile in its voice. Open your eyes.

I did. Slowly, I lifted one bruised arm. And it was *gone.* I twisted my arm this way and that, wincing at the pain. But though the arm hurt, I couldn't see it. It, and my other arm, and my torso and my legs, had gone completely translucent. I felt the weight of my clothing on my body, but it too had disappeared.

"Merciful Mother," I murmured.

I crawled from bed to stand before my dingy mirror. Only logic told me where I was. In the mirror, I saw nothing but the faintest flicker of movement, even as I stared at the space where my body should've been.

In channeling the relic's power, I had made myself truly invisible.

The shock of my own sudden success broke my focus, and the feeling of cool water fell away all at once. I watched in the mirror as the invisibility and its curious magic drained out of me, then fell back on my bed in a daze.

"What changed?" I wondered. "I couldn't do that before."

I THINK IT MAY HAVE SOMETHING TO DO WITH YOU TRUSTING ME. THE MORE TIME WE SPEND TOGETHER, THE LESS I FEEL YOU DOUBTING AND SECOND-GUESSING MY INSTRUCTIONS. YOU TRUST ME MORE NOW THAN YOU DID WHEN YOU FIRST DONNED THE RING. I THINK, TOO, THAT YOU'VE GROWN STRONGER AS WELL. I FELT HOW TERRIFIED YOU WERE LAST NIGHT IN THE NORTH WING, SISTER. HOW MUCH YOU SUFFERED WHEN THE HORRID ABBESS PUNISHED YOU. BUT YOU ENDURED, AND SURVIVED, AND EMERGED THE OTHER SIDE STRONGER FOR IT. POWER RECOGNIZES POWER.

The relic's words sent little shivers of goosebumps up and down my arms. It *was* right, in a way. I'd activated the relic to help me with my own aims, but I hadn't expected it to nurture me as a person as well. I'd been caught and punished for rule breaking, something that, in the past, would've sent me into a meltdown and left me emotionally volatile for days. Instead, I'd cried, and I was sitting with the pain, and I had no intention of abandoning my goal.

I had been rewarded with a taste of the great power I sought, and oh, did that power sit sweet and satisfying on my tongue.

YOU ARE CAPABLE OF GREAT THINGS, added the relic. SOMEWHERE DEEP DOWN, YOU KNEW THAT ALREADY, OR YOU WOULDN'T BE FIGHTING TOOTH AND NAIL TO SNATCH BACK THAT AWARD.

Smiling, unfamiliar with the fragile buzz of joy in my limbs, I wrapped my arms around myself. I knew now how capable I was—I had successfully channeled the power of a holy maternal relic.

Three days of confinement, and then I would be back to my task.

I would return to the North Wing, and this time, it would not deny me the answers I sought.

Chapter Fifteen

"What I saw in the aftermath was this: Sister Anika, dead on the floor. The evidence of some sort of dark ritual gone wrong. And the Acosta demon, sprawled in the middle of it all, feigning injury."
—Sister Vanessa, regarding the North Wing incident of Year 542, in a testimony to the Order Council

When my punishment came to an end, I felt born anew. The forced stagnation of the last three days had chafed at me. Despite mastering the relic's invisibility for short spurts of time, I couldn't maintain it for long, which ruled out a forbidden journey to the archives.

I'd been delivered food and drink at regular intervals and permitted to indulge myself in solitary prayer. The relic had kept me company as best as it could. But I hadn't been able to stop my thoughts careening toward the archives, the North Wing, and the mystery that I now knew existed.

The next morning, I bolted to the archives after breakfast, determined to make up for lost time. I needed to share what I'd seen
in the North Wing with the demon and see what he made of
my findings. Halfway buzzing out of my skin, I stole down the
basement steps and quickly lit all the candles, as had become my
ritual.

When I approached the demon's cell, I found him sleeping.

Had anyone brought him food while I'd been confined? Did I
even care? I wasn't sure.

I paused. He certainly kept an irregular sleep schedule, and I
couldn't fault him that, being surrounded by consecrated stone that
was likely a near-constant torture upon his unholy frame, but I felt
a flicker of irritation. Here I was ready to move forward, and he
was *asleep*.

It would be simple enough to wake him. I raised a hand to rap
a knuckle on the bars, then froze. My dream from a few days
ago drifted back to me, mingling with my present like milk with
coffee, and I found myself suddenly overwhelmed with an intense
curiosity about this demon. So I brought my candle to the bars
instead, for a better look, and simply watched him. He slept soundly
on the stone bench and lumpy pillow along the back of the cell,
curled up on his side. Steady, slow breaths lifted and lowered his
chest. Slackened with sleep, his sharp features seemed somehow less
threatening. He looked normal. Human, even, though I knew he
wasn't.

One of his breaths lifted an unruly chunk of dark hair from
his forehead. Watching him, I felt a stirring in my middle, and
admitted to myself, finally, what it was about him that so drew my
eye.

I wanted to touch him again. I still remembered the brush of his fingertips against mine, our hands clasped through the bars of his cell. The demon's face, and the way he'd seem to *know* me with a few hours' observation, appealed to me.

Before the relic could latch on to that thought, I shuddered and made to turn away.

WAIT, WHAT'S THAT? asked the relic. It gave me a gentle nudge from within. I moved my candle where its attention was focused, angled it for a better look. Just inside the cell, to my right, a sheaf of papers lay strewn across the floor.

Where had that come from? Had the papers always been there, and I'd simply overlooked them in the dim light?

"I didn't see those before."

NEITHER DID I. The relic paused. ONLY ONE WAY TO FIND OUT WHAT THEY ARE.

"Relic, I cannot walk through walls—" I began in a whisper.

YOU DON'T NEED TO. I frowned. REMEMBER WHAT I TAUGHT YOU? The invisibility, of course, but I didn't see what that had to do with anything. Then the relic tugged my gaze to the set of keys that hung on a hook outside the cell door. USE YOUR INVISIBILITY IN CASE HE WAKES. WHATEVER THOSE PAPERS ARE, HE'S KEPT THEM OUT OF YOUR SIGHT FOR A REASON. WOULDN'T YOU LIKE TO KNOW WHAT THEY SAY?

There was a sly curiosity to the relic's voice that I felt mirrored within myself. Yes, I did want to know what the papers were, and why the demon had them in his cell. As a prisoner, there should have been nothing inside. I considered a few seconds more, then closed my eyes to tether my focus. I felt for the relic's presence in my body and imagined slipping into it like cold water. Power rose up from my feet in an icy spill. When I opened my eyes again, my candle appeared to be floating. My arm, and the rest of my body, had vanished.

EXCELLENT. NOW UNLOCK THE CELL. QUIETLY. AND TAKE THOSE PAPERS WITHOUT WAKING HIM UP.

I nodded, set the candle down. Invisible fingers grasping the key ring, I moved slowly to avoid jangling the metal. There were only two keys—one for each cell—and by some stroke of good fortune, my first try worked. The lock gave with a polite *snick*, and I eased the door open inch by inch, hoping it wouldn't creak.

It did not. The demon slept on.

Crouching, I slid through the door and into the cell. A wild thrill stole over me. I was inside the demon's cell, invisible, as he slept. At any moment, he could wake and discover me, and—and what? How would he react? Would my actions make him angry? Would he attempt to harm me? I swallowed. I didn't want to find out. Two quick steps, and I had reached the papers, which I gathered into my hands. Then I retreated, locked the door, and dropped to my hands and knees. My heart was racing, my body going lightheaded as I released my grip on the relic's shared power.

SISTER?

"I'm fine."

I sucked in great gulps of air. I didn't think I had breathed at all the entire time I'd been in the cell. Once I'd recovered, I took my candle to one of the work tables and spread the papers along a relatively empty surface. The relic's vision sharpened behind mine as we both looked.

THESE ARE. . .fINANCIAL RECORDS, the relic observed.

The cover sheet indeed detailed a long list of budget items, dating back nearly twenty years. Each few lines were more or less the same: *Prisoner accommodation, Prisoner meals, Prisoner interrogation.* I frowned. Someone here had interrogated him? When? And where were those records?

I kept reading until I came to what looked like an old personal file.

MORIAH ABBEY, YEAR 542

PRISONER NAME: RIGOBERTO ACOSTA

COUNTRY OF ORIGIN: SULVA

NATIONALITY: DEMONKIND

REASON FOR IMPRISONMENT: ACOSTA WAS PRESUMED GUILTY OF THE MURDER OF SISTER ANIKA PIERRE AND THE ATTEMPTED THEFT OF A HOLY RELIC.

I stumbled back. Bile rose in my throat. The very same demon I'd brought food and water to and trusted to help me in my quest had gotten himself locked up here for *killing a nun.*

What a fool I'd been to trust him at all.

"Relic," I demanded. "Did you know about this?"

It hesitated, distracted. It seemed to be scanning the text on the pages anew. I—

Filled with a righteous rage, I didn't feel like waiting for it to respond.

I stormed over to the demon's cell and banged on the door. The demon's concerned and sleepy face appeared behind the bars a moment later.

"What," I hissed, "is this?"

I held up the papers. To his credit, his expression didn't change, but I knew from the slight droop of his shoulders that he recognized the papers I held, and knew he'd been caught.

"Sister, I can explain," he said slowly.

"Then explain." I kept my anger leashed, but only just. "And I expect the whole truth this time, demon, or I'll cut out your throat with my nail file and tell the others you attacked me."

He flinched. Nodded, in a small, resigned way. With a heavy sigh, he began. "Those records are both correct and incorrect. The length of my sentence is correct. I've been here for nearly twenty years. But the *reason* for my imprisonment is incorrect. Yes, I unlawfully gained entry to the abbey. But I did it with the express purpose of finding my brother, and stopping him."

Understanding flashed through the relic, lightning-quick. There, and then gone.

When I said nothing, only deepened my frown, the demon went on.

"My brother was. . .problematic. I never found out exactly what he was up to, but from what I pieced together, he was working with someone, an Order nun, to complete some sort of ritual. He's always been skeptical of church-demon relations, never bought into the ideals the rest of our family holds so dear. He wanted to see the abbey, and the Order, hurt. Only I never figured out why." He paused, eyes slipped closed as if reliving the memory. "I came to try and stop him from doing something he'd regret. But he'd already killed a nun and stolen from the abbey. When your Order found us, he fled, leaving only me to answer for his crimes. And with him gone, I had no way of disputing the accusations."

As I let the papers flutter to the floor, I crossed my arms across my chest and tried to sort through this. I'd left my candle on the table. Without it, I could hardly see the demon, which made this feel more intimate, somehow. My anger had cooled to something tepid as curiosity battled logic, fact, and reason.

"Where did he go? Your brother?"

"I'm not sure. He's in hiding, that much I know. He never returned. His disappearance, and my capture, has surely devastated our family all these years. As of now, I'm sure they believe I've betrayed them. Only the Order's version of events is public knowledge, and with me stuck here, no one will ever know the truth."

"So you—*that's* why you want the relic. To bring yourself back to full power, track down your brother, and clear your name, after all these years."

The demon gave me one single, solemn nod.

"How did you get your hands on those records?" The idea of him being able to leave his cell unnerved me to the core. "Did you escape, however briefly?"

He shook his head. "I persuaded Leonora to give them to me. She grew rather scatterbrained as she aged."

My mind was racing. "Did you kill her?"

"No. I swear to you, I did not. She died of old age."

"And why should I believe your account of what happened to Sister Anika over the official Order record?"

Now he narrowed his eyes at me, and the intensity in them sent a shiver down my spine.

"Do you have any idea what this has been like? Years of imprisonment, knowing my family has turned their backs on me, and for so long, I had no way to stop it. I was trying to do the right thing and keep the two halves of our world from going at each other's throats again. Instead I let my brother escape and got myself imprisoned for his crimes. I'm a failure to my race, and I deserve this punishment. But I also deserve to make it right, now that I have a chance." His gaze bored into mine. And despite the eerie blankness of his eyes, I couldn't look away. "It's the cruelest irony in the world to get fucked over despite being a good person. You'd know something about that, wouldn't you?"

Now I felt hot and nervous, caught off guard once again by how easily he'd seen through me. We were more alike, this foul-mouthed demon and I, than I cared to admit.

"You don't have any reason to believe me," he added. "You could leave me here to die while you go and chase your revenge, and no one would ever know. But, as I believe we've already established, you're something of an anomaly among the other nuns, aren't you? You spoke to me. Bargained with me. Shook my hand, and accepted my help. If you're half the person I think you are, you'll forgive my lying by omission. You'll set aside our differences. And we'll work together, to get what we both want."

I studied him for a long moment, letting his many words sink in. The fervor of his speech and his piercing look had set my pulse to pounding, but I had to push that away, had to make sense of this.

I hated him for not telling me the whole truth to begin with. I'd chosen, despite my initial misgivings, to trust him because I'd needed his help. And in confirmation of my worst nightmares, he'd already betrayed that trust. Though he had a good reason, I was unable to shake the comparison: the relic had yet to betray me. It was evasive, sure, but that was it. The relic had nurtured me, cared for me, kept me company, and taught me to use its power.

And yet. The demon's situation was pitiable. If what he said was indeed true, then he'd been imprisoned here for twenty years on a crime he didn't commit, and I was the only one who could help him. I didn't *want* to help him—I was still prone to disliking him on principle. But I kept picturing myself in his shoes. I knew how feral and desperate I'd be for justice, knew the lengths to which I would've gone to prove everyone wrong. I was already there, ready to burn the abbey down to keep myself warm.

"Relic?" I prodded. "**What do you make of this?**"

I felt it there, considering, presiding over my thought processes and the conversation with the demon. I would've thought it might have an opinion. When it did speak, though, it remained carefully neutral.

THE CHOICE IS YOURS, SISTER. I CANNOT TELL YOU WHO TO TRUST. BUT I DO RECOMMEND YOU PROCEED CAREFULLY.

I looked up at the demon. He'd been quiet, watching me, allowing me the time I needed to make sense of his admission. Thoroughly unaccustomed to being given the courtesy of time to corral my thoughts, I respected and admired him for that. He looked at me now the same way he'd studied me in my dream—black eyes devoid of pupils peering carefully into my own. And though I still hated him, wanted to spit and curse at him through the bars, I felt some of my indignant resolve crumble like loose soil along the shore.

I should have cut him out of my plan completely.

I didn't want to.

Instead I took a step forward, and met his piercing look with a steely one of my own.

Slowly, I told him, "I am choosing to believe you." Relief softened his features. "But no more secrets, or I swear on the Mother I'll—"

"—Cut my throat out with a nail file, got it."

I shot a glare in his direction. "If we're going to do this, I need your absolute loyalty. You *must* promise me. No more lies, demon."

"I can certainly promise you that," he responded. "Only, you don't seem entirely willing to accept it." Another pause. "I *am* sorry, Sister Annette."

The relic whispered an idea to me then. I listened and accepted, nodding.

"Then prove it."

The demon's nose scrunched in confusion. "How?"

I reached for the keys next to the cell. Held them carefully in my hands like ripe fruit. "I need to return to the North Wing to have another look around. I was caught and punished last time, and I could use an extra set of eyes to keep watch."

The keys jangled. The demon's eyes widened with the possibility of escape, however brief.

"Be my lookout, and prove to me how sorry you are," I proposed to him, holding up the key that would unlock his cell. "Prove to me that I can trust you."

Chapter Sixteen

"I am supposed to be a servant of the Mother. But diary, if I am being truthful, sometimes I feel more inclined to serve only myself instead."
—The true diary of Novice Rosalind, Year 537–542

It was the strangest thing to walk the halls of the abbey with a demon at my side.

Though the abbey had betrayed me, I still felt like I was breaking every rule I'd lived by for the past fifteen years. Speaking to the demon through the barred door of his cell was one thing—it was altogether different to unlock his prison and walk beside him as an equal.

He was about a head taller than me, with long limbs and a stretched-out look to him that reminded me of a stick bug. He wore a tattered old tunic and loose pants full of holes. To my surprise, when he brushed close, I smelled only a hint of earth, like the whiff of a recently tended garden through an open window. I had not expected demonkind to smell better than humans. Especially not after rotting in a basement cell for two decades.

"You're staring."

I yanked my gaze away from him. Heat rushed from my neck to my cheeks. "I am *not*."

He scoffed. "What were you expecting? Horns? Claws? Flaming leaves shooting out of my ears?" I didn't respond, just quickened my step to put him behind me. "Would you appreciate it if I stared at you like I was wondering what was beneath your robes?" he added. My shoulders stiffened, every muscle in my body going taut, though I wasn't sure if it was due to offense at his impropriety or something else. From his resulting laugh, my reaction hadn't been as subtle as I'd hoped. "That's what I thought."

I rolled my eyes fiercely. Still, I said nothing.

The relic chose then to cut in. IT SURE SEEMS TO ME LIKE YOU ENJOY THE WAY HE LOOKS AT YOU.

I made sure to respond to it in my thoughts. If Rigo heard this, I would die.

"Relic, please, not now—"

SISTER, I THINK YOU FORGET THAT I'M INSIDE YOUR HEAD. I EXPERIENCE WHAT YOU EXPERIENCE. AND RIGHT NOW YOUR ELEVATED BREATHING AND HEART RATE ARE BETRAYING THE ATTRACTION YOU KEEP TRYING TO SHOVE UNDER THE RUG.

Shocked, I stopped short. **"Excuse me?"**

YOU LIKE HIM, said the relic, with a hint of a laugh in its voice. IT'S OKAY, SISTER. YOU'RE ALLOWED TO find PEOPLE ATTRACTIVE—

The accusation was so offensive to me, and so uncomfortably accurate, all rational thought fled my mind. What remained was a feral defensiveness that grew like a tidal wave in me until—

"Be fucking silent!" I snarled at the relic.

It fell silent. Its own shock at my words trickled through me, matching my own. A beat, and then it burst into laughter, a high and joyful cackle.

I'M RIGHT, AREN'T I?

"I hate the both of you," I muttered to myself, and decided to ignore the relic for as long as I could.

I resumed walking. Rigo had just caught up, but now slowed again, falling further behind, and braced himself with a hand on the wall, trying and failing to hide a slight wince.

"I'm fine," he muttered, in response to my questioning look.

"You don't look fine." The regular sustenance I was bringing him had certainly helped, but it would take more than a few days to heal from his yearlong abandonment. How long had it been since he'd had the opportunity to walk the length of a space longer than his cell? He was still struggling. I was torn between irritation at him slowing me down and a sense of pity I tried to convince myself was misplaced.

"I'm weak, that's all," he added, straightening once more. He was breathing heavily, though he tried to disguise it. "But I'll do your bidding, Sister, don't worry."

"You can just call me Annette." I wasn't sure where the words came from.

The demon seemed just as shocked by them as I was, looking over at me with a bewildered expression I saw only through flashes of candlelight.

"Annette?" he repeated. In his accent, my name had a bite to it. It sounded strong. Powerful.

"Yes."

He looked away, the slight edge of a smirk vanishing into the dark. "I thought I was meant to call you Sister."

Now that he was making a big deal of this, I wanted to take the words back. "This is my attempt to be polite," I snapped. "Would you prefer I be unpleasant instead?"

That smirk still present, he shook his head.

We started walking again—slower, now, and sticking to the shadows. Borrowing the relic's invisibility, I'd stolen the master keys once more from a sleeping Sister Colette, and this time I'd checked with my own eyes to ensure Mother Vanessa was sleeping and wouldn't sneak up on me, but the dangerous and forbidden nature of our task was still a heavy weight on my shoulders. The last thing we needed was to be spotted. And I did not feel comfortable showcasing my ability to channel the relic's invisibility in front of the demon.

Soon, the doors to the North Wing loomed before us, and I shoved down the memory of my last visit's disastrous end. Though the bruises from Mother Vanessa's caning had faded, the pain was not entirely gone, and it seemed to all come roaring back as we stood upon the space where she'd punished me. I suppressed a shudder.

Rigo was watching me.

"You mentioned that you were caught and punished last time," he said. I could barely see him, but I had the sense of his eyes skipping around my body, looking for proof of injury. Gently, he added, "What exactly did they do to you?"

I didn't want to talk about it. Pain was something secret and shameful in my eyes, and even if I wanted him to care, I wasn't comfortable showing him the bruises. Instead I made sure the sleeves of my robe were tugged down to my wrists and moved to unlock the door, ignoring his question.

"Let's just get this over with."

The muffled snap of the doors behind me was far less unsettling now that I was no longer alone.

Last time, I'd frozen upon stepping foot in here, paralyzed by the weight of my wrongdoing. I'd needed the relic to prod me along. Now it was tucked away in my mind, chuckling to itself, giving me the space my thoughts screamed for. It was just me and Rigo. And I refused to show him any more weakness on my own.

I forced myself into the main hallway, candle thrust forward as a light against the dark. The demon followed behind me with slow, shuffling steps and the ragged breath of someone recovering from a long convalescence. We paused as we came to the common area with the old fireplace and dilapidated furniture.

"This place. . .hasn't changed at all," Rigo remarked. "This section, the other area we walked through—it's as if it were frozen in time. What do you nuns have against a little interior design?"

I was ready to glare at him. Then I noticed the easy way he moved around the hulking shapes of the furniture.

"Can you see? In this low lighting?"

"Yes."

"Then guide me through this room. Even with this candle, I'm half blind."

Rigo sighed and muttered, "Glad to know I've been reduced to a mere guide."

"Consider it a promotion from lookout."

With a small laugh, he did as I requested. He cut a slow path across the common area, glancing only briefly at the circular scorch mark on the floor. I supposed demons were used to such things.

"My first trip here, I investigated that hallway," I said, pointing, "And found little of note, save for a room burned beyond recognition. I'd like to explore the hallway on the left this time."

"All right."

Once we'd reached the mouth of the unexplored hallway, Rigo leaned against the wall once more. "I'll wait here."

I nodded. He was exhausted, that much was obvious, but I'd let him pretend to loiter on excuse of keeping watch.

"Let me know if you hear or see anything," I said, and slipped away into the dark.

With the demon's backup, I felt less on edge. My focus seemed stronger and less prone to dissolving in the face of sudden skittering panic. Time seemed to slow within the darkened hallways as I drifted from room to room at my leisure, looking for anything that seemed out of place. This side, like the other, was composed mostly of acolytes' rooms, though none of them were as thoroughly decimated as that other one. At the end of the hall, I swung the candle over one last room, expecting it to look the same as all the others. Instead, it was an office.

Possibility sparked in my chest. I went in.

Dust-caked and laced with cobwebs, the office had clearly once belonged to a superior nun, perhaps the assistant to the abbess or even the abbess herself. I had no idea how differently things might have been arranged all those years ago. The desk that squatted in the center of the room was larger and grander than the one in Sister Colette's office, made of heavy wood that emitted a dull *thunk* when I rapped my knuckles over it. Bookshelves lined three of the four walls—both a blessing and a curse. Something could be hidden among these shelves, but there was no way for me to sort through it all in the space of a single night. And I wasn't sure how many more times I could risk venturing into this forbidden wing.

"Relic," I said. "Help me. Where should I direct my focus?"

It roused with a stretch and a sensation like the fluttering of great wings. With a smirk in its voice, it said, OH, YOU'RE TALKING TO ME AGAIN?

An exasperated sigh fell from my lips. "I'm sorry, all right? I shouldn't have cursed at you. It won't happen again. And no, I don't want to talk about it. Will you please help me?"

It made a gesture like a shrugging of its shoulders and took in the room around us.

UGH, THIS MISERABLE PLACE.

"I need your help. The recertification records from the missing folder, if they haven't been destroyed, are likely to be here. But I don't have time to search each book on each shelf."

HMMM. The relic borrowed my vision and started to look around. I felt part of its attention, its consciousness, lurch toward the demon waiting at the end of the hallway. I had the sense of the relic curling its lip in disgust. HAVE YOU TASKED THE DEMON WITH KEEPING WATCH?

"Yes. . ." I responded, frowning. "It was your idea."

OH, YES. THAT'S CORRECT.

It didn't remember? I had never given much thought as to what the relic did when it went inactive. Now I found myself wondering. To what extent did it have the capacity for memory? There seemed to be no rhyme or reason to the patter of its remembrance. I had more questions, but I kept quiet, not wanting to distract it.

After a few minutes, it reported, ONLY THE MIDDLE SHELF IS UN-USUAL. THE OTHERS ARE JUST REGULAR BOOKS, BUT ON THE MIDDLE SHELF, I SENSE SOME PARCHMENT. I SUGGEST STARTING THERE.

"Thank you."

I set out in search of the recertification records. The shelves were stuffed full of all manner of books: withered scripture texts, books in Old Demonic, historical treatises on the abbey and the Islands. I had half a mind to stuff a few of the more interesting ones into my robe to peruse at my leisure later. But I forced myself to look for any book that had parchment sticking out of it. Several of these were false alarms—ancient letters in the old nuns' famously terrible script or copies of particularly accomplished student essays. Still, nothing like what I really sought. Then, halfway down the tall shelf, an oddly sized book caught my eye. It was easily half as large as most of the others, and lacked the thick ornate leather spine marking it as an academic text. On instinct, I reached for it.

It came loose with a cloud of dust, which I quickly waved away. The front cover, which held no title, was made of simple black leather, and held a litany of burn marks, like someone had dropped it briefly into a fireplace. I flipped it open to the first page. The interior appeared intact. Rich, creamy parchment lay below the title, written in a careful and neat hand.

THE TRUE DIARY OF NOVICE ROSALIND, YEAR 537–542

A diary wasn't much use to me, but the years. . .the year of the missing recertification records was included in the range listed. What if this Rosalind person knew something, anything, that could help me find those records?

I turned to the next page.

—Diary, today was as dull as ever. Morning prayers, break-
fast, then hours spent in the garden beneath the hot sun. I find
myself lamenting my choice of gardening over brewing. At
least with brewing, I'd be indoors, away from this wretched
island heat.
I had my gloved hands in the dirt for what felt like hours.
Pruning, weeding, trying not to sneeze at all the pollen
wafting through the air. Finally, before lunch, I took that
morning's haul into the laboratory to hand over to the next
available brewer. Of course, it was Ratface. She snatched the
plants from my arms with hardly a glance and tossed them
onto her work table. I could see already that she'd bruised
the delicate bulbs of the foxglove I'd been cultivating for two
years. But before I could say anything, the lunch bell rang,
and she darted for the refectory with all the rest, no doubt
hoping to get first choice of meals—

Rosalind's daily life was eerily similar to my own. I had no doubt
she had been an acolyte, a novice, and then an avowed Sister, just
like me. Only, why had she kept a diary? And why had she not
maintained possession of that diary, leaving it instead tucked into
a bookshelf in the abbey's forbidden North Wing?

WHAT IS THAT? the relic said suddenly, with a jolt. It had been
using its expanded consciousness to do another sweep of the other
shelves.

"What?"

THE BOOK IN YOUR HANDS.

I opened it again, wincing as the relic used my eyes a little too forcefully. "It appears to be a diary."

Some unrecognizable emotion bubbled up in me from the relic. Just as quickly as it came, it faded neatly away, leaving me to wonder if I'd imagined it.

THAT HARDLY SEEMS WORTH YOUR TIME, SISTER. A pause. YOU STILL HAVE SEVERAL MORE SHELVES CLOSER TO THE GROUND TO SEARCH. I WOULD KEEP LOOKING FOR THOSE RECERTIFICATION RECORDS.

I nodded, agreeing, though I tucked the diary into my robes all the same. The relic said nothing.

The remaining sections of the middle shelf turned up nothing more of note. I had just turned to the shelf on the right, ready to begin my search anew, when exhaustion hit me like an errant wave and I stumbled.

SISTER, YOU'RE EXHAUSTED. AND IT'S NEARLY DAWN.

The relic's reminder sent a bolt of reality and fear through me. I had indeed spent longer here than intended. Who knew if Rigo had even lingered? I wouldn't have been surprised if he'd simply slipped away, leaving me to fend for myself.

I needed to leave this wing before the abbey's other inhabitants started to wake up.

Taking a quick mental note of where I'd left off on the shelf, I made my way back down the hallway to where I'd left the demon. He had not, in fact, fled, but instead lay slumped against the lower half of the wall, looking barely awake. His eyes flickered up to me.

"Did you find anything?"

I took out the diary. "Perhaps. There was a bookshelf full of things that could prove useful. But I didn't get through searching the entire thing."

Rigo quickly stood, as if he didn't want me to see him in such a weakened state for too long.

"What is that?"

"A diary of some sort." He stepped closer as I opened it to the first page. His arm pressed into mine as he peered down to read. At the touch of his skin, a shiver went through me. Goosebumps rose on my skin in a polite riot of desire. To distract myself, I said, "Can you read Moriahan?"

He shot me a look. My surprised tone had offended him. "Can *you* read Old Demonic?

"I can, actually. We're all trained—"

"Look at this." He pointed to the year.

"That's exactly why I grabbed it. Maybe it's not a direct answer, but if this woman was around during that time period, her diary might shed some light on that year's recertification, whose records I still can't seem to find. And—" I dropped my voice, realizing all of a sudden that the relic had faded away as soon as I'd gone near Rigo again, "—the relic seems wary of it. I'm not sure what that means."

Rigo's brow furrowed. He studied me thoroughly, as if searching for evidence of the relic's presence behind my eyes. The weight of his stare pinned me to the spot. I had never been this close to him without bars between us.

"Where is it now?"

Pretending I wasn't affected by his presence, I shrugged. "Sometimes it just. . .goes away."

"And it can't hear us when it's away? Or hear your thoughts?" he asked, frown deepening.

"I don't think so. Earlier, it helped me look through the bookshelves, and seemed surprised you were here keeping watch. But it's the one who encouraged me to bring you along in the first place, and it was here when we first entered the wing. Sometimes it doesn't remember things quite well."

"That's. . .strange."

And it was. It was the first real break I'd encountered throughout this entire effort, and the relic didn't seem to care, or think this was worth my attention. Rigo, on the other hand, was making a concerted effort to repair my trust, even as it cost him physical strength to exert himself like this.

Why had the relic chosen now to shy away, while Rigo was fully on board?

I did trust the relic, but the fact that it seemed so uninterested in a diary that struck me as very important had raised my suspicions. The relic's reluctance to engage with the diary had me almost certain I was on to something, though I couldn't quite identify what.

The next time we were alone, I would have to ask it. And refuse to allow it to slither away from my pointed questioning.

If both the relic and the demon were to be my allies, I needed to have full confidence in them both. Right now, despite his major omission, I trusted Rigo more.

He was still watching me. I got the sense he had further thoughts on the matter, but instead of voicing them, he refocused on the diary.

"So we read it."

Did Rigo really trust me to hand over the relic as payment after all of this, as promised? Or was he playing me like I was playing him? And did I trust myself to break my promise to him, knowing what I did now of his situation?

All I knew for sure was that this diary could be the thing I had been looking for all along. The key to bringing down the abbey, and getting back the award I was owed.

"We read it," I agreed. "And soon."

Chapter Seventeen

"Please do not repeat this, my dear Sister, but—has it occurred to you that something may be quite wrong with our Abbess?"

—An unsent letter from the office of Sister Colette, Assistant to the Abbess of Moriah Abbey, in the Year 563 of Order Record

I crashed in my room just before dawn, sleeping for maybe thirty minutes, before waking reluctantly for morning prayers. It wasn't enough sleep, not after being up all night, and I felt it. Fatigue pulled my eyelids and limbs toward the ground and left my mind a mess of scattered focus. But what choice did I have?

After prayers and breakfast, I returned to my room—and froze in the doorway as panic spilled through me.

The demon sat on my bedroom floor with the diary in his lap, looking just as exhausted as I was.

I yanked my door shut and advanced on him.

"What are you doing here?" I demanded.

He looked up. "You left me here," he said slowly. "Last night, remember?" When I only looked at him with increasing panic, he sighed. "No, you don't. I'm not surprised. You were all but dead on your feet."

"Explain," I barked, crossing my arms over my chest.

"You fell asleep before taking me back to my cell. I thought it unwise to go wandering the halls on my own during the daytime, so I remained here. Slept on the floor."

I stared at him as this sunk in. Had one sleepless night truly rendered me so careless? I'd been so focused on maintaining my usual routine this morning, I hadn't even noticed him in my room. Sharp pinpricks of alarm needled me, though I tried to hide it.

Merciful Mother, I was so tired. I couldn't believe I'd forgotten to return him to the basement. He'd slept next to my bed, and I'd been so exhausted and distracted I hadn't even noticed. I was surprised the relic hadn't woken me cringing with disgust. Why hadn't it said anything to me? Had it also not noticed? Whatever the reason, this couldn't happen again.

What if Rigo decided he no longer needed me to clear his name and escape the abbey? There was nothing stopping him from taking the relic from me by force and fleeing. I shuddered, pushing all of this aside.

Rigo's head tilted sideways, studying my reaction. "Is that a problem?"

"No," I snapped. "No problem. I just forgot." I inclined my head at the diary, eager to move away from my own glaring lack of observation. "Have you found anything interesting?"

Diary in hand, Rigo stood and stepped closer, holding a page open with his thumb. "Not particularly. The writer appears to have been a nun here like yourself. The first few entries detail her very boring personal life. But the years of the diary's range include the year of the missing recertification. I think it's possible she wrote about something that might help us."

"That's what I was thinking, too."

Nodding, I took the diary and flipped through the pages he indicated, quickly scanning their contents. His hand brushed mine, and again his proximity rioted through me. The mere fact of him standing in my room like this felt forbidden in a way that set me on edge—and yet, I didn't want him to leave. I *liked* having him here, in my space. The urge to reach for him built in me, a strong yearning with the momentum of a rogue wave.

A glance up revealed he was watching me patiently with an unreadable expression. Warm sunlight through my window cast its rays across his dark hair and brought out all sorts of minor hues and undertones. What I'd thought was black was actually a kaleidoscope of darkest brown, and the effect was stunning. *He* was stunning. I'd never seen him in the light like this. The shadows, I realized, did not do him justice.

Unbidden, my gaze fell to his lips, plump and medium-brown.

I had never kissed anyone before. And the realization that I wanted to, right now, sprawled through me like the sweet warmth of hot tea with honey.

Instead, I dropped my eyes to the page once more, glued them there, while my heart thudded.

Shoving my pesky feelings aside, I returned my efforts to the diary. Something about the name Rosalind felt familiar, only I couldn't place where I'd heard it before.

"Does she ever state her full name?" I asked.

If Rigo had noticed the way I'd been ogling him, he didn't show it.

"Yes, it's Rosalind Carey."

Suddenly, my focus sharpened. Rosalind. Rosalind *Carey*.

"That's the Prioress," I whispered.

"The *who*?"

"Our highest-ranking Order nun. She's in charge of abbey re-certification. She's—" I broke off, the significance of this discovery rendering me temporarily stunned. "She's traveling here right now."

Rigo's expression smeared into grim confusion. "That's one hell of a coincidence. She's on her way here to recertify the place, and we just found her diary?"

It wasn't a mere coincidence. Couldn't be. I could not think of a single reason the Prioress might have left an old diary in Moriah Abbey's forbidden North Wing, unless she'd simply forgotten it.

Or, unless she had something to hide.

The demon and I stared at each other. "So—the recertification records from Year 542 are missing. We go looking for the records in the forbidden wing and find instead a diary from that time, a diary that belongs to the woman who now leads your Order." He was silent for a long moment before speaking again. "Do you think she had something to do with the missing records?"

Dread had settled its claws deep into my chest. I nodded, feeling sick. All this time, I'd been bent on revenge, looking for something

I could use to invalidate this year's recertification. It had never occurred to me that the evidence I sought might come in the form of the Prioress's diary from one seemingly ill-fated recertification twenty years ago.

"Nothing else makes sense," I added. "Whatever's in that diary, she left it behind for a reason. And judging from where it was, she never meant for anyone to find it."

Bells chimed throughout the abbey, then, signaling the start of the next class period for the younger acolytes. It was enough to jolt me back to reality. I'd released the demon prisoner from his cell and accidentally left him in my room all night. I'd gone snooping in the forbidden North Wing twice and now held Prioress Rosalind's novice diary in my hands. I felt tantalizingly close to real answers, poised on a knife's edge of everything unraveling around me.

Appearances, I reminded myself. *Keep up appearances.*

I was supposed to be in the archives. No one had come looking for me as of yet, but if they did, and I wasn't there? And they came to my room and found the demon inside?

"I'll return you to your cell tonight," I told him, ignoring the rush of sudden heat that swept my cheeks. "I've got to get down to the archives before anyone notices I'm late. Keep reading."

"All right," Rigo agreed.

I made to leave, then paused. "Can I trust you to stay here and not cause any trouble? And stay out of sight if anyone comes?"

He quirked a crooked grin at me. "There's no trouble for me to cause. And only you can decide your own level of trust toward me."

Infuriating. Rolling my eyes, I left.

I spent the rest of the day in the archives, mindlessly shuffling papers around. I should've kept looking, just in case the Prioress's diary turned out to be a total wash, but little sleep and a lot of stress kept my focus slipping through my fingers. Somehow, the hours passed. After dinner, as the sun began to set, I swiped a handful of biscuits and a container of pineapple juice for the demon, and made to return to my room.

As I climbed the stairs, I felt a shuffling inside my head. The relic roused itself and stretched like a cat after a lazy nap in the sunshine.

YOU'RE NOT OFF TO KEEP READING FROM THAT HORRID OLD DIARY, ARE YOU?

The condescension in its tone, coupled with how long it had been gone, made me bristle. "**And who are you to care?**" I snapped mentally. "**You keep disappearing whenever you so please. Excuse me for finding something that seems worthwhile and chasing it. You don't think the diary is worth my time? Fine. Then stick around and help me find something that is.**"

The relic's shock filtered through me. I knew almost immediately that I'd hurt its feelings. I sensed it backing away inside me in a quiet sort of outrage.

THAT WAS QUITE UNKIND, SISTER. It spoke in a detached, wounded sort of tone, like it *wanted* me to know I'd upset it, but only just a little. VERY WELL. I'LL LEAVE YOU TO YOUR EFFORTS.

"**Wait, that's not what I—**"

But it was already gone. It hadn't tucked itself away entirely—if I really poked and prodded, I could feel it huddle in the corner of my mind like an affronted child. But it seemed it absolutely did not want to speak to me at the moment.

Sighing, I shook off my frustration and kept on to my room. I could try to apologize later.

When I entered, Rigo looked up from the floor, almost exactly where I'd left him.

"I brought you these. I'm sorry I couldn't sneak away more. Once you're back in the cell, I can go and request another tray of food like before. I'll try not to forget this time."

Rigo said nothing, just took the biscuits and juice and wolfed them down. Then he thrust the diary at me as he wiped crumbs from his mouth.

"Here, look." He'd found a bit of pencil and made a bunch of markings throughout the first chunk of the diary. He continued, "The whole first bit is just Rosalind detailing a never-ending conflict she has with another novitiate."

"Who?" I asked, frowning.

"She calls her 'Ratface,'" he said with a shrug. "I guess she didn't want to risk badmouthing the girl by name."

I perched on my bed and flipped through the bits he'd marked.

—*Ratface was in fine form today, as usual. On our way to breakfast after morning prayers, she tripped me, pretended not to notice, then laughed at me with her friends as I only barely righted myself. It was just luck that kept me from falling on my face. I still don't understand why she hates me so—we were such close friends as girls, all the way up to last year. When the Sisters sat us down to discuss puberty, I knew things would change, but I never imagined this. I thought Ratface and I would always be best friends, close as always.*

A few pages later, Rigo had circled:

—It truly baffles me how suddenly and thoroughly the other novitiates have snubbed me, and for no concrete reason I can discern. Mother forgive my vanity, but I am prettier and more likable than Ratface—who is quiet and bookish and smart—and yet our peers flock to her. What does she have to offer that I do not?

Rosalind's diary went on and on in a similar fashion. Each entry was a long, depressing treatise in her bitter feelings toward this girl she called Ratface, whose very existence seemed to cause her offense. I doubted Ratface was relevant, but I didn't want to skip anything. We needed to scour the entire diary if we had a shot at untangling this mystery that had suddenly sprung up before us.

By the time true night fell, I could hardly keep my eyes open.

"Sister, you need to sleep," the demon remarked. "It's dark enough now. I think we can risk you escorting me back to my cell."

Fighting a yawn, I studied him. We were both seated on the floor next to each other with my bed at our backs. Razor-edged fatigue had bled away my already low reserves of politeness. "Why haven't you tried to run away?" I wondered. "You've been free from the cell for nearly twenty-four hours. I must admit I'm a little shocked that you've stayed at my side and that you're requesting to return."

He blinked. "My escape from this place is meaningless if I cannot clear my name. So I'm with you, Sister, until we find the truth we both need."

"Annette," I corrected.

Rigo offered me a tentative, but true, smile. "Annette."

The way my name fell from his lips felt entirely different when we were seated this close, half asleep on the floor of my bedroom. Warmth bloomed in my middle. Selfishly, I considered asking him to stay the night here again if only for the comfort his presence brought me.

But the risk of discovery was too great.

I tried not to think about his dirt-damned lips as I sleepily escorted him back to his basement cell without incident, and promised to return in the morning. I intended to keep reading the diary, which he'd left with me so as not to arouse suspicion should someone find it in his cell, but as soon as I returned to my room, I nearly collapsed. The relic all but forced my barely awake body beneath the sheets. Before I could think about asking it where it had been all day, I fell asleep, so quickly I didn't even remember to blow out my candle.

At the next day's morning prayers, I felt marginally better with a solid night's sleep beneath my belt. Prayers drew to a close, and I readied myself to grab a brief breakfast on my way down to the archives. Rosalind's diary wasn't very long, and with enough discipline, I suspected Rigo and I could read through it all today.

But instead of Sister Colette stepping away and leading us to breakfast, Mother Vanessa took her place at the lectern.

I, along with every other acolyte, novitiate, and avowed Sister in the chapel, froze. Some were half out of their seats, others nearly at the door. A murmur of confusion fluttered through the space.

"My apologies for the disruption," said Mother Vanessa. "I have a matter I'd like to briefly discuss with you all. Please take your seats."

The murmurs only intensified. I was wildly confused, and relieved to see similar expressions on the faces of those around me.

Mother Vanessa had been keeping her distance from our daily routines for so long, I'd nearly forgotten her. As I looked at her now, I saw only the cruel way she'd punished me with a cane to my forearms for being caught in the North Wing. I doubted I would ever again see her as the kind and caring abbess who'd raised me.

Mother Vanessa gripped the sides of the lectern, her expression grave despite her polite tone. "It pains me to say this, but it has come to my attention that a theft has occurred within our sacred walls." Everyone exploded into chatter, which immediately trailed off at a stern look from the abbess. "As the Mother's servants, you should all know that such petty crimes and behavior are beneath you. Nonetheless, an item was stolen, and that simply will not do. Whoever recently pilfered this item from the North Wing must return it and identify themselves, or I will unfortunately be forced to enact an abbey-wide punishment as deterrent against future misdeeds."

My pulse slowed, then resumed in double time. A cold chill spread through me. Distantly, I felt the relic's concern within me, but I was still frozen to the spot with a grim sort of horror.

How did she *know*?

"Abbess?" said a small voice near the front. "May I ask what item was stolen?"

Mother Vanessa's expression softened as she trained her gaze on the young acolyte who'd asked. "I'm afraid I'm not at liberty to say." This only inspired a fresh but quiet wave of worried conversation. As Mother Vanessa returned her attention to the crowd at large, I felt, for the briefest of moments, her focus linger on *me*. The memory of the pain she'd wrought on my arms reared up as quick and scalding as a splatter of oil in a hot pan, bringing with it a flash of clarity.

Unless anyone else was sneaking around the abbey at night, I was the last person to be caught out after hours. The last to be punished for unauthorized access to the North Wing. Which made me the top suspect, if not the only one.

I swallowed.

"You have twenty-four hours," the abbess informed us. "That will be all. Please proceed with your day."

I was up and out of there the instant she dismissed us. I forgot breakfast. Forgot anything, really, but the Prioress's diary burning a hole in my robe pocket, and the urgency Mother Vanessa's announcement had stoked in me.

In the same way I knew the North Wing was significant because of Mother Vanessa's punishment, I was now convinced the diary was, too. Otherwise, why all the fuss? There was something in that stupid book that I could use, I had only to find it. This echoed on a loop in my mind as I raced down to the archival room, to the demon's cell.

"We have a problem," I announced.

Rigo stood up and listened intently as I described what had just happened. His look of alarm mirrored my own, the panic that had my heart clanging around out of control.

"How could she possibly have known?" he wondered.

"I'm not sure." My voice had started to shake. "I checked that she was sleeping before we entered the wing that night we found the diary. So she must have someone else watching, or another way to tell if anyone has stepped foot inside."

"And you said she caught you the first time?" he clarified. I nodded. "So what was *she* doing there?"

I hadn't considered that before, but it didn't feel relevant. "It doesn't matter. I have to return the diary within twenty-four hours or she's going to punish everyone."

The mere thought made me shudder. If she'd wrought such violence on me for simply being caught in the North Wing, I didn't want to think about what she'd do as punishment for stealing from it. And I could not allow the others to suffer for my own disobedience.

The diary had to go.

And the faster we pushed through it and found what we needed, the faster I could be done with Rigo. I could stop pretending not to notice the unique beauty of his features. I could get the relic out of my head, stop worrying about where it disappeared to for long stretches of time inside my mind. I could bring everything back to normal.

Time was no longer a luxury. It was now or never.

"Right, then," said Rigo. "I hope you've slept. It's time to get reading."

Chapter Eighteen

"Diary, please forgive me. What lies between these pages is damning enough to have me expelled from the Order entirely—so naturally, I tried to destroy you. I was never quite as good with poisons as Ratface, but I tried nonetheless to prepare a poison brew that might melt your paper. Only, it failed. The bizarre concoction unfortunately seems to have left you fireproof, as is evidenced by how many attempts I've made to burn you. I shall have to leave you somewhere unseen and hope that no one ever finds you."

—The true diary of Novice Rosalind, Year 537–542

I was far from prepared for another night of little sleep so soon after the last, but Mother Vanessa's search for the North Wing thief had left me with very little choice. We'd spent the rest of the day reading, but it wasn't enough. More of the diary remained, and our time was running short.

Having pilfered a pot of strong tea and a few mugs from the kitchen, I settled in and prepared to spend the night in the archives with the demon.

"You brought tea?" Rigo asked, peering through the bars of his cell.

"Yes. How else would you expect me to stay awake?"

He snorted. "Sheer force of stubborn will, like you did the other night."

"I'm afraid my 'stubborn will' can only do so much," I retorted. "Now, are you going to mock me all night, or can we commence reading?"

Sarcastically, he waved a hand as if to say, *you may proceed.*

I turned away from him, rolled my eyes, and sat down with my back against his cell door, placing a lit candlestick at my side. Though he'd already proven to me that he wasn't a flight risk—that we were twined together in our quest for the truth—I still felt wary about leaving him unrestrained without a good reason. I had needed his physical presence and assistance to keep watch while I searched the North Wing the other night. But if all we were doing was reading Rosalind's diary, I had no reason to allow him out of his cell now, and if he had any objections on the matter, he didn't voice them.

I heard him simply slide down on his side of the door with a faint rustling that told me he'd mirrored my position. If I, in perfect health, was still recovering from that recent night's nonexistent sleep, he had to be struggling.

Without fanfare, I opened the diary to the last marked page and continued to read.

—Diary, I really and truly believe today marked the end of the fragile friendship remaining between Ratface and I.

I am so angry and humiliated. I am shaking as I write this. Earlier this afternoon, I was deep into a study session in the scriptorium when I suddenly felt a rush of warm wetness between my legs. When I investigated, I found blood. My menstrual cycle had arrived for the very first time. The mere fact of it wasn't shocking at all—I am fourteen and expected this, it had to happen eventually—but I found myself surprised by its sudden arrival. Sister Letitia told us that our cycles might often be preceded by fatigue, intense cramping, and lightheadedness, so those were the symptoms I anticipated, and to receive no warning was immensely bewildering.

I stood from my desk in a sudden panic. This was a natural bodily function, but still, I hardly wanted to stain a scriptorium seat with my blood! As luck would have it, the only other person in the room with me was Ratface. I'd hoped to sneak out unnoticed. As soon as I stood, however, she looked over. For some reason, feeling small and vulnerable, and strangely teary, I blurted out, "I've just started my first cycle."

Ratface's eyes widened. "Your very first?"

I nodded. I could feel the blood beginning to drip down my inner thigh.

Ratface stood. For once, she looked like my old friend, and gestured for me to follow her. "Come. We'll go to the restroom and I'll show you where we keep the rags."

As children, she had always been the problem solver, the

mediator. She was the one I and others turned to when
something odd happened and we were unsure how to react.
We found ourselves slipping naturally back into those roles
now. I squeezed my legs shut tight and followed her into the
hallway.

Halfway to the nearest restroom, a group of novices our age
turned the corner—the girls for whom Ratface had so easily
discarded me.

"Oh, hello!" one of them called to her. Noticing me, the girl
screwed up her face. "What are you doing with Rosalind?"
I'll admit that what happened next was my fault. I panicked,
and started walking quickly toward the bathroom. The
novices erupted in a squeal of screaming laughter as I did.
"Rosalind's got blood all over the back of her robes!"
"Dirty, dirty Rosalind! Can't even keep her cycle under
control!"

Face flaming, I all but dove into the bathroom. Sure enough,
when I looked in the mirror, the back of my robes were
stained with blood. How had I not noticed or felt that? My
eyes brimmed with tears. They spilled over, blurring my
vision, as I hastily rustled around in the bathroom closet for
spare robes and the rags Ratface had mentioned. I cleaned
myself up, changed robes, and tucked a rag between my legs
to stem the flow. I was in there long enough that I was sure
they had to have gone, but when I emerged, they were all
still there, waiting for me in the hallway.

One of the girls pitched her voice high like talking to an
infant. "All clean now? No more blood on your robes?"
The others dissolved into laughter. I glanced at Ratface, who

didn't laugh, but neither did she stop them. A fresh wave of
tears flooded my eyes as I jabbed a finger at her, suddenly
realizing how convenient this was.
"You did this," I barked. "You knew they would be here. You
wanted to humiliate me."
Ratface recoiled. "Rosalind, no, I wouldn't—I was trying to
help you—"
"Why should I believe that? You've been nothing but cruel
to me this whole year."
Someone mocked my last sentence in a shrill tone, and that
was the final straw. I ran back to my room and spent the rest
of the day crying in bed.
I despise her, Diary. I really do.

"I thought you nuns were supposed to be kind," Rigo remarked, once I'd finished reading the entry. "Those girls sound like monsters."

And they were still monsters, a lot of them. "Intense faith doesn't necessarily make someone a good person," I said, sighing, and read on.

—Diary, I'm afraid things have become much worse since I
last wrote. Ratface's crew of misery seems to have united
under a singular purpose—to make my existence within
these abbey walls a living hell. They point, laugh, and mock
me whenever I am in sight, never failing to remind me of the
humiliation of my bloody-backed robes. They torment me
as we walk the halls between lessons, as it is the only time
we are not often supervised by the instructing Sisters. At

every possible opportunity, they snub me, refusing to allow me to be part of their working group during lessons. And their disdain for me is rubbing off onto some of the other novitiates who used to not take issue with me. The other night at dinner, I tried four separate tables before finding one that would allow me to sit, and even then, it was mostly abandoned. Ratface herself seems to have backed off me, but she makes no effort to corral her followers, and I often catch the twitch of a smile on her lips, like she's trying not to laugh as they ridicule me.

I don't understand what I possibly could've done to deserve this. Friendships end, I know that, but what did I do to bring on such relentless humiliation? I would never allow someone I once considered a friend to be treated in this way, and I confess I am appalled by Ratface's indifference. I hoped that somewhere, deep down, she might find it within herself to put a stop to this harassment. I now realize that even if she wanted to, standing up for me would cost her this precious social status she's suddenly gained.

Pity to me for being the fool.

I was quiet for a long while after that entry, feeling unsettled to my core. Rosalind's struggles were not unfamiliar to me. I, too, had found myself ostracized for no reason I could discern, and struggled to find my footing within the abbey's social hierarchy. While I had not been bullied quite as severely as she had, her feelings could easily have been my own.

"Annette?" Rigo's voice crept into my thoughts. "Is everything all right?"

"Yes. I just. . ." I saw far too much of myself in these pages, and I didn't like it. "Never mind."

A silent moment passed, during which I heard only his steady breathing on the other side of the door and the soft plop of wax dripping onto my candlestick. Before beginning to read, I hadn't felt so conscious of his presence. Now this felt. . .different. Both forbidden and comforting in a tantalizing way. Being this close to him and hearing his voice, but not seeing his face, engendered a certain degree of intimacy. And without really knowing why, I found myself speaking again.

"I'll admit that I can see myself in Rosalind's struggles. Her ostracization. Her yearning to belong. The other acolytes. . .don't care for me all that much." I thought back to the too-accurate observation he'd made of me on the day when he'd finally convinced me he was worth my attention. "You were correct in what you said before: I enjoy solitude. But my solitude isn't always by choice."

I would let him read into that what he wished. I wasn't going to tally all my miseries for him. We still had much more of the diary to get through, and sinking into despair would only cost me my focus.

The demon spoke finally. "For what it's worth," he said, speaking slowly, in a voice that made me feel like he'd reached a warm hand through the door to hold mine, "I don't think you're all that terrible."

An unexpected kindness. His words tugged at the heart space where I imagined normal people might experience their emotions.

Don't you feel anything? Another novitiate had once asked me. The memory came back in a brief, sickening flash. A gaggle of preteens in the gardens, me among them, all of us gawking over a dead bird. Most of the others had been crying, and I also felt upset, but all that made its way to the surface was a deep frown, which seemed to disturb the others. *How can you be so heartless?*

I did not have the words, then, to express that I *did* feel things—quite deeply and profoundly—it was just the way that I expressed myself, or *didn't*, that was different enough to make others uncomfortable.

I didn't know how to respond to Rigo's kindness. So I didn't. Instead, I turned to the diary's next entry.

—Diary, you won't believe this, but I've made a new friend! With the other girls determined to ignore me, I've spent the last few weeks diving deep into my studies. I chose earlier this year to specialize in translation from Old Demonic, and since then, my knowledge about demonkind has grown by leaps and bounds. In my search for an old reference text, I stumbled upon a demonic relic who exhibits a shocking kindness. I know this may concern you, but trust me when I say that I believe in this demonic spirit wholeheartedly. We've spent hours talking. He knows me better than I know myself. He's sensed how unhappy I am, and provided a much-needed source of companionship during this difficult time. Do not worry—I have my guard up, and I am keeping my wits about me. But I am not about to forsake a new friend simply due to their demonic nature.

So Rosalind had had a relic, too, and spoken to it much like I did with mine. Only, I couldn't help feeling disturbed by her easy acceptance of the demonic. I'd taken great pains to ensure the relic

I'd found was of maternal nature, not demonic, while Rosalind had seemingly been so desperate for friendship she'd embraced the antithesis of our very beliefs.

With a jolt, thinking of the demon sitting in the cell behind me, I realized—so had I.

Rigo didn't comment on this entry, though I felt his attention sharpen on me like a physical thing. I read on. This next entry started off much the same, but soon took on a decidedly darker tone.

> —*Diary, my relic has presented me with a thrilling idea. I've told it all about Ratface and how she is the root of my problems here at the abbey. My relic has informed me of its inherent power. When I expressed a desire to see Ratface permanently disappear, the relic claimed it could accomplish this. First, I must help it gather ingredients to perform a dark ritual. If I can complete the ritual correctly, this will free my sweet, cherished spirit from its reliquary prison, and allow him to roam our world at his leisure. He has promised me that, upon occasion of his freedom, Ratface will be his first target.*
>
> *I cannot wait until I no longer have to see her face.*

I let the diary fall into my lap in shock. Rosalind had stated this all so casually, but—

"Is she saying that she tried to have this other girl *killed?*" Rigo asked.

My hands were shaking. "Yes," I answered, "I had come to the same conclusion."

He swore, low and violent. "So her relic wants to be free, and promises it'll get rid of her 'problem.' And she wants this girl gone so badly she's willing to set a strange demonic spirit loose on the world to do it?"

"She was desperate," I said, feeling strangely defensive. "You heard the previous entries. I won't condone killing. But her desperation? I understand it."

"I'm—I'm not trying to make a value statement. Just trying to understand. I want to know more about this ritual."

His mention of rituals slid neatly into place among the scattered puzzle pieces inside my mind.

"You said you thought your brother was working toward some sort of ritual, didn't you?"

"Yes," he confirmed, sounding both weary and apprehensive.

"Do you think the two are related?"

"I am really hoping they aren't."

Picking up the diary again, I noticed that there were only a few written pages left. I relayed as much to Rigo, frowning, but he only urged me onward.

—Diary, I've ruined everything. I failed so miserably. And now everything is upside down.
Where do I begin? I spent days gathering the items the relic needed for the ritual. I sourced various locations where we might perform it, and he rejected them all. Finally, one night I was returning to my bedroom in the new North Wing, and the relic stirred. He said he felt drawn to the hearth in the common area, and felt that would be a perfect place to try the ritual. So over the next few days, I slowly snuck ingredients

to the area, hiding them inside the rarely used hearth. When it came time for the ritual, I followed my relic's instructions exactly. I hoped to see him soon freed.

But something went wrong. I still haven't figured out what. Before I knew it, a fire had started, and quickly consumed the wing. Being new, not many acolytes had moved over yet, but there were a handful in their rooms, and their screaming echoed in my ears as I fled. The relic's presence vanished. I am distraught. I haven't heard its voice since. We found out during morning prayers today that five young postulants and one Sister were killed in the fire, with many injured, Ratface among them. Of course, she was one of the few who delayed their own evacuation to try and help the others.

It was all my fault, and I don't even have anything to show for it.

I thought the relic's ritual would end with my spirit friend free, Ratface out of my sight, and happiness returning to my miserable life. Instead, I've got to attend a memorial service, and witness the postulants' and Sister's grieving parents, all while grieving my own loss of my spirit friend. I have to watch everyone fawn over Ratface for her heroic efforts. Did you know she's been asked to give a testimony about the event before the Order Council? How ironic is it that after all this, she's now more popular than ever.

I cannot stop crying. I've been forced to move back into my old rooms as the new wing is no longer fit for living. I am right back where I started, with a heart full of hatred for my onetime best friend and an aching loneliness for the life I could've had.

I think this will be my last entry for a while. It's simply too painful to revisit my misfortune so often.
But rest assured, one day, I will have my revenge. One day, Ratface will get what she deserves.

One last line was written at the bottom of the page, scribbled over and crossed out so many times it was barely legible. I squinted, running my finger along the rage-indented parchment.

One day, Vanessa Coulis, I will take everything you love and cherish and watch it burn to dust the way you did to me.

Gasping, the diary fell from my hands again.

"What? What is it?"

I had yet to read the last line to Rigo. I did now, nearly tripping over the words.

"Vanessa Coulis?" he repeated. "Is that name familiar to you?"

It was familiar. So familiar it hurt.

"Vanessa Coulis is our abbess," I told him, in a soft, shaken voice. "Mother Vanessa."

I dropped my head into my hands. A wave of dizziness swept over me, my thoughts racing to piece it all together.

The miserable bully Prioress Rosalind had written about had been Mother Vanessa all along. Mother Vanessa had destroyed their friendship, left Rosalind companionless, and driven her to the desperation of finding solace in a demonic relic. It was Rosalind's attempt to settle the score that had condemned the North Wing.

Now its forbidden nature, despite only one room having burned completely, made sense. Five postulants had died. It explained the missing class photo from that year, and I was willing to bet the incident also had something to do with the missing recertification records. Something so mundane as a recertification would not have been a priority after such a grand tragedy.

My mind whirled back around to Rosalind's relic. It had sought freedom, and given her specific instructions, only for something to go awry at the last minute.

"Rigo," I said, realization dawning. "You told me before that you came here to try and stop your brother from—from what?"

His voice was ragged when he replied. "I never knew. He only implied he was planning something terrible for the abbey." He sounded like he was slouched against the door, feeling as defeated and blindsided by all of this as I was. "I was too late."

Rigo's words from before came back to me. *I came to try and stop him from doing something he'd regret. But he'd already killed a nun and stolen from the abbey. When your Order found us, he fled, leaving only me to answer for his crimes. And with him gone, I had no way of disputing the accusations.*

"So your brother was Rosalind's relic? Their ritual went wrong, he abandoned her, and left you to deal with the aftermath."

Rigo made a pained noise of agreement. "I didn't know it was your Prioress he was working with, Annette, please believe me."

"I do." I felt his shock through the silence, through the dark. "There's no way you could've known. You were trying to save him—to save all of us."

We both stood, then, peering at each other through the bars.

Part of me stuck on how Prioress Rosalind had gone from vengeful novice to head of the Order with all these skeletons in her closet.
Then it occurred to me that the only real proof of what she'd done
lay written in this diary, which was exactly why she'd left it behind,
hidden in a bookshelf no one would disturb in the forbidden North
Wing. And for twenty years, she'd been able to keep her ghastly
secret under wraps.

But no longer.

I met the demon's depthless eyes. "This is exactly what I've
been looking for," I said. "Our Prioress cavorted with a demon
twenty years ago, attempted to summon its magic in a ritual, and
ended up killing Order servants and destroying Order property as
a result." Purpose, and righteousness, built within me like carefully
laid bricks. "It's all been a grand cover up. I'm willing to bet that
year's recertification was postponed, or otherwise exempted. That
would explain why that folder was missing."

On a desperate impulse, as the momentum of the discovery
carried on, I remembered the relic and its casual insistence that the
diary was worthless.

"**Relic**," I called inside my mind, suddenly curious. "**Did you
know about this? About Prioress Rosalind's misadventures?
Answer me.**"

Still upset, the relic didn't even bother to fully reveal its presence.
It spoke to me as if from across a great distance, on an exaggerated
sigh. I DID NOT THINK THAT PARTICULAR BIT OF ABBEY GOSSIP WAS
WORTH YOUR TIME.

For a moment I reeled, considering its response. "**It's hardly
gossip! I have the proof right here in my hand. You're telling
me you knew all of this and said nothing?**" My mind raced faster

and faster. "Is it because the truth of this reflects badly on the abbey? On our Prioress?"

The relic was quiet for a long moment. I CANNOT IN GOOD CONSCIENCE CONDONE ANY SORT OF HEARSAY REGARDING OUR HOLY-ORDAINED PRIORESS.

I scoffed. "So that's a yes," I muttered furiously, clenching a fist at my side. At Rigo's inquisitive look, I told him, "My relic knew of this, and said nothing. It claims it does not want *gossip* circulating about the Prioress."

"But it isn't gossip."

"I know."

"And it agreed to help you with your task, did it not? So why now would it claim to only want to preserve this woman's reputation?" I didn't have an answer. I would have to contend with the relic later. Rigo's expression deepened into a frown. He studied me, concern glinting in his black gaze. "What are you going to do?"

"Rosalind will be here in a matter of days, and we know now that she doesn't have the abbey's best interests at heart. It's her first year as Prioress—no one knows what to expect from her. I need to warn someone of her true nature. Show them the proof of what we've found."

Rigo's eyes widened in alarm. "I'm not sure that's wise. What if you're not believed? This could get you in worse trouble, or punished again!"

I'M NOT SO SURE I WOULD LISTEN TO HIM, said the relic suddenly. Its voice had gone low and smooth like a snake winding across cool stone. THINK OF IT THIS WAY—THIS INFORMATION ISN'T SOMETHING THE ABBEY WOULD WANT PUBLICIZED. BUT YOU HAVE PROOF, AND THAT GIVES YOU LEVERAGE YOU COULD USE TO NEGOTIATE A BETTER

POSITION FOR YOURSELF, IF NOT DEMAND A RESHUFFLING OF AWARDS
ENTIRELY.

Maybe that should've given me pause. The relic had been shifty, yes, and seemed to show a strong and sudden loyalty to Prioress Rosalind. But it had a point, and besides, if I played my cards right, no one else beyond a key few needed to know the details of this truth. As the relic had said, Rosalind's novice diary was leverage.

I saw stretched out before me a golden, glittering road of possibility. I would warn someone about the threat the Prioress posed to the abbey, and once they saw the proof, I could demand from them what I wanted.

"Annette." Rigo grabbed the bars and shook them in frustration, rattling the door. "The relic is talking to you, isn't it?" I nodded. I wasn't going to admit what it had said to me, though. "Whatever it's telling you, just stop for a moment and listen. Something's not right. If you want to go tell one of the other Sisters, we should talk about a strategy for this first so you don't—"

"Rigo, I'm sorry, but I don't have time for this!"

Mother Vanessa's deadline for the thief to return the diary would come due in a few hours. And the longer I waited, the less time I would have to make my bargain.

I turned from Rigo and strode for the stairs. For the first time in a long time, I held all the cards, all the power.

And now, no one would take it from me.

Chapter Nineteen

"One anonymous source shared, 'When I joined the Order
later in life, I had grand aspirations of becoming an Abbess
one day. I abandoned that dream quite quickly. Inter-abbey
politics were some of the most brutal, harsh, and cruel
experiences I ever endured, and this was after fifteen years
of military service.'"

—Excerpt from An Exploration of the Order of the
Revenant Mother and Other Island Religions

O nce again, I found myself outside Sister Colette's office just
after dawn. She took one look at me and gave a weary
sigh, then waved me in. Maybe it was my restless, wild energy, or
her own early-morning fatigue—unlike the other nuns, she wasn't
known for being an early riser—but neither of us spoke until she
had perched herself against the edge of her desk.

"I'm assuming whatever it is that's brought you to my office so early another time is important, so out with it," she said, with a hint of impatience, though not unkindly.

I fished Prioress Rosalind's diary out of my pocket and held it in my hands like an amulet that might give me strength. Hesitating, I considered how best to approach this. Somehow, I needed the conversation to help me figure out what to do with Rosalind's diary. Mother Vanessa was expecting it returned, and soon, or she would punish the entire abbey.

Sister Colette liked me and was sympathetic to my concerns, but that could only carry me so far. Even I knew that the accusations I had against the Prioress were outlandish, despite being true.

To be believed, I would have to state my claims confidently, and back them up with the evidence I held in my palms. Only then might I stand a chance at using this information to my advantage.

"Sister, I have reason to believe that the Prioress's visit may put the abbey in great danger."

At this, her eyebrows shot up to her hairline. "That's a very serious concern, Sister Annette. What makes you believe this?"

"I will warn you that this will sound unlikely," I said. "But I have proof, and I only ask that you listen to me."

When Sister Colette said nothing, just continued to look at me with slight alarm, I breathed deep, took care to arrange my words carefully, and began.

I told her of what I'd discovered in the archives—a set of recertification folders missing a certain year—and laid out a false path of discovery that led me to the diary. I couldn't tell her I'd gone snooping around in the North Wing, of course, so I brushed over certain parts of the story with an artist's care, creating the illusion that I'd come across all this knowledge during my recertification preparation tasks in the archives. I claimed that I had opened the diary in order to briefly peruse and better categorize it, but felt compelled to keep reading upon realizing what its contents implied. I told her of the teenage conflict the diary detailed between Mother Vanessa and the Prioress, the failed demonic ritual that had backfired and cost the abbey six lives, and what it might mean for our immediate future.

Sister Colette listened to all of this with a furrow in her brow. When I finished, she muttered a quick prayer under her breath.

I was relieved to see that she at least did not appear to find me insane.

"To be sure I have this correct," she said, speaking slowly, "You believe this diary is evidence of an attempt by Prioress Rosalind to *murder* her fellow novitiate using a demonic power?"

I nodded, feeling suddenly ashamed. How ridiculous it all sounded, when summarized so succinctly like that. If she saw fit to banish me from her office—or from the abbey entirely—over fears of insanity, I can't say I would've blamed her.

"And where is the proof you speak of?"

"Here." I thrust the diary at her. "It's all in there."

Sister Colette took the diary and opened it to the first page. "The true diary of Novice Rosalind, Year 537–542," she read aloud, then looked up at me with a start. "That is indeed the Prioress's name." She inspected the diary a moment longer before handing it back to me, rising, and beginning to pace slowly across her office floor. "These are very serious accusations, Annette," she said. A pause. "But I believe you are right to be concerned."

Mentally, I'd been preparing how to steer the conversation once more, this time toward my proposed bargain—the information in the diary in exchange for the return of my award. I'd expected skepticism, or outright hostility. I'd expected to have to wield the threat of divulging the diary's secrets as some sort of weapon.

But Sister Colette's words shocked me to my core, sending all my carefully laid thoughts skittering away.

"You do?"

Sister Colette glanced at me, suddenly very serious. "What I'm about to tell you must not be repeated. Do you understand?"

She seemed to imply that she meant to *investigate* the claims, not simply sweep them under the rug. No part of me had been prepared for that.

I nodded, eyes wide.

"Mother Vanessa hasn't been herself for quite some time, and I haven't been able to figure out why, though I have my suspicions. Nothing I can prove, however. But if what's written in this diary is true, and she's aware of the Prioress's dislike, then that may explain why the upcoming recertification is affecting her so. She may believe the Prioress has some sort of ill intent toward her or the abbey, but this is not a visit that she, as abbess, can refuse." Sister Colette swallowed. "I've suspected for a while that something was strange here, and this only further confirms that."

I nearly collapsed with relief. She'd noticed the sudden change in Mother Vanessa, too. It was so refreshing to be taken seriously, after so frequently having been brushed off as inconsequential. And I could see now that I'd made the right decision by coming to Sister Colette with this. Though she had worked here for many years, she had not been raised in this abbey, and possessed none of the particular childlike loyalties that often lingered among other Sisters and could cloud their reasoning. She seemed genuinely alarmed by what I had shared with her.

She had been candid with me. I appreciated and respected her for it. So I decided to take a risk and be equally candid with her.

"I want my award," I ground out. I was still growing used to advocating for myself, and my heart began to race. But I continued on despite my discomfort. "You and I both know Chief Poisoness was meant for me. I want it back, or I share the truth of Prioress Rosalind's misdeeds."

Sister Colette abruptly ceased her pacing to gawk at me. Her mouth had fallen open into a perfect "o".

"You—You mean to blackmail the abbey?"

I swallowed. Now, especially, I could not back down. "I'll do what I have to in order to take back what I'm rightly owed."

As if truly seeing me for the first time, she stared at me for a long stretch, then went to her desk and sank heavily into the chair.

"Mother help us all," she murmured to herself, pressing a hand to her forehead. With a great sigh, Sister Colette met my eyes once more. "Mother Vanessa is in charge of the awards, Annette. You know that. Any trades you'd like to make, you'll have to do so with her."

"What? But you just agreed with me that she's been behaving strangely. Mother Vanessa—"

"—is our abbess, and this is a matter she must be aware of." At the look on my face, she added, "I understand your reluctance. If Mother Vanessa had a role to play in the Prioress's scheme, might she not prove dangerous in possession of this information? But I urge you to think of the other possibility, the far more likely one—that Mother Vanessa, knowing the Prioress has our abbey in her sights, will fight with everything she can in our defense."

"But she—" I clamped my mouth shut. I couldn't admit to Mother Vanessa's punishment without also admitting to my trespassing in the North Wing.

"You must trust in the abbess, dear. We all must. She is the Mother's highest servant in this building. Even if it appears she may be somehow compromised, and it does—we must trust in the Mother's ability to work through her." Sister Colette paused, dropping both her eyes and her voice. "If it were proper for me to act on my own, I would. But I cannot step on the abbess's toes in such a manner without consequence."

Realization dawned. As assistant to the abbess, Sister Colette couldn't, or wouldn't, openly accuse the Prioress. And she couldn't grant my award back without undermining Mother Vanessa's authority. Both options could jeopardize her career. And if I lost Sister Colette, who else in the abbey would I have on my side?

I felt a brief flare of righteous anger toward her for being so self-centered, then as quickly as it rose, it vanished. Who was I to accuse a self-serving Sister of selfishness when I had made it my mission to sabotage the abbey's recertification over a failed injustice? When I had come here demanding my award in exchange for keeping the abbey's secrets?

Sister Colette and I studied each other. My eyes welled with a sudden rush of frustrated tears that I blinked quickly away.

"Mother Vanessa won't listen to me," I said finally in a small, sad voice. "She hasn't for a while now."

Softly, Sister Colette responded, "I understand. But you must *try*, and quickly. The Prioress arrives tomorrow morning."

I bit back the scream rising in my throat. The last thing I wanted to do was talk to Mother Vanessa. But it seemed that was my only option.

Struggling to put my hesitation into words, I forced a nod, then held the diary out to her. "Can you keep this?"

Leaving the diary with Sister Colette was safer than with me or Rigo.

"Yes." Sister Colette tucked the diary beneath one arm and studied me, her gaze a mixture of complex emotions I didn't have time to untangle.

Though this still felt unfinished, I made for the doorway. I needed to catch Mother Vanessa before she decided to punish everyone for the diary I alone had stolen.

"Stand strong, Sister. If this is truly as important as it sounds, the abbess needs to know," intoned Sister Colette as I left. "May the Mother guide you."

Chapter Twenty

"Part of what renders a demonic relic so insidious is that the true effects of its power are often not seen or felt for quite some time."

—Excerpt from An Exploration of the Order of the Revenant Mother and Other Island Religions

There was no answer when I knocked on Mother Vanessa's office door. I tested the knob, finding it unlocked, and let myself in. Soon, I'd have to go to morning prayers for the sake of routine, to keep up the illusion that everything was just fine. I could only hope that the abbess stopped by her office on the way to the chapel, as she often did.

I stood for a moment within her quiet space, watching the previous night's candles burn low in their holders. It occurred to me that this was the first time I'd ever been alone in her office, and the only time I'd ever had a reason to go poking around. Still, I hesitated. Not only was it an invasion of privacy, it was a violation of the abbey's most stringent rules to disturb the elder Sisters' personal effects.

I'd broken so many rules already. Could I live with myself if I did one more?

I SEE NO HARM IN MERELY HAVING A LOOK AROUND, noted the relic.

Its voice made me jump. Just as I'd gotten used to it, it had grown unfamiliar all over again in its recent absence. "Where have you been? I haven't heard from you much as of late."

It was quiet for a long moment. YOU'VE BEEN SPENDING A GREAT DEAL OF TIME WITH THAT DEMON, it said finally. AND I DON'T LIKE HIM.

Frowning, I tried to make sense of this. "You're the one who encouraged me to befriend and later betray him. Why bother, if you dislike him?"

I felt strangely defensive of the demon all of a sudden, but shoved it down before the relic could pick up on it.

Instead of responding to that, it plucked at my eyes, double vision searching Mother Vanessa's office. NEVER MIND THAT. AREN'T YOU CURIOUS WHAT SECRETS THE HORRID ABBESS KEEPS IN HERE?

I was, but that was hardly the point. I was growing tired of the relic's clumsy misdirections when I asked it questions it didn't want to answer. I would speak to it later about this, but for now, I needed to use my time wisely.

"Fine," I told the relic. "But we'll be discussing your evasive nature later."

Shuffling through the papers atop the abbess's desk, I looked for anything that might catch my eye. Then I saw Narissa's name peeking out from the bottom of a stack of parchment. She wasn't relevant—but curiosity tugged me toward the bit of correspondence, and before I knew it, the letter was in my hands. It was dated over a month ago, right around the time I'd begun to loathe Narissa for singing my song at morning prayers.

Dear Mother Abbess Vanessa Coulis,
Thank you for your kind outreach to our institution, and your inquiry regarding Novice Narissa Clee. Unfortunately, I can find no record of any novice under such name here at St. Elizabeth Abbey. Nor have I ever heard mention of Helene Abbey, at which this novice also claimed to you to have studied. To my knowledge, Helene Abbey does not exist. Is it possible the girl has taken a new name? That may explain our lack of proper records on her. If there is additional information that would aid us in your records request, please feel free to include that with your next response.
I am sorry I could not be of more help.
Yours in the Mother's light,
Sister Vidya Leela Ramsumair
Assistant to Abbess Althea Lochan, St. Elizabeth Abbey

Blood rushed in my ears. One of the abbeys at which Narissa had claimed to have studied didn't exist, and the other had no record of her attendance. Mother Vanessa had been curious enough about the girl to write to other institutions—but why?

I pushed the letter aside, hoping to find more correspondence. Countless papers were strewn across the desk, layers and layers. It was uncharacteristic of the abbess—I'd known her to be neat and tidy for years.

Sister Colette's earlier statement came to mind: *Mother Vanessa hasn't been herself for quite some time.*

I kept digging. Seeing something about the Ceremonial Profession, I grabbed it. A task list unfolded before my eyes, complete with assignments for each of the avowed Sisters on the first few pages, a list of all who would become avowed this year on the middle pages, and finally, information on award recipients on the final pages. Each award listed out its criteria, and beneath it were written the possible contenders among the novitiates, along with a brief explanation of how they met said criteria.

My eyes bulged toward my own name.

I blinked. Blinked again.

NOMINATION FOR CHIEF POISONESS: NOVICE ANNETTE BOODRAM

The paper dropped out of my suddenly shaking fingers.

I'd been *right.* The proof was right here in Mother Vanessa's office, buried beneath the clutter atop her desk. The Chief Poisoness award had been mine by rights. I'd always been meant to win. Only, something had changed.

I went to grab the paper again, thinking I would compare the other named nominees to the actual awardees. But as I did, my hand brushed up against an open cardboard gift box and—

A many-fingered, inhuman hand grasping at an ash brown throat. An array of faceless figures hooded in gray. A dark and winding forested path, stretching onward into nothing, tree branches arching overhead like a gnarled head of silvery hair—

Stumbling back, chest heaving, I stared at the cardboard box. Like my relic's box had all those weeks ago, this box had an energy of its own, one I felt even just while looking at it.

And I knew, even before I reached for the gift tag—carefully avoiding touching the box again—that Mother Vanessa now had a relic of her own.

Dearest Vanessa,
As your abbey's recertification visit approaches, I look for-
ward to seeing you once again. Much has happened since our
last meeting many years ago, and we have much to discuss.
Please enjoy this gift. Do take care—the bracelet's clasp
pinches.
Rosalind

Sure enough, inside the box was a faint splatter of old blood. My mind conjured up the image of the night I'd first noticed Mother Vanessa acting wildly out of character—it was the same night I'd first noticed her new jewelry, too, a tarnished golden bracelet she'd never worn before. That bracelet had come from the Prioress, who I now knew hated Mother Vanessa enough to have tried to kill her when they were younger.

If the Prioress had attempted to have a relic do her bidding then, what was stopping her from trying again now? Was the relic she'd sent Mother Vanessa poisoned, or otherwise malicious? Clearly, it was affecting her behavior in some way.

But why go through all the trouble of sending a gifted relic if the Prioress was planning to visit in person?

I had so many questions, and far too many concerns. I'd come here against my will to try and force Mother Vanessa's hand. Now, my world felt like it had been shaken on its axis. To my surprise, all I wanted to do was run down to the archives, tell Rigo what I'd discovered, and seek his council.

Naturally, Mother Vanessa chose that exact moment to arrive.

The patter of her footsteps in the hall gave me mere moments to set her desk back to rights. With a rush of dizziness and panicked nausea, my heart slammed up into my throat. Fingers trembling, I hastily reorganized the papers on her desk, then dashed around to the front, where I stood innocently, hands clasped as I awaited her entrance.

The door swung open.

Mother Vanessa stopped short upon sight of me. "Annette," she said, her lip curling slightly. "How did you get into my office?"

"The door was unlocked, Abbess."

Slowly, she closed the door, and stepped closer. "Were you or were you not taught that this office is a sacred space to be respected?"

"I was, Abbess, but this is important."

There was nothing of the abbess I knew in her gaze. She looked at me with fleeting curiosity, as if inspecting an odd-looking insect she intended to squish.

"All right. To what do I owe this pleasure?"

The sarcasm in her tone needled at me. My over-sensitive nature left me highly attuned to slights like this, and any other day, I might've backed down. But not today.

I held my head high and tried to remind myself what had brought me here in the first place. "I have some grave concerns regarding the Prioress's upcoming visit."

Mother Vanessa coughed out a laugh. "Do share."

I felt a brief flare of deep-seated panic. I knew that I had to do this—I didn't have a choice. But all I could think about was the cruelty Mother Vanessa had recently shown me, first following the disastrous award ceremony, then upon her catching me in the North Wing. I'd once thought that cruelty arbitrary. Now I knew there were greater forces at play, but that didn't lessen my fear any. If the Prioress's gifted relic was powerful enough to alter the abbess's behavior, what degree of sentience did it have? Did it have powers of its own, like my relic? Was it sympathetic to the Prioress's aims? Would it interpret my accusations as a threat?

In the end, I could not prolong the task any longer. I sucked in a deep breath and let my discoveries spill forth.

"Abbess, I've uncovered evidence that suggests a personal vendetta the Prioress has against you. Her teenage diary details an attempt to have you killed using the power of a demonic relic—only, the attempt failed, and damaged part of the North Wing instead." When she said nothing, I went on. "I worry that she plans to use her upcoming visit to try again."

Mother Vanessa received this all impassively. "Our Prioress would do no such thing," she said mildly.

I met her gaze again, looking for any trace within of the woman who had raised me. How much of the true Mother Vanessa remained, and how much had been overpowered by the relic completely? I wasn't sure, and—

Another possibility crossed my mind, one that froze me momentarily to the spot. If our abbess could be corrupted by a relic to the point where it changed her behavior, the same could happen to me.

A chill swept through me. Later, later, I kept telling myself. I'd deal with the relic later—with all of its lies and misdirections. But if I waited too long?

Swallowing, trying to grasp at my rapidly unraveling composure, I tried again.

"You taught us from a young age to lead with courage and conviction. I've seen the proof with my own eyes—and I've shared it with Sister Colette—and I am telling you that you, and the abbey as well, are in danger. I do not think the Prioress has our best interests at heart."

Now the abbess's face changed, becoming ugly. In seconds, she advanced on me, setting my heart to pounding. "You presume to put forth lies against our highest holy Sister? Heinous lies, unfounded accusations—"

"Abbess, I speak the truth—"

"*Lies*," she hissed. She turned her back to me, facing her desk. Her shoulders rose and fell with her heaving breath. "I'll ask you to reconsider your statement."

I shook my head, biting back tears. Even if she didn't believe me, I had to keep trying.

"I'm sorry, Abbess, but I will not reconsider. I have proof in the form of Prioress Rosalind's diary. And if you refuse to acknowledge these claims, I'll go public with its contents."

The moment Mother Vanessa's attention snagged was tangible. All her many candles began to flicker in an eerie unison. Her shoulders stilled.

"So it *was* you," she said, quite calmly. For a moment, her voice shifted, changed, as if a more gnarled and scratchy tone briefly peeked through. "I knew someone had been poking around where they didn't belong."

The sudden change in her demeanor unsettled and disarmed me.

"Yes," I admitted. I wasn't sure how else to proceed. "I—"

Then, suddenly, she whirled, seizing me by the biceps.

Her grip on me was white-hot with pain. I cried out and tried to wrestle away. Searing heat dripped toward my forearms, and I looked down in a panicked haze to find she'd seized handfuls of hot wax in her bare hands, which she now pressed to my skin.

It was a brutal, unrelenting pain, so much worse than the cane. All my instincts screamed to put distance between the wax and my skin, and I tried, pulling and yanking and thrashing about. She held me fast, her grasp made of iron.

I could do nothing but endure. I couldn't even scream. As she pressed harder, and the pain intensified, I froze like a wounded animal in a trap.

Mother Vanessa held the wax to me, heedless of her own skin, until I began to sway. When she released me, I collapsed to the floor, whimpering. My vision blurred. Black spots danced in the corners.

"Abandon this subject, Annette, if you know what's good for you."

Then she stepped over my prone form and left the room without even a backward glance.

Chapter Twenty-One

"The manchineel tree, otherwise known as the Tree of Death, is plentiful in the region. Nearly every inch of this tree—its sap, bark, fruit, and leaves—-are utter poison to humans. The practical uses of the tree have not proved to be worth the risk."

—A Phytotoxicological Treatise on the Plant Life of
Manzanilla & Moriah

I had no memory of how I'd returned to my room. I remembered only waking in fits and starts, pain flaring with an ugly frequency. My fingers wouldn't stop twitching. My arms were being dipped into cool water, which soothed the worst of the sting. But the agony beneath lingered, and I tumbled again into the dark.

When I finally woke for good, it was nighttime outside my window. A single candle flame flickered on the far edge of my night table. Someone was sitting with their back resting against my bed, a familiar swath of dark hair facing me.

Frowning, I ground out, "Rigo?"

He whipped his head around. A stream of what sounded like curses in Old Demonic fled his lips. On his knees, he turned around, then rested one forearm on my bed. His face hovered close to mine as those black, pupil-less eyes searched me intensely.

"How do you feel?"

I considered. I could tell my body had been through another great shock. Internally, I felt waves of a soothing sort of cool analgesic, along with a weak rush of pity from the relic. Quickly, I understood. It was doing what it could to help me, though it itself was suffering, too.

In my weakened state, I slowly oriented myself. I was in my own bed, head on my own pillow, lying on my side with my arms stretched out in front of me. They were covered in layers of bandages. An experimental movement sent a flash of pain through them, making me hiss. The skin felt like it had been repeatedly lit on fire.

"Awful," I answered finally.

Rigo nodded. "That's what I expected. But you'll live."

He kept staring at me, saying nothing. There was an unfamiliar rigidity to the set of his full lips. He wasn't blinking, hardly breathed. It took me a moment to process—he was *worried*. And *relieved* that I'd regained consciousness.

Uncomfortable with his piercing observation, and unsure how to handle his proximity, I cast my eyes around the room, seeing my water basin and a pile of old robes that had been torn apart to create my bandages. As I did, I noticed that Rigo's other arm hung at his side at an unnatural angle.

"Wait a minute," I said, my brain finally catching up. "How did you escape your cell? How are you here?"

His mouth pressed into a grim line. "When you didn't return, I had a horrible feeling something had gone wrong. That you might need help. So I dislocated my shoulder and elbow in order to reach the keys and release myself. Then I came looking for you. I found you here, unconscious. Your wounds were. . ." He trailed off, looked away. The candlelight framed the cut edge of his jaw as a muscle tensed there. "I waited until everyone was in their classes to go looking for medical supplies."

My thoughts felt slow and sludgy, several steps behind. "You dislocated a limb?"

"It'll heal," he said with a shrug.

So it had been *him*. The cool water, the bandages, all of it—from the demon I hadn't wanted to trust in the first place. He'd injured himself for me, risked his own discovery for me.

I couldn't recall the last time anyone had cared so much. And I didn't know how I felt about that.

"What about my wounds worried you so much?" I asked. The memory of Mother Vanessa's attack returned to me in muted recollections. "They're only wax burns."

Rigo shook his head. "No. Not only wax. I spent ages plucking torn bits of manchineel leaves from you. Whoever did this to you did not just want you injured—they wanted you dead."

The horror of that sliced through me like a rusty knife. The manchineel tree was arguably the most poisonous plant native to the Islands. We were meant to take great care in handling it. How had I not noticed a cutting of its leaves on Mother Vanessa's desk? Had she simply had the leaves in her pockets? I couldn't believe

I'd missed that. I replayed my visit to her office over and over, as quickly as my mind would allow. All I could theorize was that she'd seized the leaves, along with the wax, when she'd had her back to me. I'd been so foolish—I hadn't seen it coming.

That was the final piece of evidence I needed to confirm my suspicions. Mother Vanessa was no longer the woman I knew.

And whatever nasty spirit the Prioress had sent her in the form of a relic? It was now in charge.

For a moment, I screwed my eyes shut tight, overwhelmed. My thoughts circled back to the poisonous leaves. I'd touched them. I should've been dead, or at least well on the way to it.

"You mixed an antidote," I said, as the realization careened through me.

"I did."

Though he'd left so much unsaid, I understood the broad strokes. And I had the strangest urge to reach for him in return. Too exhausted to fight it, I did.

The slightest shift of my arm brought my hand to his. I reached out with my fingers, cautiously, unsure how he might respond—

His fingers curled smoothly and instantly around mine. Such a simple, ordinary thing. We'd grasped fingers like this not long ago, bargaining through the bars of his cell. But this felt entirely different. There was a comfort to his touch that grounded me, steadied me against the rough waters of the turmoil surrounding us.

I waited for him to pull his hand away. He didn't.

Rigo studied me more sharply now, like he meant to peer right through to my soul. A reflection of the candle's flame danced in the black depths of his eyes. It mesmerized me. If I kept looking at him, bathed in dim light like that, I was going to do something stupid like reach for his face.

So instead I trained my eyes on the corner of my pillow.

"Thank you," I told him, and I meant it.

He gave one brief nod in acknowledgment. Then he asked, "What happened? When you went to tell someone about the diary?"

A fresh rush of tears filled my eyes, and with it came a sickening wave of shame and vulnerability. I did not cry before anyone, as a rule. But right then, I was too exhausted, and in too much pain, to care.

And so with his hand still in mine, I told him about going to Sister Colette and her shocking faith in me. This seemed to hearten him. When I reached the subject of Mother Vanessa and what she'd done, however, a new and chilling darkness came into his gaze.

"Listen to me," he said in a low and dangerous tone. "That woman will not touch you again if I have anything to do with it. Understand?"

The sudden intensity in his voice made my thoughts stutter. I knew there was an intent there, I just couldn't figure out what it was he meant to tell me.

"Understand *what?*"

A half-exasperated noise, somewhere between a laugh and a sigh, fell from his lips. His thumb traced over the backs of my knuckles. "Nothing. Never mind. I'll tell you later." Before I could linger too long on what that meant, he spoke again. "Earlier, before you were fully awake, you kept mumbling that this was hopeless. That you'd ruined everything."

I wasn't surprised. Even now, I felt the same. Once again, I'd placed my foolish, misguided trust in the abbey, and once again, it had let me down. *Mother Vanessa* had let me down.

"It *is* hopeless," I said. "I've ruined my chance to right the Prioress's wrongs. Only Sister Colette believes what I've discovered, and she alone cannot do anything. Not without undermining Mother Vanessa's authority, and the abbess herself is compromised. The Prioress arrives in the morning." The reality of my inconvenient injuries dawned on me. "And I probably can't even hold a candle."

"Nothing is ever hopeless," Rigo murmured in a faraway voice. Coming back to himself, he added, "Can your relic do anything to aid your healing?"

I shook my head. "It's trying. It's doing its best, but there's only so much it can do. It feels my pain, too."

"All right. I'll see if I can find something to help. If not, I'll go back to your gardens and mix something myself."

He stood with a grunt and a wince. Something tender and fragile swelled in my chest, oddly touched by his care for me. All of this sneaking around in the shadows, all of this risk.

All for me.

"Rigo, what am I going to do?"

He paused just before my door. "First, you rest. Then we try again. If your Prioress arrives tomorrow morning, that means we have one more opportunity. We watch her, and we try to find irrefutable proof of our claims."

The prospect of even that flimsy plan comforted me. If I had recovered enough by morning, maybe I could use the relic's invisibility again to search the Prioress's personal effects.

Rigo reached for the doorknob. My eyes fluttered closed, my body tipping once more toward exhaustion.

"Don't get caught," I warned, halfway to sleep.

I could've sworn he smirked and rolled his eyes at me on his way out.

"I won't."

The memory of the lingering tenor of his voice lulled me to sleep.

Chapter Twenty-Two

"The desecration of a corpse is unforgivable. It is considered a most heinous sin."
    —The Gospel of the Order, Book 3, Testament 9

Despite my injuries, I slept like the dead, and woke with a start just after dawn to the sound of horses' hooves on stone.

I pushed myself up on one elbow, my burns smarting, to peer out the window. My room overlooked the abbey's front yard. A massive gray carriage pulled by four magnificent black horses clattered over the cobblestones up the long front drive. The carriage was decorated with ornate curlicued designs in glimmering black, along with a highly detailed etching of the face of the Revenant Mother. A black-robed woman manned the horses from the carriage's exposed front seat. Behind the carriage, clouds loomed, gray and low and close.

The Prioress had arrived.

I shivered. A wave of sick foreboding riled through me, all the worse for having mixed with my persistent wound pain and the general exhaustion of the last few weeks. A night's sleep had done wonders for me, and I felt better, though still nowhere close to my usual self. In fact, I wanted nothing more than to crawl back beneath my sheets and continue sleeping for another week. But today would be my last chance to unmask the Prioress's evil. I could not falter.

As I gathered myself, trying to ignore the still-stinging pain on my wax-burned arms, I saw a note on my night table.

I've returned to my prison. Will keep searching for answers.
Do not take your eyes off that woman.
Also, drink this.
-R

The fact that he'd left me a note brought a smile to my lips. His handwriting was neat and refined, which surprised me—Demonic used a different script. I took his terse message to me that he would continue a last-minute combing of the archives for anything we had missed before. The rest—keeping the Prioress under careful scrutiny—fell to me.

Next to his note stood a small, cork-stoppered bottle in a shade of deep amber that reminded me of his skin. On opening it, I gave an experimental sniff, and my smile only grew. He'd mixed an analgesic tonic for me, and a good one at that—strong and long-lasting. I wouldn't need another dose until the evening. It was almost exactly what I would've made myself.

I downed the whole thing, dressed quickly, and changed my bandages as best as I could. Then, before fear could overwhelm me completely, I headed downstairs.

We were expected to greet the Prioress as if she were the Mother herself. I noticed, now, all the work my fellow Order acolytes had accomplished while I'd been sequestered in the archives and sneaking around the abbey at night. While the archives were clean and tidy now, they were nowhere near as organized as I'd hoped to have them by this time, and they certainly couldn't compare to *this*.

The front hall was so tidy it nearly sparkled. The black-and-white stained glass windows lining the front door gleamed and shone. The scent of lavender-sage cleaning fluid tickled my nose. Large vases of our prettiest nontoxic tropical flowers lined either side of the entrance hall, exploding against the dreary stone walls in riots of aqua, magenta, and scarlet.

As I passed the kitchens, I picked up the scent of a magnificent meal—all sorts of luxurious meats, likely stewed chicken and oxtails, along with pigeon peas, rice, and roti. We would serve the Prioress the finest fare our kitchen hands could muster, all of it so much richer than what we were accustomed to.

We lined up in the entrance hall to formally receive our Prioress. Two Sisters pulled open the great front doors, and the Mother's holy-ordained right hand stepped into Moriah Abbey with all the pomp and circumstance of a royal returning to their kingdom.

Prioress Rosalind was a tall, sturdy woman who reminded me of Sister Denise in the kitchens. She wore robes in the same style as ours, only hers were a deep gray. Her skin was umber, a dark yellow-brown, and her headscarf pinned so securely around her face that not even a glimpse of her hairline was visible. She had an oval-shaped face with a wide, flat nose and dark eyes whose color I could not distinguish from this distance. The retinue that accompanied her consisted of two black-robed High Nuns who stood behind her, gazes averted.

A hush fell over the hall. Mother Vanessa stepped forward.

"On behalf of Moriah Abbey, and our devoted Order, I welcome you, Prioress Rosalind."

The Prioress dipped her chin in acknowledgment. "Thank you very much, Abbess Coulis. I'm pleased to be here." Her voice was high, clear, and commanding. Her eyes darted around in a brief assessment. "Such lovely flowers."

It all felt so *normal*. Knowing what I did, it unsettled me. I half expected the Prioress to unsheathe an elaborate ceremonial dagger and attack Mother Vanessa with no warning. But there were no such theatrics.

Instead, Mother Vanessa simply swept out an arm toward the chapel. After she and other Sisters ushered the Prioress inside, the rest of us filed in quietly and took our seats.

Today's morning prayers were special. Mother Vanessa held forth for longer than usual, emphasizing what an honor it was to have the Prioress in our presence. It made me furrow my brow. Of course it was an honor—but it was not as if we had a choice. By the time the extended prayer service was over, my stomach was growling. But then, instead of dismissing us like normal, Mother Vanessa ceded the lectern to the Prioress.

"I'd like to offer a brief overview of the recertification proceedings. I'll be residing here for the next three days, during which time I will assess this abbey in numerous ways. Please pay no mind to myself or my retinue and carry on with your daily routines as normal."

She went on to provide a few more details, but I had stopped listening, focused instead on the fact that her stay here was so limited. Three days to find irrefutable proof of her evil, and prevent her from carrying out the plans I still did not fully understand. As she spoke, she swept her eyes across all of us assembled in the chapel, seemingly looking at each of us in turn.

For a moment, when her eyes met mine, I felt as if she had seen straight into my soul. I froze, seized by a terrifying and wild certainty that she could read all of my misdeeds with a single glance. As my heart raced, a flash of emotion swept up from the relic. There and gone before I could even identify the feeling. It said nothing, and the Prioress looked away.

My heart raced. I could not shake the uneasy feeling that had speared me from the Prioress's gaze.

The ceremony concluded soon after. Slowly, everyone began to filter out of the chapel and toward the refectory. Eyes glued to the Prioress, I watched her linger near the lectern for a moment with several of the high-ranking Sisters. Then she and Mother Vanessa angled themselves toward a door in the rear of the chapel. I stood, blended in with the flow of breakfast-oriented bodies, and exited the chapel. While the others went to the refectory, I veered left instead, drawing the relic's invisibility around me almost effortlessly.

The chapel's rear door led to a back hallway used mostly for transporting prayer items from the storeroom before our services. It was this hallway in which Mother Vanessa and the Prioress stood now. I approached as silently as I could and waited discreetly around the corner. The Prioress looked up and down the hall as I poked my head around, but with the relic's invisibility, her gaze passed right over me.

Prioress Rosalind had left her retinue behind in the chapel. Whatever the nature of this discussion, she did not want them to overhear. A long moment of silence passed during which she merely stared at Mother Vanessa, as if inspecting her. Finally, she reached for the abbess's chin and inspected her more closely, tilting her head this way and that.

"So. It appears to have worked after all," said the Prioress. She released Mother Vanessa with a pat on the head, not unlike how one might treat a stray animal. "How go the preparations?"

Mother Vanessa had gone oddly still. Her arms hung loosely at her sides. She stared straight ahead as if she had no thought behind her eyes. "Proceeding as planned, my Prioress."

Prioress Rosalind folded her arms across her chest, nodding as she took this in. "And the girl?"

"She suspects," said Mother Vanessa tonelessly, her voice utterly foreign. "I have physically dissuaded her from the subject multiple times. I believe this to have been successful." A pause, and then she added, "No matter what she suspects, there is little she can do."

"Very good."

Now the Prioress turned, and I saw what I had not before: a third person stood in this back hallway, previously blocked by the Prioress's large frame. A third person with honey-gold curls peeking out of her scarf and a small, pinched face in the color of golden clay.

Narissa.

My stomach dropped. I'd *just* seen her in the chapel, acting perfectly normal. I thought she'd already gone to breakfast with the others. What could Narissa possibly have to do with any of this? How did she know the Prioress?

At the Prioress's expectant look, Narissa, who had also gone as still and lifeless as Mother Vanessa, added, "Yes, Prioress. She knows something is amiss. The award was meant for her, after all. But I do not believe her intelligent enough to work out our true aims here."

The *award*. The *girl*.

Were they talking about *me*?

For a moment, the shock of the revelation wiped my mind blank. Then thoughts came rushing in like water filling a cavern. I'd already seen evidence both of the award belonging to me, and of Narissa not actually having hailed from the abbey she claimed. Now Mother Vanessa and Narissa stood before the Prioress like brainless puppets, and she'd treated them like pets. I knew from the Prioress's note and the gifted reliquary box on the abbess's desk that she had Mother Vanessa in her thrall to some degree.

What if she now controlled Narissa, too?

Prioress Rosalind accepted this report with another nod. "And has there been any sign of my old friend?"

Both Mother Vanessa and Narissa shook their heads in unison.

"No, Prioress."

This alone seemed to distress her. Her shoulders sagged. She quickly pulled herself together, however. "That's unfortunate, and not what I had hoped, but very well. We'll proceed as planned." She looked between them. "I'll check your relic bonds briefly, then we'll return to the proceedings. I am quite looking forward to abbey porridge again."

The Prioress raised her hands, and I saw then the array of rings that adorned her fingers. She touched one, which matched the bracelet she'd sent Mother Vanessa, and the abbess gave a shiver. Still touching the ring, Prioress Rosalind swung her hand gently back and forth in the air.

And Mother Vanessa swayed along with the movement.

When the Prioress gave her hand a violent shake, so shook Mother Vanessa. They were tethered, somehow, bound by relic jewelry and dark power that had all the hairs on the back of my neck standing on end. When she released the ring, Mother Vanessa sagged, returning to her previous listless state.

"Acceptable," remarked the Prioress. She turned to Narissa. "And you?"

At her gesture, Narissa pulled down her scarf and dug her fingers into her forehead, just below one errant golden curl. With a flap of skin in hand, Narissa pulled gently backward, her hair and scalp rolling back onto itself to slowly reveal the bald and gray skull of a corpse. Wisps of hair in an indeterminate shade mottled the bony head beneath. The skin on the top half of her face flopped lazily down to reveal the rest. Eye sockets gaped, empty and black, one lone maggot wriggling where her left eye should have been.

And yet, from the neck down, she looked fully whole and human and alive.

I gagged as the awful wet stench of pungent death reached me. My invisibility shimmered, likely the result of a lapse in focus, so I breathed through my mouth and tried to keep my wits about me. I could still *taste* the death smell, though, which was somehow worse.

So Narissa Clee had never existed. She was a puppet corpse reanimated in human skin, with a stolen identity, sent by the Prioress to infiltrate our abbey.

Prioress Rosalind was unaffected by this whole display. She peered closely at the corpse beneath the skin, all while Narissa herself inhaled and exhaled patiently in an unsettlingly human fashion.

"Hmm. More decay than I'd hoped for. Still, I think you'll do for now." She tapped another ring this time, twice, and the thing that was Narissa carefully folded its skin back into place. With another tap to the rings, both Mother Vanessa and Narissa perked up, losing their listless nature. "Let's go."

They walked away. I slid down the wall to a seated position on shaking legs. Unable to hold the relic's invisibility any longer, it faded cleanly away, but I knew now the chapel and the hallway were empty, and I was alone. My stomach roiled, the stench of the corpse beneath Narissa still lingering in my throat.

Everything that had recently caused me trouble—all of it—led back to the Prioress. She had gifted Mother Vanessa a relic in order to control her, and she had resurrected something unholy and covered it in Narissa's skin like an artist molding clay.

And me—they knew about *me*. From the way it sounded, Prioress Rosalind had been behind this from the beginning. Her denying me my rightful award was all part of some unseen plan. My life, destroyed in a single moment as collateral damage to her aims.

My mind raced. I was on the verge of throwing up, but I fought it.

I needed to speak with Sister Colette, figure out what to do next. The Prioress's evil had to be proven, and without any opportunity for doubt. But how?

"Relic," I said. "I need you."

I waited. There was no response.

"Relic?" I said again. I closed my eyes, focused, and prodded its presence in my mind. It was undoubtedly still there. So why wasn't it responding to me?

"Relic, I need your counsel!"

Again, no response. Frustrated, I groaned. Of course it would choose, now out of all times, to go dormant and do whatever it pleased.

But I didn't have *time* to wait for it to resurface. I had to trace out my next steps immediately, and I needed to consult someone first, since I had failed so miserably before.

I stood, Rigo on my mind, and headed for the archives.

Chapter Twenty-Three

"Prioress Rosalind Carey, the Order's newest and most high-ranking nun, is something of a legend among Order scholars. In the twenty years leading up to her ordination, she became known for her research into and in-depth knowledge of relics, both maternal and demonic."
—Excerpt from An Exploration of the Order of the Revenant Mother and Other Island Religions

No sooner had I closed the door to the archives behind me than searing pain swept through my head, bringing me to my knees. My vision blotted gray, then black. Everything smeared sideways into a whirling miasma of confusion.

When it finally abated, I came back to myself, hands on the stone floor, shaking like I'd been exerting myself for hours.

The archives were utterly silent. One mere candle flickered from its holder in the corner, rendering the whole room in sepia-toned flashes.

"Annette?"

Rigo's voice, from the corner. I couldn't see him.

"What happened?"

My tongue felt strange. All of me felt strange, in fact, nothing connecting together in quite the way it should.

Slow footsteps approached me. Rigo came into dim view. A bleeding scratch crossed one of his cheeks. In his hand, he held my metal nail file—gripped tightly, and angled as if to attack me if I made any sudden movements.

Like he was *afraid* of me.

"Rigo?"

I tried to stand—he flinched—and I only fell back to my knees again.

Rigo dropped to kneel next to me. He peered at me in that intense way of his, the one that told me he was trying to make sure I was okay, but there was something more to it this time. A careful wariness that made dread curl its fingers around my intestines.

"You attacked me," he said simply. "You walked in and came at me with the nail file."

"*What?*" I had no memory of this. I did not even remember journeying to the archives, only my initial intent to. When I probed my memory for what he claimed, I found no recollection—just a blank, gaping space. "I-I don't remember doing that, I'm sorry, I—"

His expression mirrored the urgent horror I felt. Mouth setting into a firm line, he brought the nail file up into the space between us like a sword's barrier. Glinting metal bisected his face.

"Ask it." Rigo's voice trembled. "That thing inside you? Ask it its name."

I shook my head. I couldn't stand him treating me like this. "I already *know* the relic's name—"

"What is it?"

"It told me I could call it Jay, but I've just been calling it 'relic'—"

"Just Jay? That's all?"

I nodded. Frustrated tears wet my eyes. "Why? What's—"

"Ask it its *full* name," Rigo commanded, and in that moment I had never heard him sound more like the dangerous bit of demonkind he was.

Gooseflesh stippled my arms. I had never asked the relic's full name because I'd never had reason to. Now I knew, with a deep, unsettling certainty, that I'd erred.

My stomach seemed to fall out of my feet as I reached within, prodded the relic's presence, and found it waiting, vibrating with a kind of unholy glee.

"**Relic?**" It thrummed in response. "**Tell me your name. Your *full* name.**"

I felt a sensation like the relic breathing deep, shedding the weight of an identity it had never wanted to begin with.

Sister, I've been waiting so long for you to ask me that. Its voice had changed, becoming something slimier and uglier that caressed my insides like spoiled honey. My full name is Julián Acosta.

He said it with the Sulvan pronunciation, the J sounding like an H. But it was the last name that stuck in my head.

Acosta.

I only knew one other person with the surname Acosta, and it seemed no coincidence that he was also in the room with me.

"What did it say?" Rigo said.

"It said its name is Julián—"

The words had hardly escaped my mouth before Rigo tackled me. Panicked, and terrified, I curled my arms around myself protectively. The nail file clattered across the stone out of sight. For a moment, I was so sure I was about to die. I imagined that this had all been an elaborate setup between the two demon brothers and that now was the time it would come to a head. Rigo grabbed at my arms. Kicking and screaming, I cried out, certain he was trying to strangle me. Then, finally, his palm closed roughly around the finger that wore the relic ring, tearing it roughly off my hand.

The ring bounced twice and came to rest not far away. Silence descended for a split second that felt like it lasted forever.

I broke, my composure shattering into one loud, messy sob. I scrabbled backward away from him as fast as I could.

"Sorry—I'm sorry—I just needed—" Rigo's attention split between me and the ring as the latter began to vibrate of its own accord, producing a high, tinny sound.

It was unnatural, unholy. Wrong to the bone.

The ring stilled. "BROTHER," said the relic's voice from the ring. "HOW LOVELY IT IS TO MEET YOU AGAIN."

Rigo stiffened. I had never seen him look more otherworldly, nor more deadly. Meanwhile, I struggled to reconcile the fact of the relic's voice—which I was so used to inside my head—filling a real, live space, one that allowed another to hear what had long been mine alone.

The ring did not move, and no apparition appeared before us, yet I *felt* the relic turn toward me. Its regard felt somehow so much more sinister now that it did not come from within. I wanted to recoil, though I fought the urge, unsure how to proceed.

"And Sister Annette. My, isn't this exciting."

Recovering, Rigo snatched up the nail file and stepped in front of me. "Dispense with the pleasantries, Julián. Why are you here? What are you doing?"

A pulse of mirth came from the energy surrounding the ring. Like Julián had *smirked* at us.

"Is it not obvious?"

"You lied to me." The words snapped from my mouth of their own accord. Now that my brain had caught up to my body's hot terror, I was furious. "You told me you were a shard of the Mother's spirit. But you're not. You're—you're—"

"A demonic entity, yes, Annette. Congratulations for finally realizing what should have been so obvious to you all along." Julián's voice dripped with condescension. No matter that the voice was disembodied, emanating from a ring on the ground—the words hurt all the same. "You were so desperate for revenge—parched for it, actually, in a way that felt very refreshing—that I scarcely had to lie at all. You asked of me only what you wanted to ask, and heard only the answers you wished to hear."

"Did you target her?" Rigo demanded. When Julián only laughed, it enraged Rigo further. "Answer me!"

The candle in the corner went out with the force of his ire, then slowly re-lit itself once more.

Julián was still laughing. "Of course not. The nun found her way to me. Unfortunately for her, she never stopped to consider that the mysterious relic she found in these very archives might have an agenda of its own."

I felt sick. The bodiless voice, the candle, the darkness—it all felt off-kilter and threatening, like all that I knew was tilting sideways out of control.

"Stop this," snarled Rigo. "Tell me why you possessed Annette. Start from the beginning."

Julián's laughter paused to a silky, perilous silence. "OR WHAT?"

"Or I'll toss your vessel into the ocean, you miserable sack of shit. Only one of us is corporeal here. You can't do anything without a body."

Now it was Julián's rage that was palpable. It swelled with a feeling like rapidly-shifting air pressure during a storm, crackling with myriad dangerous possibilities, then dissipated. "VERY WELL." Its focus swiveled between the both of us. "ALL THOSE YEARS AGO, WHEN YOU SPOILED MY RITUAL, YOU BELIEVED I FLED THE SCENE ENTIRELY. I DID NOT."

"You've been here the entire time?" Rigo said.

"INDEED. YOUR INTERFERENCE WEAKENED US BOTH. I FLED INTO THE FIRST RELIC-WORTHY ITEM I COULD SENSE NEARBY. BY THE TIME THE NUNS CAME TO COLLECT THEIR DEAD AND LOCK YOU UP, I WAS ALREADY TUCKED INTO THIS RING, CONSUMING ITS ESSENCE AS FUEL FOR MY OWN HEALING."

"But it's a maternal relic," I cried. I had sensed no evil from the ring. I would have known if the entity inside had evil intentions, I was sure of it. "How did you get inside?"

MY DEAR, I SIMPLY MADE ROOM. THE MOTHER'S SPIRIT SHARDS ARE NOT AS STRONG AS YOU MAY THINK. THOUGH THEY MAKE TASTY FUEL.

I clenched my fists at my sides, struck by the sudden urge to punch Julián's nonexistent form.

"Keep talking," ordered Rigo. He caught my eye as he did. It seemed like he was trying to signal something, only I couldn't figure out what.

"I REMAINED IN THE RING FOR YEARS, CONSUMING THE MATERNAL SHARD TO KEEP MYSELF ALIVE. THEN ONE DAY, A LONELY NUN WITH VENGEANCE IN HER HEART STUMBLED UPON ME BY ACCIDENT. WITH A SINGLE TOUCH, I KNEW HER DARKEST DESIRES, AND I PROMISED THEM TO HER ON A PLATTER. SHE WAS ALL TOO WILLING TO ACCEPT MY TERMS, SHARE IN THE WIELDING OF MY MAGIC, IF IT MEANT SHE COULD RIGHT THOSE WHO HAD WRONGED HER."

I had been so stupid. Of course it had all seemed too good to be true. I'd had suspicions about the relic and its occasional lack of forthcoming, and I'd overlooked that willingly in the name of my own aims, but I had never expected this. Never imagined that, in trying to seize a bit of the Mother's power to aid me during my time of need, I had welcomed a demon into my soul instead.

Rigo's knuckles were white around the hilt of the nail file. "And just now? She's been wearing your ring since I met her. She's never attacked me before."

A low, drawn-out chuckle came from the ring. "SHE SIMPLY GOT A BIT TOO CLOSE TO THE TRUTH."

The truth. Was that why the relic—or what I'd *thought* was my relic—had disappeared as of late?

All the evidence rushed rapidly through my mind. He'd gone strangely quiet upon my discovery of Rosalind's diary. He'd offered no help following my realization that the Prioress was controlling both Mother Vanessa and Narissa with her own cursed relics. Now that I revisited its actions, the relic had only been present, and cooperated with my requests, when it felt like it—when, I imagined, it was able to serve its own interests.

It occurred to me suddenly, with a gasp.

"It was you," I said. "Rosalind was working with *you* to try and kill Vanessa."

"Very good, nun. It sure took you long enough." Rigo bared his teeth, but Julián seemed unfazed. "Yes, Rosalind and I are close, though we haven't been in contact since the incident. It was so nice to see her again, even if through your miserable eyes."

"So. . ." I grasped wildly for focus, fitting the pieces together. "You helped her twenty years ago, but Rigo stopped your ritual. Why is she back now, after so long? Why not seek you out first for help?"

This seemed to irritate Julián. "As you've seen, Rosalind has recruited others to her cause. She likely has no need of me. But that doesn't mean I won't do everything in my power to help her."

At Rigo's brief look of confusion, I added, "I saw Rosalind with the abbess and another Sister. She has them in her thrall somehow, controlled by the rings she wears." How simple and full of possibility this all had seemed mere moments ago. "That's what I was on my way here to tell you."

He absorbed this with a nod, never removing the bulk of his attention from the ring. Then he stepped sideways, again and again, until he was close enough to me to slip an arm around my waist and press his mouth to my ear.

"Destroy it," Rigo said in a barely audible whisper.

My gooseflesh returned. He'd already stepped away, resumed talking to his evil brother imprisoned in the ring. I understood—he would keep Julián occupied.

But that meant I had to find a means to destroy Julián, and I had no idea where to start.

Could a relic even be destroyed, and how might one go about that? I knew of no weapons down here other than the nail file and a rusty pair of scissors, and neither of those could make a dent in the ring's sturdy craftsmanship. Perhaps burning it, melting it down to its base parts might work, but we had no massive central forge, and I doubted we had time to experiment with candles. I thought briefly of the ring box in which I'd originally discovered the relic. If I could shove it back inside, that might provide a temporary solution. But I'd thrown away that box and that envelope over the course of my organizational efforts, deeming them useless trash.

An image came to mind, of another box—the gift box in Mother Vanessa's office. The very one Prioress Rosalind had used to send our abbess her cursed gift.

Everyone was likely to still be at breakfast. If I could get back to that box, and back to the archives, quickly and without being seen—

No, not *if.* The relic had been with me all along. It knew my plans, my proof. It could ruin all of this if I didn't destroy or incapacitate it. And with no relic to cause trouble for me, I would still have a chance to make my case against the Prioress. I could not allow myself any *ifs.*

I began to back slowly away toward the basement door. A few hundred steps, and several floors, were all that separated me from the abbess's office. I would run. I would be quick. Rigo could manage against his ring-imprisoned relic brother for a few minutes.

I could do this. I could *fix* this, bring everything to a neat resolution before it unraveled further—

As I touched the doorknob, it twisted beneath my hand. Panic closed my throat.

I could do nothing but watch as it swung open to reveal the Prioress and her retinue, Mother Vanessa, and the handful of other Sisters assigned to assist with the recertification.

Chapter Twenty-Four

"To trust is to be holy, to act in the Mother's image. But that trust must be placed wisely."
    —The Gospel of the Order, Book 4, Testament 5

I gaped at them all like a dying fish stricken with panic.

The Prioress, her retinue, Mother Vanessa, and Sisters Colette and Edna stared back. On some distant, darkly comedic level, it struck me that we made an interesting tableau—a handful of the Mother's holy servants, along with a demon and his evil brother imprisoned in a ring on the ground.

A moment passed, held in the grasp of a shocked, tense silence.

Prioress Rosalind recovered first. In a voice like a silky soft hiss, she demanded, "What exactly is going on here?"

"I—" I opened my mouth. Grasped for an explanation. The effects of having the relic suddenly and forcibly removed from me chose then to hit, several minutes delayed. My vision swam, head spinning with a dreadful bout of vertigo. It took all my effort to remain standing, let alone speak.

Sister Colette's voice. "Why is the prisoner out of his cage?"

"I can—I can explain—"

But I couldn't. My mouth felt full of cotton, my tongue foreign and unwieldy. My body repeatedly searched for the relic's presence, found none, and revolted. I stumbled back a few steps until I was leaning against the wall. If there was ever a time to overcome my signature struggle to quickly articulate my thoughts, it was now. There *was* a way to explain all of this away that didn't end with me in loads of trouble. I knew it, knew I was smart enough to find it, but it seemed all of my abilities remained stubbornly out of my reach.

"The prisoner?" repeated Prioress Rosalind. I watched through dimming vision as her attention fell on Rigo. He stood very still, making no sudden moves, waiting to see what would happen. Julián, to his credit, had fallen silent inside the ring. It looked completely innocuous on the floor. "Ah, yes. Our demon friend. The one who murdered my classmates so long ago."

Not true. I wanted to shout it. Rigo had tried to *stop* all of that.

"Annette." Mother Vanessa's voice cut sharply through the tension. "Explain yourself."

Countless pairs of eyes fell on me. I had to get it together. I couldn't afford to be ill, not now, when everything I'd worked so hard for stood on the edge of unraveling.

"I—"

My stomach roiled. I dropped to my knees, retching, and brought up a small quantity of yellowish bile. The effort nearly knocked me flat. My vision pulsed alternately light and dark. Voices overlapped within the small space like seagulls competing for attention. Hands on my arms, my shoulders. I knew that wherever the Sisters were taking me, it was nowhere good, but I was powerless to resist, all my strength having fled my limbs with the relic's departure.

The last thing I saw before they dragged me from the archives was the Prioress plucking Julián's ring off the floor. When she thought no one was looking, she kissed it tenderly, then tucked it into her robes.

I looked for Rigo—but he was gone. I'd missed his departure entirely.

For what felt like miles, I stumbled along between my captors, drifting in and out of consciousness. I hated Julián more in that moment than I ever had—he'd taken my strength and agency from me at the time when I needed it most.

Eventually, we came to a stop. A familiar creak, a rush of wet wind, and I found myself falling to my knees on damp stone.

I looked up. Blinked. Moriah Abbey's front courtyard stared back at me beneath a slate gray sky. Rain poured from dark clouds in a sudden storm typical of the Islands, pelting my robes. I'd assumed I was being taken to Mother Vanessa's office for another bout of punishment. Why had they brought me *here*?

"Sister Annette." I whirled to find Mother Vanessa behind me, and behind her, Sister Edna and Sister Colette. Their faces looked grave. Where was the Prioress? "You have cavorted with our demon prisoner and risked the safety and security of the entire abbey."

I lowered my head. Spit trailed from my slack jaw, and I half wanted to retch again. Instead I forced myself to speak.

"I—I will accept any p-punishment you deem fit, Abbess."

Mother Vanessa's following silence was heavy and telling. I kept my gaze averted, muscles tense and waiting for pain, but it never came.

"There is to be no punishment," she said softly. "You will leave the abbey, Sister Annette, and never return."

The sounds of the rain, and its damp persistence on my robes, suddenly felt very far away.

"What?"

Her response was simply, "We cannot abide a demon sympathizer in our midst."

But I wasn't a demon sympathizer.

Or was I?

Everything I had done might have been driven by vengeance, but my efforts to expose the Prioress's misdeeds were done with the abbey in mind. I wanted to save myself, earn back my award, yes, but part of that meant keeping the Prioress and her evil from whatever her nefarious plans would be. Her diary proved as much—

The diary. I cast my eyes to Sister Colette in a desperate plea.

"But you *knew*—you knew of the demon, Sister. I reminded you, and you directed me to ensure he was given food and water. His presence was not a surprise."

It was the longest sentence I'd managed to string together in minutes, and it cost me. Black spots danced along the edges of my peripherals.

Sister Colette's normally kind mouth tightened into a thin line. I had never seen her look at me with such disapproval. "Yes, Annette, this is true. But you made the choice to release him from his cell, knowing full well what risk it brought, and that choice was your own." I thought then of the Prioress's diary in her possession, proof of everything I'd told her. But who would listen to me now that I'd been caught outright with the freed demon? "I'm very sorry, but there is nothing I can do for you."

Sister Edna said nothing, just looked down her nose at me and made a ward against evil.

I was on my own. I understood that then. There would be no opportunity to redeem myself or my award, nor to prove that the Prioress had come here with malicious intent and hate for Mother Vanessa in her heart.

The Sisters left. Mother Vanessa studied me for one long, final moment, while I looked up at her. I felt ten years old again, sobbing at the thought of being dragged into the abbey against my will, only now the situation was reversed—I was an adult now, fully in control of my own capacities, and I would've done anything to get back within those walls and prove what I knew in my heart to be true.

When Mother Vanessa turned away to return inside, it was as if the last vestiges of hope keeping me afloat sunk suddenly like a bag of rocks. She was under the Prioress's thrall, after all—I'd been a fool to expect any mercy from our abbess. But that didn't make it hurt any less.

The front doors snapped shut behind her, leaving me on the steps of the only real home I'd ever known. The rain chose then to pick up in intensity. It pelted harder, and the wind grew greedier, plucking at my robes. My scarf flew sideways, revealing my hair to the elements.

I was miserable, utterly dejected, and becoming more soaked by the minute. Part of me seemed content to crawl into the front gardens and simply lay there to die. Then I remembered—the

Prioress had Julián's ring now. She'd been reunited with her old friend. And if she didn't already know that I had delved into her shady past, Julián was sure to tell her. He'd been with me all along and knew exactly what I knew. He could even warn her of the extent of my knowledge so that she could better defend herself against my accusations.

And I couldn't risk her coming after me in an effort to keep her secrets hidden.

Though my body felt like old chewing gum, I forced myself to my feet. I took one last look at the abbey. Then I fled.

I fled into the city that, for all intents and purposes, should have been my home. But my parents had abandoned me to the abbey at such a young age that I'd never had a normal child's opportunity to wander the streets and learn their hometown. The rain-sodden streets were labyrinthine around me now, foreign and unfamiliar much like vague shapes in the dark. Trams and carriages of all shapes and sizes trundled along. Their wheels spat rain up toward the sidewalks. People hurried along beneath umbrellas or jackets, hunched against the wind and rain. A few puzzled glances came my way—my dirt-colored robes gave me away as a member of an Order cloister, something strange and unusual amid the pastel vibrancy of these streets.

Still recovering from the relic's withdrawal, I felt weak and off-balance, and the unrelenting rain soaking through my robes rendered me colder by the minute.

Panicked, I simply ran.

I kept running until I could no longer. Then I walked, and then I stumbled, leaning against the front walls of storefronts and businesses when I could. The few people left on the streets in this weather veered away to avoid me. I knew I must look terrible. But still I kept going, picturing the Prioress on my tail. I went until I'd turned so many corners and wandered so many streets that nothing looked right anymore. I could've been miles from the abbey, or one street over, or on another world entirely.

Ducking into an alley, I found an alcove over a building's side entrance that provided a bit of shelter, and leaned my miserable bones against that closed door. Here on the Islands, a storm like this could last either fifteen minutes or six hours. I needed somewhere to wait it out. My tired mind raced frantically, examining the situation from all angles.

I soon realized that this was the worst possible outcome. For all the abbey's faults, I was nothing without that place. I *had* nothing without it. All of my belongings and my meager savings were still in my room. I had no idea how to get back, and they would not let me in besides. All I had on my person were my robes.

A sob worked its way out, and I didn't bother choking it back. What was the point? Each of my carefully laid plans had gone completely off the rails. Once again, somehow, I had ruined everything. Now I would never be able to expose the truth about the Prioress or negotiate my award as deserved.

Sinking to the ground, I wrapped my arms around myself. Despondency draped itself over me like a blanket. It pressed me firmly down toward the wet earth.

I was soaked to the bone, sitting in a wet, dirty alley in a city I didn't know how to navigate, and there was nowhere I could go, no one I could ask for help.

I wasn't sure how long I cried. I just knew that I began to shiver uncontrollably. Wet clothing upon wet skin upon still-pelting rain was a sensory torment that I would've turned my skin inside out to escape. It only made me cry more—my breath coming in pathetic gasps, my abdomen trembling against the force of emotions I usually tried so hard to keep at bay.

If not for the heavy footsteps I heard then, I might have died there.

Thick boots splashed through large puddles, heading from the mouth of the alley in my direction. I looked up to find a strange figure in a raincoat. Perfect. Now, on top of everything else, I was going to be robbed.

I opened my mouth to tell the would-be thief that I had no money, nothing worth stealing—

"Annette?"

I blinked. Swiped at my tear-swollen eyes. Looked again. The hood of the raincoat lifted slightly to reveal the person beneath: Rigo.

Never had I been so happy to see his stupid demon face. Cautious relief swarmed through me, a welcome warmth.

"I've been looking for you for hours," he said. His brow furrowed as he took in my sorry state. "You're soaked. Have you been outside all this time?"

I didn't know what to say. How had he escaped the abbey without getting himself caught again? How had he found me?

Why bother spending time looking for me at all?

"I thought you left," were the first words that emerged, and they were half a sob at that.

The furrow grew deeper. He shook his head. "Your Sisters were more concerned with throwing you out than they were with my whereabouts. I saw an opportunity and took it."

A whimper crawled its way out of my throat. I hated him seeing me like this, but all my defenses were down. I had no energy left to conceal the worst of me.

"Why bother spending time looking for me at all? You could've just fled. I don't understand why you care so much."

His face pinched into a pained expression. Slowly, as if choosing his words carefully, he said, "Is it so hard to believe I might be fond of you?"

My addled mind stumbled over his words. Did that mean what I thought it did?

Without waiting for a response, he extended a hand toward me, a gesture that meant everything in the world. "Come on. We need to get out of the rain."

I stared at his hand. Reeled, from the offer it represented.

He was not supposed to be the one I fell back on. I was supposed to handle everything myself. But I'd ruined everything on my own, and no one else would be coming to look for me. Only Rigo stood at my side now. I had two choices: trust him, or let everything I'd worked so hard for fall apart.

To his credit, he gave me time to think. He stood there waiting with his hand outstretched for so long his arm must have started to ache.

Until, finally, I took his hand, sank into the comfort of his touch, and let him pull me up.

Chapter Twenty-Five

"To prevent conception, mix one part stoneseed root, one part wild carrot seed, and one part thistle. Boil in water to create a potent tea. Serve hot."
—Excerpt from an unofficial compendium of recipes, developed by Order acolytes

Despite being a demon, Rigo was surprisingly street-smart. He knew, somehow, which areas were a good idea and which ones were not. I didn't know how he navigated so successfully—was this some sort of demon power I'd overlooked in my studies? Or was he simply noting the city's directional cues I was too overwhelmed to parse? Either way, I was beyond grateful for his presence. I stumbled along behind him like a baby duckling for nearly half an hour.

Finally, he stepped into a restaurant.

"Look like you know what you're doing," he murmured, and addressed the hostess. I felt like a drowned rat. But I smiled all the same, and we found ourselves being shown to a table in a far corner.

Inside, the space was crowded with people and the smell of wet clothing and wet hair. It was delightfully warm after the rain's chill. At the table, Rigo unearthed a stack of clothing from his raincoat and pushed it at me.

"Did you steal this?"

He shot me a dark look. "Do you really want to know the answer to that?" When I just sighed, exasperated, he continued. "Go change," he said. "You can't wear wet clothes all day."

I nodded, grateful for the instruction. I felt hopelessly adrift, suddenly unmoored in the raging sea that was my life. In the corner of the building, I found a restroom, and there I stripped off my soaking robes and underthings, slipping into the blissfully dry clothing Rigo had procured. Within the stack he'd handed me were also a few lengths of bandages, which I used to replace the sopping wet ones covering my arms. As I did, I finally took a good look beneath. The skin on my forearms was blistered and raw, shiny and tender to the touch. More proof of the fake Mother Vanessa's handiwork. I put it out of my mind. Thanks to Rigo, I would heal.

There was also another pain-relieving tonic, which I drank.

I've been looking for you for hours, he'd said. He'd brought me clothing, too. He'd been thinking of me this whole time, all the while I was falling completely apart. I couldn't put into words how much that meant to me—to be taken care of like this.

It had been years since I'd worn anything other than my abbey-issued robes or nightgown. The clothes he'd given me—long linen pants and a shirt with sleeves that reached to my wrists—were comfortable if unfamiliar, the fabric chafing in places I'd forgotten to be used to. Weirder still was removing my headscarf. I knew why he wanted me to change—the wet clothes were a health risk, and a dead giveaway that I was a nun, making it easier for us to be found. But I still hesitated, looking at myself and my dripping wet twists in the mirror, unused to seeing myself so exposed.

I felt both like my truest self and like a stranger, and I wasn't sure what to make of that.

Joining Rigo back at the table, I discovered that he had a menu in his hands. We'd already been brought two steaming mugs of hot tea. I cupped my hands gently around one and sipped, letting the warm liquid revitalize me. Around us, the restaurant was full of the hum of conversation.

"How are we going to pay for this?" I asked, as the thought suddenly occurred to me. "I have no money. It's all back at the abbey."

He grinned up at me over top of the menu. "Don't worry about it."

I studied him. He, too, wore what I assumed were stolen bits of clothing, only he looked completely at home in the garments. A new energy suffused him. He seemed brighter, somehow, more whole and himself.

"You're in good spirits," I observed. "Considering."

"It's the first time in twenty years I've been outside of that abbey and those miserable consecrated walls. I can *breathe*," he said, meeting my eyes for a moment. The intensity in his dark gaze felt so much more tantalizing without the abbey's protection surrounding us. Dropping his gaze back to the menu, he added, "I am actively restraining myself from doing cartwheels in the street."

I snorted, choking on my tea. Freedom suited him, I had to admit.

He ordered for us: a warm soup of split peas, dumplings, and yams, flavored with a piece of salted pork. The dish was so familiar to me, comforting and warm and soothing, that I had to swallow down a lump in my throat as I ate and it chased away the storm's chill. It was simple, hearty food like this that I'd grown up eating at home with my parents before they left me to the abbey. And I'd grown to love the abbey's food, too, but something about this meal in particular left me feeling teary and vulnerable.

Was Rigo doing this on purpose? How could he know the effect these simple, kind gestures would have on me?

We ate quietly, and I tried not to stare at him as I puzzled out his motives.

At one point, looking up over his tea, he caught my eye again. His attention flitted about my face, lingering on the clothing he'd given me, on the twists that hung soaked on my shoulders.

"You look nice," he said quietly. "It's a shame this is the first time I'm seeing you out of your robes. In normal clothes, I mean."

I flushed and dropped my eyes. "I'm a nun. Before this, I never left the abbey's walls. What reason would I have to wear normal clothes?"

"Good point." Rigo drained his tea.

Itching to shift his attention off me, I changed the subject to what had been weighing on me since we'd stepped into the restaurant.

"I need to know," I ventured. "Did you know my relic was your brother this whole time?"

At the mention of Julián, shadows seemed to sweep across Rigo's face. He seemed to feel about his brother the way I felt about

Mother Vanessa. Betrayed. Abandoned. Brimming with fiery rage. "No," he said, with a quick shake of the head. "I suspected there was a possibility it could be him, but I couldn't be sure. Not until he chose to act."

"So that's why you wanted the relic. In exchange for your freedom, I mean. You needed it from me for closer inspection."

"Yes." A moment's silence. "And as for why I didn't mention it to you, I wasn't sure what he might do to you once he knew I was onto him. I hoped I could help you secure your award before he chose to put you in peril, but that didn't happen."

Again, I stared at him. He'd saved me countless times, and I hadn't even realized. And while I was immensely grateful to him for that, it hadn't been enough. Julián was in the Prioress's clutches. The very things Rigo had failed to stop his brother from all those years ago seemed only hours away from happening again.

"What are we going to do?"

I didn't have to clarify. He knew.

"We go back, of course. But not right now. Not yet. You need to recover. Taking the relic from you took its toll—I'm sorry about that."

I nodded, still feeling the withdrawal as a lingering malaise. "But how. . ."

It all seemed so lost, so grim. I couldn't see any purpose in going back.

"We find Julián's relic," Rigo said firmly, "Before your Prioress can try to release him to harm your abbess or anyone else. We prove her transgressions. We get you your award back."

He sounded so confident, so sure, but I just couldn't see how we would accomplish that. "And how are we going to do that?"

Now he paused, wringing his bottom lip between his teeth.

"I'm still working on that part," he admitted. He gestured at my half-eaten bowl of soup. "Eat."

I wanted to figure out our next steps. It seemed pointless to eat when so much was at stake. For all I knew, the Prioress could have released Julián and slaughtered half the abbey by now. But Rigo was right, I was in no state to be making serious decisions.

So I ate. Out of the rain, with warm food in my stomach, I began to feel better. Less like a sobbing husk and more human. Clouds shifted across the sky out the restaurant's nearby window as the storm moved through. In time, the rain calmed, and the city came alive once more, the sidewalks filling with people and animals and street vendors. I was seeing my own city in a way I never had before. I felt horribly exposed and unnatural without my robes, but at the same time, oddly calm and at peace.

I swallowed the last of my soup around the time the first fingers of dusk began to streak across the cloud-swept sky.

"Where are we going to sleep?"

For that, too, Rigo already had an answer. "I know of a place where we should be safe. An inn, not far from here. There are places in your world where my kind know we can go and find a friendly face."

That was good enough for me. We were brought our bill. Rigo hunched over it, using his upper body to shield it from view as he waggled his fingers. A slew of coins appeared atop the bill tray with a faint bronzed sparkle. I gawked at him. I'd never seen demon magic before, and doubted I would again.

"Have you always been able to do that?"

"Consecrated stone, remember? I could hardly breathe inside your abbey. Here, I feel like a god," he said with a wink. "Let's go."

I was still thinking about the wink and the effect it had had on my middle as we spilled back onto the sidewalk. The road surface now shimmered gray and reflective, massive puddles mirroring the sunset back up toward the sky. Combined with the rising humidity after the storm, it gave everything the fuzzy, muted look of an old oil painting. At the corner, there was a cart selling goolab jamoon—fatty fritters of flour and cardamom glazed with sugary ginger syrup. Wanting tugged at my chest.

"What's the matter?" Rigo had slowed next to me. He followed my intent gaze on the cart. Without my having to ask, he understood. He stepped up to the vendor. "Two, please."

I wanted to cry, and not because I was upset. How was it that he knew my own desires better than even I did? When he passed me my serving a moment later, I hardly knew what to say. I waited until he'd paid—with money produced by a furtive wave of the hand—and we were walking away before saying anything.

"Thank you."

Rigo just grinned at me in response.

We ate and walked. The fritters were a delight to all the senses, a riot of sugar and spice and sticky ginger tang. I let the simple pleasure of the sweet lull me into complacency as I followed behind him on the way to the inn. He had said it wasn't far, and I was already looking forward to the prospect of a warm bed.

Then we turned a corner and Rigo froze, becoming a solid wall of unmoving muscle. I smacked into him.

"What—"

Then I, too, froze. At the end of the street was the Prioress's carriage. Though she herself was nowhere in sight, the carriage squatted near the sidewalk like a jungle cat looking out for its prey. My heart galloped into my throat.

She was here. She had come for me.

"We need to move," Rigo said, and took my hand.

I let him pull me along through different streets, cutting a wide berth around the Prioress's carriage. But I felt it at my back all the while, as if she could see me no matter where I was. I half expected her to reach down from the sky and pluck me up with giant taloned fingers. Though we put distance between us and the carriage, it never felt like enough. While we'd been eating, the Prioress had had her people searching for me, and we were at a disadvantage.

Several blocks from the carriage, we finally slowed, winding through a narrow side street. It dumped us out into an intersection. A black-robed nun—one of the Prioress's servants—prowled along the next street over, squinting against the coming dusk.

"Rigo—"

His hand tightened on mine. "I know. I see them."

Stepping sideways into the next alley, he pushed me behind him. While I waited, heart hammering, he poked his head around the corner to keep an eye on the Prioress's retinue.

"Are there only two of them?" he asked.

"Yes. As far as I know. Unless she's recruited some of the other nuns."

Another moment of watching. Then he stiffened.

"They're coming this way."

My stomach dropped into my toes. Rigo had whirled around, and it was only his fierce determination that kept me from simply dissolving into terror. His urgent gaze devoured me, something calculating creeping in.

He swallowed. "Do you trust me?"

"Yes," I said without hesitation, surprising even myself. And I did—I trusted him to keep us safe more than I did myself.

"Good," he said.

Then he stepped toward me, took me by the waist, and brought his lips to mine. The frantic heat of him blazed a path from where our lips met all the way to the tips of each of my limbs. My lips parted on a sigh. I drew him in, searching deeper, wanting more. One of his hands came up to cup my jaw right by my ear. His fingers sank into my wet hair, tugging me closer as his kiss grew more insistent. Knees weak, I backed into the alley wall and he followed, pressing me to the damp stone. My head spun with the warmth of his body against mine, the soft press of his lips, and my own hungry mouth moving on his in return.

I'd never kissed anyone before. Had never cared to. I found the lack of knowledge didn't matter. Touching him, giving in to this growing heat between us, somehow felt as natural to me as breathing.

This was forbidden, meant to be a distraction only. I knew by how he angled his body to keep me from view. But I didn't care, didn't push him away. I didn't want to. His kiss woke something in me that I'd long pushed aside—the attraction to him I'd been determined to ignore because it could only spell ruin. His kiss unsettled me in the best way possible. As the moment stretched on, I put my arms around his middle as well, fingers slipping on his slick raincoat, and held him as if that alone would make him mine.

He pulled away what felt like a lifetime later, brown lips swollen and chest heaving against mine. We were pressed so closely I could feel his heartbeat—no, heart*beats*. Two distinct sets. I stared at his chest, my question unspoken.

"Two hearts," he said, his voice rough.

Looking at him felt so different now—changed, and *charged*. The demon had two hearts. He'd kissed me in an alleyway, his tongue had been in my mouth, his hand in my hair. I took stock of my body. Warmth and longing between my legs, heat in my middle, and above it all, an almost magnetic yearning for more of his touch.

I wanted to kiss him again. I wanted him any way he would have me.

"Are you all right?" he asked. I nodded. His eyes scanned the street. "They've gone—for now. We need to get off the streets while we can."

He could have asked me for anything, right then.

And once more, I let him take my hand, tugging me along.

Chapter Twenty-Six

"No Order text will admit to this outright. However, just as there is an established history of acolyte–demon collaboration, there is also a strong and underestimated record of acolyte–demon relationships, ranging from dear friendships to much more. Given the Order's ingrained prejudice toward demonkind, we will likely never know the true extent of such close relationships. For what Order acolyte would willingly own up to their friendship—or more—with a demon?"
—Perspectives on the Below: A Scholarly Approach to the Demon Mirror World and Its Inhabitants

The inn was calm and quiet. It was an unassuming place tucked into a sleepy corner of town, sandwiched on either side by a small bookshop and a tailor's storefront. Inside, there was a small reception desk, one skinny hallway leading back to what I assumed was a dining room, and a narrow, rickety staircase leading up to the second and third floors.

Night had fallen, but every inch of me felt like a flower in full sun, blooming with heat. I tried to keep my wits about myself as Rigo exchanged quick, hushed words in Old Demonic with the innkeeper. We were granted a key and ushered upstairs. The room was not large, though well-appointed, with a small bathroom off to the side and a bed just big enough for two made with gauzy white linens.

I should have been ready for sleep. This had felt like the longest day of my life, full of horrors and revelations, most of which I would've given anything to take back. But my insides felt restless and insistent, buzzing like a colony of bees beneath my skin. Rigo had brought us here so that I could rest and recover from the relic's withdrawal, so that we could prepare for what we would have to do tomorrow.

I did not know how to tell him that rest and recovery was the last thing I wanted at the moment.

Once inside, Rigo shut the door and shrugged out of his stolen raincoat. He hung it carefully on the coat rack, avoiding my eyes.

"You can use the restroom first, if you'd like. I suppose you'll want to rinse the rain from your hair?"

Nodding, mumbling something in the affirmative, I closed myself into the restroom.

There, I shut my eyes. My skittering pulse had returned, though this time I did not fear capture—instead, it was something else entirely. I stared at the door for a long stretch before forcing myself to disrobe and bathe. There was a pedestal sink, along with a rudimentary toilet and a clawfoot tub with a privacy curtain rigged above. At the abbey, we were encouraged to use as little water as possible. I was used to tepid baths. Here, the water was steaming hot, and I luxuriated in it. Taking care to keep my bandages out of the water, I let the heat soothe my sore and tense muscles and wash away the day's stress. Then I wrapped myself in a towel and returned to the bedroom.

Rigo stood by the window, looking out onto the darkened streets. He'd lit a few candles. Their glow now cast flickering light throughout the room. Still warm from my bath, and with his presence a welcome fog to my senses, everything felt hazy, gilded in butter-yellow candlelight.

"Your turn," I said. He whirled around. His eyes skated over me head to toe, then quickly darted away from my bare legs. "I need to comb out my hair, and don't want to wet my clothes," I added by way of explanation.

"Of course," he said, and brushed past me. I heard the water start again a moment later.

I'd gathered my clothes from before and now set them down. With my fingers, I combed through my hair, and redid my twists as best as I could without any product. But I did not put my clothes from earlier back on. I remained in the towel, sat instead on the edge of the bed, and tried to breathe. The buzzing beneath my skin grew more insistent, building to a fever pitch. I was beginning to feel like I might explode if he did not touch me again.

When Rigo emerged from the bathroom, dressed in the same clothes as before, I was waiting for him. He paused in the doorway, one hand frozen halfway with a small towel against his wet hair.

"Annette." There was a note of surprise in his voice, along with something else—something darker, more heated and inquisitive. His gaze lingered on my hair. "I thought you were combing your hair?"

"I did."

A pause. Then: "Where are your clothes?"

Heart hammering in my chest, I pointed. "Over there. On the floor."

"And why is that?" he asked slowly, a bit breathlessly.

I couldn't get the words out. There wasn't enough light to see his face from here. Just the set of his shoulders, and the curve of his bicep as he lowered the towel from his hair.

"You're still in that towel," he remarked, walking over to me.

Now he stood before me. Tilting my head up, I forced myself to look at him. His mouth hung open, lips slightly parted. I remembered the feel of those full lips on mine. Noticed, now, his attention lingering on all of my exposed skin. There was something in his gaze that told me all my wanting was not one-sided.

I shouldn't have wanted him. He was a demon, the very type of monster I'd been taught to fear. But he'd been nothing but kind to me, and I was slowly learning that not everything I'd learned at the abbey was true. More than ever, I felt like I was coming to know myself apart from that structure. I was giving in to all my basest desires. Rigo would not be the exception.

"I. . ." My throat felt parched, and my hands trembled where I held the towel closed across my heart. "I-I want. . ."

Rigo took another step closer. Softly, he said, "What?"

Say it, I told myself. *Be brave.*

I breathed deep and released the words with my exhale.

You," I said finally. "I want you."

The demon's jaw went slack. I watched as he realized what I was asking, what all of this was about. His expression shifted from curiosity to plain hunger. His chest rose and fell, his breathing the only sound that felt like it mattered.

"And what is it you think this will accomplish?" he asked, in his signature inquisitive tone.

I recognized the challenge. So many of our conversations in the archives had taken a similar bent, me proposing something and him poking and prodding until I fully formed the thought. He was doing the same now—giving me the opportunity to make my desires clear.

All this time, I had planned to use him, only I had come to depend on him instead. Tomorrow, we would face off against his brother and the Prioress. I felt very aware of the fact that this could be my last night of freedom. My last night alive. If we failed. . .there was no telling what the abbey would do to either of us.

Finally, I said, "I just. . .want to know what it's like. Just once."

Rigo's steady breathing hitched. The intensity of his stare was such that he didn't so much as blink.

"And you've never. . ."

I shook my head.

"Are you even allowed?" he asked, as if it had just occurred to him.

Yes, we were. Popular acolytes with normal social skills easily formed bonds with the locals who did business with the abbey. Sometimes those relationships were mere community ties. Other times, they went far beyond. I'd spent many nights fireside in the parlor, pretending not to listen to the others' stories about spending a discreet evening with this person or that. Those types of things had just never seemed like a possibility for me.

Until now.

"The Mother demands no celibacy from her servants," I told him. "We're all free to. . .do as we wish. I just, I'm very particular. And I haven't felt like—I haven't felt like I ever wanted to, until you."

His next inhale went ragged, his eyes widening.

"I see," he said.

His tongue darted out to wet his lower lip. The sight of it left me feverish.

And he had not yet given me an answer, so I went on, letting my thoughts spill out as they came to me. "We could die tomorrow. You and I both know that. There's no telling what might happen."

Rigo's eyes never wavered from mine, even as he swallowed, stepped closer. "Do you doubt your own ability to succeed so thoroughly?"

I nodded. "I don't know if I'm strong enough. To defy the Prioress. Mother Vanessa. All the other Sisters. And if I'm not. . ."

"Then we die." Now he stood very close. His knees touched mine. He seemed to be weighing my words. After a moment, he said, "If it makes any difference.. . .I have faith in you."

I couldn't help but quirk up one side of my mouth into a smile. That word again: faith. Like the two of us weren't already a gross abomination just sitting here.

"So is that a no?"

"I'm not going to refuse you, Annette."

A hot flush went through me. My palms began to sweat where they were clasped around the towel.

"You're not?"

In a voice like velvet, he said, "Did you think I did not desire you?"

Goosebumps stippled my flesh. "I. . .I wasn't entirely sure."

Rigo gave half a scoff, half a grin. "That kiss we shared out of necessity in the alleyway was not just a ruse, little nun. I wouldn't have tasted you then if I hadn't already considered it."

My eyes grew wide as the truth of this skittered through me. "You. . ."

Rigo, a demon of unknowable age, who'd likely had thousands of lovers, was interested in. . .me?

He bent at the waist and placed his arms on either side of where I sat on the bed, bringing our faces very close together. This close, he smelled of the same soap I'd used, and the ghost of his breath over my lips left my head spinning. "I've been trying to show you how I feel all this time. You've captivated me, Annette. Every time I think I know you, you surprise me again." He dropped his head to press a kiss to my shoulder. My eyes fluttered briefly closed at the contact. "You're so fucking intriguing, I can hardly stand it."

I swallowed. "I am?"

A slow nod. Slowly, he reached for the silk tie that held my twists together, pulled, and let my hair fall free. Fingers curling, he gathered a handful, his hand brushing my collarbone. I shivered with pleasure at his touch.

"And the way you react when I touch you?" An inhale, shaky and slow. "Fuck. I can't get enough."

His gaze dropped to the makeshift knot I'd made to keep the towel closed. Beneath the heat of his stare, I loosened it, removed my fingers, let the towel fall open to reveal my nakedness beneath. I felt like my heart was beating out of my skin. Could he sense how badly I wanted him? It felt like it, as he drank me in with a look, leisurely and unhurried.

It was torture. I wanted his lips on mine. I wanted to know what his skin felt like beneath his clothes.

Finally, I whispered, "Please."

"Well," he murmured. "I suppose if you're going to beg. . ."

I tipped my lips up to meet his, and as before, he claimed them as natural as breathing. But this time, given what I'd asked, there was an undercurrent beneath it all, something banked and heated and more than ready to ignite. He sipped at me with delicate, measured kisses, both firm and sweet. Soon I was gasping into his mouth, tasting his own ragged breathing. My hands curled hungrily into his hair. I fell back onto my elbows, bringing him with me, and he pressed me back against the bed. The solid warmth of his body on mine was a delicious shock. I moaned into the kiss, and he stifled a curse against my lips, fisting a hand in the sheets.

"Annette," he gasped. "*Fuck*."

He broke the kiss, and I would've despaired, until I realized where he was going. Slow and deliberate, Rigo trailed his lips down my body, putting his mouth on my collarbone, my breasts, the hollow of my stomach. Finally, his weight left me and he sank to his knees on the floor, his head lingering near the apex of my thighs. Those dark, depthless eyes bored into mine.

"Can I taste you?"

Nodding, suddenly shy, I opened my thighs and exposed myself to him. I had only ever let my hands wander a handful of times. I'd never considered what his mouth might feel like there. The moment Rigo's mouth closed around the bud at my center, my back arched, and a breathy, high moan tore its way from me. I was not prepared for the wet heat of his tongue laving over my most sensitive spot. My body tingled with a fierce chorus of electric shocks. I ground my hips against him, chasing any and all pleasure he could give.

Humming an amused chuckle, Rigo gripped either side of my hips and held me in place. As the pleasure built, and he continued to worship me with his tongue, sweat broke over my skin. My fingers knotted in his hair and clutched him to me. I could barely breathe. My heart felt like it might burst through my ribcage. My eyes rolled back in my head, eyelids fluttering, until—

Breath bottled in my throat, I careened over a wild edge, gasping his name. He didn't relent. Instead, he kept his mouth on me, prolonging the pleasure until tears formed at the corners of my eyes. It was too much, it was not enough, it was everything I'd ever dreamed.

"*Fuck*!" I cried, drunk on pleasure.

As the aftershocks faded, Rigo lifted his head from between my legs, his gaze heated and heavy-lidded. I reached for him, and he crawled back over me, a wicked grin transforming his face.

"What I wouldn't give to hear you use that word again," he said.

The grin was infectious. It spread to me. I felt limp and loose-limbed, my body still tingling from what he'd done to me.

"Something to strive for, then," I murmured.

I pulled him ever closer into another deep kiss. His hands roved my body, exploring me with a hungry intensity that only stoked me hotter—hands on my neck, my breasts, the curve of my hip. His hunger for me was delicious, dizzying. I'd never felt so wanted in my life. I twined my legs with his until I could feel his stiffness against me. Curious, I ran a hand along his length, and he groaned into my mouth, letting loose with an Old Demonic curse.

He kissed me more fervently, then. In between open-mouthed kisses that left me breathless, he shed first his shirt, then his pants, until I was looking at him as naked as I was. My hips arched toward him. I whimpered, craving more. I could not get enough of him, could not get close enough. My thighs were trembling with need. I felt hot and empty and aching, and I wanted him inside me.

In a whisper pressed to his ear, I told him as much.

"You're sure?"

"Yes. Very."

Slowly, eyes on mine the entire time, Rigo aligned himself with my entrance. His tip swirled around my sensitive and slick folds, leaving me with pebbled goosebumps all over.

"Rigo," I whined.

He obliged, sinking gently into me on a prolonged moan. There was only the briefest flare of pain, and then a shocking pleasure, shivering up my spine as the length of him sank deeper. I'd never imagined I would feel him this deep, or that it might feel *this* good. I felt full to bursting, open from within by a molten heat that left me trembling. His lips found mine once more, one arm cradling my hip while the other cupped my jaw, and rolled his hips into mine with a tantalizing slowness. My breath caught in my throat with each thrust. Fingers curling around his muscled upper arms, I clutched at him like he was the only thing keeping me tethered to this world.

"Am I hurting you?"

"No," I told him, but I could hardly speak. I felt blind with pleasure, all my thoughts split open and spilled out of me. His next thrust was more intense, and I cried out, shocked by how good it felt. "Please. . .more?"

My mouth fell open on a moan as he increased his pace. His ragged breathing, and the hot slide of our bodies together, were music to my ears. His hand found its way down between us to stroke me, and that was about all I could take. A few more snaps of his hips to mine, and stars burst bright and blinding behind my eyelids. Sobbing a filthy curse into the crook of his neck, I clamped down on him as waves of pleasure swept through me, leaving me boneless. Rigo twitched inside of me, gasping, his chest heaving, and collapsed against me.

I felt sated. Content. My pulse thrummed along in my fingertips, the top of my head, between my legs where Rigo still filled me. Residual pleasure left me dizzy and blurry-eyed. When he finally slid from me, he stretched out on his side next to me and tucked me against him. I went willingly. Wanting more, I tugged his lips to mine again. The way he took my face in his hands and reciprocated the kiss told me he was far from done.

I found him to have an insatiable appetite. It made sense to me. He'd been locked up, alone, for twenty years, and if he needed an outlet for all that misplaced passion, I was happy to provide. And as long as he was kissing me, sliding inside me so gentle and tender, I found I could not refuse him. I wanted anything and everything he was willing to give. I managed maybe one or two more times before at last, with the pleasure too great and my senses thoroughly over-stimulated, I pushed him gently away.

Chuckling, he went into the restroom and brought a warm cloth, which he used to gently clean the mess between my thighs. I felt some soreness already, and suspected it would only intensify by morning, but I'd handle it then. I felt zero regret for what we'd done. And I wouldn't have changed it for the world.

I must have dozed off. Sometime a few hours later, I woke. Rigo was curled around me like a warm blanket, his head nuzzled against my neck. He was singing quietly, some sort of demon song. And though I couldn't parse the words, it sounded the same way I felt—like for a moment, we were all that existed, and tomorrow would never come.

Like my heart was floating free, untethered from all the burdens of the world.

Chapter Twenty-Seven

"Many Order abbeys are known to take in unwanted or otherwise unruly children from across the Islands. As far as what becomes of them afterward, very little is known."
—Excerpt from An Exploration of the Order of the Revenant Mother and Other Island Religions

When I finally woke again, for good, early morning sunlight draped the inn's gauzy curtains in soft yellow. The sounds here were all different from what I was used to at the abbey. Faint laughter, conversation, the *whirr* of someone cranking a coffee grinder in the distance. It was the first time in years that I hadn't woken up on my lumpy mattress behind those walls. The world felt novel and different, subtly changed.

Then I remembered the awful task that lay ahead.

The previous day's events came back to me all at once. The Sisters tossing me out of the abbey with nothing to my name. Wandering the city during a downpour, thinking I would never find my way to safety. Rigo rescuing me, consoling me, and accepting my offer when I invited him to bed. . .

Groaning, I opened my eyes and sat up, reaching automatically for Rigo. My hand passed through empty air.

He was gone. The bed next to me was empty, the pillow still sunken from where his head had been. I pressed the back of my hand to the skull-shaped indentation. Still warm. So he'd only recently left.

I swallowed. There was nothing to indicate he was gone for good. And yet, I couldn't shake the nagging, anxious unease beginning to climb my esophagus like the gradual onset of a sore throat. He wasn't *here*.

I'd been left alone. Again.

The pads of my fingers pressed into the sheets in desperation. This early in the morning, I was used to Grounding myself, but there was no pot of dirt here, nothing for me to sink my toes into. My uneasiness climbed higher.

I'd given myself to Rigo last night, wholly, body and mind. And I still felt the physical evidence of what we'd done—a pleasant ache between my legs, light bruises on my hips from where he'd gripped me tightly, tender spots on my neck where he'd suckled at me with his teeth. I wasn't supposed to care for a demon, but I did.

On top of all of that, I still needed his help. I was depending on him to help me stop whatever evil the Prioress had planned, to keep Julián from assisting in her aims. Only I could act on the danger the Prioress posed—and I couldn't do it alone.

Had I made an error trusting him with my affections?

I'm not sure how long I sat there, panicking. Only when the door swung open an indeterminate amount of time later did I feel like I finally breathed again.

Rigo stepped inside and set down two steaming mugs on the side table.

He had barely closed the door before I was up and out of the bed, tripping over the sheets that entangled me, and locking my arms around his neck with a wordless cry.

Caught off-balance, he staggered. Dressed and carrying with him the scent of baked bread and sugar, he had something else in his hands that he quickly set down on the side table. I didn't care what it was. He'd come back, and that was all that mattered to me.

"Whoa! Is everything okay?"

I inhaled, but no words would come out. Seeing him again had unstoppered all the emotions brewing in my chest, and now, like the most fast-acting poison, everything swept through me at once. Trembling, I stepped back, taking in the welcome sight of him.

"Annette?" Now he was frowning, concern rising. "What's wrong?"

My chest clenched tight. A rush of heat, then cold, swept me from head to toe. He reached for me, but my legs buckled, and I found myself on the floor, back against the bedframe, knees pulled toward my chest. I was gasping, convulsing with a sudden swell of feeling that seemed to come from nowhere. Panic and relief and a heavy, suffocating fear—all emotions I usually kept private.

"I—thought—you—left—" I managed.

Now there were tears streaming down my face, so embarrassing, and I wanted to fling myself out the window to an untimely death.

Rigo's frown deepened as he peered at me. Snagging another sheet from the bed, he wrapped it around me, perhaps sensing I needed the comfort. And I did. I clung to the smooth feeling of the clean fabric on my skin, tried to breathe. Slowly, he lowered himself to sit next to me.

"You thought I left? Why would I leave?"

Before him, being left was all I knew. I squeezed my eyes shut tight. "Because everyone does."

A long silence.

Then: "Annette. Look at me." That much I could manage. When I opened my eyes, Rigo sat facing me, cross-legged, open and vulnerable while I was all closed up. "I'm *here*."

I nodded. "I know."

Why couldn't I stop breathing like this? What was wrong with me?

"I'm not going anywhere." He reached for one of my quivering, sweaty hands, and I let him have it. "Why did you think I left? Where would I go?"

I shrugged. I didn't have an answer.

The open wound of my childhood gaped anew, a gnawing, bloody mouth ready to swallow me whole. I didn't know what it was about his brief absence that had sent me spiraling, or why I struggled so hard to regulate myself afterward, even now that he'd returned. It all felt so silly, and yet I couldn't snap out of it.

Rigo reached behind him with his other hand and dragged down a brown paper bag, with something wrapped in parchment paper poking out the top.

Shaking the bag, he explained, "I went across the street to the bakery as soon as they opened."

"Oh, Mother." I laughed, still crying. I felt ridiculous. All I could do was repeat my own pathetic refrain: "I thought you *left*."

His dark eyes fixed on mine. He squeezed my hand, and I felt myself start to relax. Clasped hands were where it had all started for us. The reminder of that, the comfort of it, was a Grounding all on its own.

"Why?" he asked. A brief pause. "Tell me about it."

Resistance reared up in me. I never understood why it went against my nature to share pieces of myself with others. Left to my own devices, I preferred to curl inward, keep everything locked up tight inside. I struggled to volunteer even bits of information so benign as my favorite color. But Rigo's hand in mine gave me strength, and courage. When Mother Vanessa had kicked me out of the abbey, my only home, and thrown me onto the streets, it was Rigo who kept me safe. Rigo, who stayed, and swore to help me fix the grand mess I'd made of the abbey.

If I couldn't at least let *him* in, what hope did I have?

I inhaled, and it all came rushing out, like I'd been waiting my whole life to tell someone about this hurt inside me.

"When I was ten," I began, "I got in trouble at school. I was messing about with plants at recess and handed over my concoction to a classmate. She fell ill, and I got expelled. The school thought I'd done it on purpose. My parents—well, mother and stepfather—didn't know what to do with me. I begged to go live with my older sister June on the other side of town, to try and attend school there, and they seemed to agree. But on the day I thought we were going to June's house, they brought me to the abbey instead."

Even just thinking about it was enough to nearly tear me in two.

"They lied. Misled me. I was told then that I was being given over to the abbey's care. I'd thought I was going to live with my sister. Instead, the Sisters dragged me inside and beat me for causing a fuss." Those early days at the abbey were a dark blur in my mind, all but swirled out of existence. "I never saw my parents again after they walked away that day. I haven't spoken to my sister in years. There was nowhere else I could go. I was so miserable, but what other choice did I have? I was *ten years old*."

Rigo cursed, low and drawn out. "So, when I wasn't here—"

I nodded. "I figured you were gone for good."

"I'm so sorry." His expression was wretched, warped with what I was sure was pity for me. "I was coming right back. I didn't realize you'd be so upset."

"It's not your fault."

"No," he murmured. Now he shifted, pulling me to him, and I went like a needy moth to a flame. With one arm beneath my knees and the other around my back, he held me curled in his lap like an infant as I cried. "But I can assure you it won't happen again."

"What do you mean?"

"I'm not going anywhere. If I do, you'll know why in advance. I won't ever leave you, Annette. Not for long. If I do, it'll be temporary. And I promise you that I will always come back."

I was so shocked, I stopped crying.

Rigo wasn't my family. I'd been holding him and everyone else around me at a distance as if they were. For so long, I'd taught myself that I was the only one I could depend on. But my family's abandonment wasn't necessarily a cycle doomed to repeat.

Here I was in a demon's arms, in a strange inn in the center of the city, miles away from the abbey that had raised me.

Here, for the first time, I felt at home.

I knew then that I could depend on Rigo, at least. With him, I had only ever been entirely myself, and not once had he turned away. And as much as I didn't want to believe it, as strongly as my mind tried to convince me otherwise, it was Rigo's kindness and tenderness toward me in the face of the horrible things I'd done that proved to me I was worthy of having around. Of simply being *wanted*.

Finally, I exhaled, my breath returning to normal, and the tension fled my body all at once.

"Oh," was all I said, and Rigo chortled.

As I relaxed, Rigo's arms tightened around me, holding me closer. I let my eyes flutter shut to savor the calming effect of the deep pressure. With my ear pressed against his chest, I heard his two demon hearts beating wildly out of rhythm as they had before in the alley, and ironically, I'd never felt more human, or more whole.

"Thank you," I whispered to the space under his chin.

He *hmm*ed in acknowledgment. For a while, he just let me lean on him, and that space and time was exactly what I needed.

When I at last sat up, he searched my face, and I offered him a small, hesitant smile, feeling marginally better.

"So," I said timidly. "About those baked goods?"

Grinning, he reached for the bag. As I was closest to the side table now, I slid off his lap and carefully fetched the drinks he'd brought. Steam still curled upward from the tops of the mugs.

"And these are?" I gave each an experimental sniff. One was obviously coffee. The other, a tea, left me momentarily frowning as I puzzled out its contents. "Wild carrot seed, thistle, stoneseed root. . ." Years of schooling on various plants and herbs crystallized at once. It was a contraceptive tonic. Heat rushed to my cheeks. "*Oh.*"

Unwrapping the parchment paper, Rigo handed me a slice of rum cake that left my fingers sticky with syrup. "I am very impressed by your ability to identify herbs by scent."

I couldn't help the smile that stole across my lips. "I was top of my class, after all." Biting into the cake, its sweetness mixed with yet another kind gesture from Rigo to suffuse me with warmth. "I hadn't even thought about *that.*"

"You had a lot on your mind," he said simply, eyes on mine. He seemed to be holding back a smile of his own. "And you were. . .distracted."

The heat in his words had me flushing all over again. Laughing, I tossed out, "Shut up and eat your cake, demon."

We fell into easy laughter, then comfortable silence, soaking up the last bits of something *good* before we would have to face the great evil on the horizon.

The task before us stretched wide and daunting. But somehow, with Rigo by my side, I'd never felt more capable.

Chapter Twenty-Eight

"To guard against demonic evil, the walls of each Order abbey are consecrated upon construction with the application of blessed water and fervent prayer."
—Excerpt from: An Exploration of the Order of the Revenant Mother and Other Island Religions

I had dreamed about leaving the abbey, and returning to it, many times. None of those dreams had included a demon by my side.

"I saw Rosalind put the ring into her robes," Rigo told me as we rounded the corner onto the last street that would bear us upon the abbey. "She'll want Julián with her, as close by as possible. That dark ritual she once tried to use to free him? She might try it again."

I nodded my agreement. From what I knew of the Prioress, that all sounded plausible. "So we need a way to distract her long enough to get the ring back."

A thick fog had rolled across this corner of town after last night's storm. It was eerie, and certainly made me no less nervous.

My shoulder bumped his as we ambled down the sidewalk. It brought to my mind the memory of other touches from the previous night, and I had to remind myself to focus on the task at hand. How surreal this all felt, coming back to an abbey unchanged, whereas I felt like a different person entirely.

"Hopefully, before she frees him," Rigo said. He added, "Freed, he'll be that much harder to capture. And I need him to clear my name." He fell silent for a stretch. Our shoes, which still had not fully dried from yesterday's downpour, made squeaking noises as we navigated the streets. "Once we have him, we'll need to contain him somehow. Keep him from causing more harm."

"There was a box in Mother Vanessa's office," I remembered aloud, "From where the Prioress gifted her the cursed bracelet. It should work. I'm not sure if it's still there, but I could check."

"And the other relics she controls?" I had told him what I'd seen the other morning—the Prioress directing Narissa and Mother Vanessa like puppets, all with a simple touch of her rings.

"She'll want those close to her too. They'll be wherever she is." I was sure of it even as I spoke. Now that Rosalind was here, and thought she'd gotten rid of me—the one person who knew what she might be planning—I suspected she'd try to draw everything possible under her control. And the recertification provided the perfect cover. "We'll need a distraction. Something big. Then I can get the ring, get Mother Vanessa's bracelet, and find a way to subdue Narissa so she can't interfere—"

Rigo came to a sudden stop, and I broke off. Though the sidewalk had ended, a stretch of road still remained to cross before stepping on the abbey's grounds. I looked hurriedly around, half expecting to see the Prioress stepping out of the fog.

He'd been silent for too long. My stomach dropped to my toes. "What is it?"

"Something's wrong," he said, after a pause.

He shot me a worried look, and we both hastened for the main gate.

We had planned to sneak in, avoid drawing attention. A narrow alley framed the abbey's exterior, used by the locals who delivered for our food stores and sought—by appointment—to peruse our remedies. As the main gate and front gardens were seldom frequented, this alley was what we'd intended to follow around to the back to enter unnoticed. But as we approached the main gate, a sense of sudden *wrongness* arrested me and drove every thought of the alley from my mind.

The gate was open.

I had never seen it open without explicit reason. Without one of the Sisters standing immediately nearby to oversee its entrance and admit any visitor who'd come to call.

Panic tapped against the hollow of my throat. For a moment, I wasn't thinking only of my award. I thought of all the younger girls, innocent and afraid, who had no idea of the danger in their midst. I thought of the other Sisters who were likely too busy keeping a handle on the recertification to notice that anything was amiss.

If there was no abbey—if Rosalind and Julián's ritual went wrong again—there would be no award.

For all the many little wounds and indignities the abbey had inflicted upon me, it was my home. And I felt, with the Mother's holy conviction, an all-consuming duty to save it.

I stepped through the open gate—

"Annette, wait!" Rigo cried.

—And with one dizzying, brutal lurch, the world twisted upside down.

Shaking, I fell to my knees. Everything had gone very still. Not an ounce of wind swept through the courtyard. The unsettling fog had vanished. Inside the gate, the sky had an eerie, blood-red tinge to it, the sun a luminescent black dot. And that sky sat where my feet should've been.

"What the—" I blinked rapidly. My mind struggled to parse this new reality. "What *is* this?"

It was the strangest sensation—I knew I'd fallen on solid ground. I felt gravity's gentle press rooting me to the spot. But the ground and the sky had changed places, and the abbey loomed large and wrong ahead like its own mirror image on the surface of a lake.

Rigo kneeled next to me. "We're too late," he said, grim. I looked at him. His face was a mask of horror. He gestured. "He's already free. This, all of this, the sky and the upside down, it's a rift into my world. The demon world. Whatever ritual Rosalind used tore open the border in-between. Anyone, or any*thing*, could come through."

He helped me to my feet. What he said felt true. I had the slightest sense of persistent vertigo, like my own body reminding me I wasn't meant to be here. How strange it was to know I was so close to the demon world.

"So what do we do?"

"It'll close on its own soon enough. But for our sake, we need to make sure Julián is on the other side." Rigo swallowed. "He'll be with Rosalind. But if he's free? He's more dangerous now than ever. Stay alert."

I nodded. Clinging to him to orient myself in this inverted world, we trudged forward.

There was no point to sneaking in if Julián was already free. We'd lost the element of surprise we'd hoped to use to prevent the Prioress from releasing him. Now, we could only hope that we could find and subdue him before the rift closed and trapped him on our side.

The front doors were open, too, one more wrong thing in a sea of many. I nearly gagged as we stepped inside. The smell reminded me of that burnt room in the North Wing. Old smoke, and an acrid bitterness. Not a single candle flickered in the wall sconces, leaving the unholy blood-red light all we had to navigate by. And on the walls, from the ceiling, black sludge oozed, like the burn marks left on the North Wing's common room come to life.

"Magic remnants," Rigo remarked. "Demonic. Don't touch it."

We pressed on through the unnatural environment. Each step seemed to take a grand amount of effort. I kept my eyes trained straight ahead, sure that if I looked down toward where the ceiling lay, I might start screaming.

"Where is everyone?" Rigo asked, moments later.

We'd come into the main hall. He was right—it did feel empty, deserted. Which only concerned me more, because the abbey was *never* deserted.

I squeezed my eyes closed against another wave of panic and thought hard. "Emergency protocols," I murmured a moment later. "Communicated via the chapel bell. If anything goes wrong, we shelter in place."

I could only hope that Julián's release had come about when most acolytes were still in their beds, and that someone had been able to ring the bell at all.

Minutes later, my hopes were dashed as we came across a young acolyte slumped against the wall outside one of the classrooms. Her face and robes were gray with dust, and her hands were a mess of fresh scratches.

She whimpered at the sight of us, and all of my own worries fled as I rushed to her side.

"Are you hurt?"

"N-No. Just m-my hands," she stuttered out. "I-I don't know what happened—"

"Where were you? When the explosion happened?"

The acolyte screwed her face up in concentration. Despite her proclamation, she was clearly wounded, perhaps with a blow to the head. Her eyes were glassy and unfocused, the pupils blown. "The scriptorium. There was a loud bang, and then the whole building shook—I woke up on the ground and had to claw my way through. The entrance collapsed."

Following her pointed finger, I looked. Indeed, the archway surrounding the scriptorium entrance was now a pile of rubble. This girl was lucky to have survived.

I exchanged a look with Rigo. We couldn't bring her with us, but I didn't want to leave her, either.

"Where is she? The Prioress?" I demanded.

The acolyte frowned. "In the chapel," she said, seeming confused, which told me she did not yet know what the Prioress intended. "She's reconsecrating the chapel as part of the recertification."

"All right. Thank you. Stay here."

"But—"

The girl cried out briefly behind us, seeming to just now notice that the ceiling wasn't where it should be.

"She's injured," Rigo said as we moved away.

"I know that. And she'll be worse off if she's with us," I fired back. "I won't let anyone else get hurt because of me."

He frowned, but accepted this. I angled us in the direction of the chapel. Unwilling to go in through the front, I took us instead to the back hallway, which would open up into an entrance behind the lectern and a small storage space. The same place I'd seen the Narissa-thing peel open her skin the previous morning. My stomach gave a lurch at the memory. Now, unlike then, I did not have the relic's invisibility. There would be no second chances if we were seen.

Voices tiptoed through the opening as we approached.

The Prioress, unamused: "Silence, demon."

We crept closer. Each of us on one side of the doorway, we poked our heads around to see in.

The Prioress stood next to the lectern with her back to us. Next to her was the long wooden table upon which we normally displayed prayer items. But all that had been shoved to the floor, and instead, a *person* lay atop the table, strapped down with thick cording around their arms and legs.

Mother Vanessa.

The abbess whined and pulled at her restraints. The voice that left her mouth when she spoke was not her own.

"*You promised, mistress,*" said the demonic relic within her skin. It had a high, wheedling voice like some sort of rodent. "*You promised me my freedom before you would harm this vessel.*"

The Prioress shifted to the side, revealing more of the lectern, and the various gardening implements that sat atop it. Mildly, she said, "Are you not strong enough to abide it?"

"*I am, but—*"

"Then *silence*. Your presence will keep her alive longer. Allow me a sweeter revenge." Prioress Rosalind took up a small, pointed trowel between her fingers and began to draw the sharp edge along Mother Vanessa's exposed bicep. My stomach churned, nauseous saliva filling my throat. Now I could see countless stripes of red drawn along the abbess's skin, and the blood that dripped from them to pool beneath her sleeves on the table.

Prioress Rosalind was torturing her. Casually, like simply going for a stroll in the garden, and while making conversation with the demon she herself had trapped inside the abbess.

I wanted to scream. How had this all gone so wrong, so fast? By sheer brute force of will, I kept my wits intact.

"Where is Julián?" I whispered.

"I don't know," Rigo responded, looking worried. "I can't sense him. But he must be here."

It wasn't the answer I was looking for, and it was almost worse, somehow, that Rigo *couldn't* sense his brother. It meant Julián could be anywhere. The hasty plan we'd managed to cobble together was rapidly becoming irrelevant. Once again, panic bubbled in my throat, and I shoved it down.

Later, later. I could fall apart later, once this all was over.

"Find him. I'll handle the Prioress."

"Are you sure?"

Splitting up hadn't been part of the plan. But what other choice did we have? "You said we have limited time until the rift closes.

We can't both be in two places at once, and there's too much to do." I eyed the gardening tools laid out along the lectern. "I'll figure something out."

With his hesitation palpable, Rigo started to back away.

"Find Sister Colette," I told him. "She'll help you."

With a nod, he disappeared around the corner, back the way we'd come.

The sudden loss of him nearly set me screaming. Rigo was smart and capable, I told myself. I sucked in a rapid, deep breath.

So was I.

I set my shoulders and slipped silently into the chapel.

"*Mistressssss*—" The thing inside Mother Vanessa was truly distressed now, thrashing her body around like a dying fish. Prioress Rosalind was wholly unconcerned.

"You are strong, demon. Can you not handle a little pain?"

My footfalls light, I crept into the opposite corner, crouched behind a squat cabinet. The Prioress straightened to admire her work. She was on the other side of the table now, her back to me, as she plucked a pair of pruning shears off the lectern.

Ignoring the relic's wails, she took the shears to the tip of Mother Vanessa's finger. A gush of blood fell from the wound.

This sent the demon into agony.

I swallowed the saliva pooling in my mouth. Mother Vanessa had caused me a world of pain, but it had all been at the Prioress's hand. All her cruelty had been by proxy. The abbess didn't deserve this—I didn't know if she would survive it. I didn't know how much longer I could wait.

With the Prioress distracted, I snatched the first tool from the lectern. A pair of forked tongs. Not my first choice, but it would work.

From Mother Vanessa suddenly came an uncanny, guttural cry. Her body convulsed, then stilled, and a gray wisp of irate spirit flew upward off the table.

"You awful bitch," hissed the wisp. *"You promised me."*

Prioress Rosalind sighed. "Very well, then. On with it."

And she seized a string of prayer beads from nearby and drew the spirit into battle.

It had never occurred to me that the Prioress knew how to fight a demonic spirit, though in that moment I was glad that she did. They matched each other blow for blow, the spirit weakened for having shared in the abbess's pain. It was then that I saw my chance. Prioress Rosalind had her back to me again, preoccupied with fighting off the angry spirit. I moved forward, lifting the tongs. It would take only one sharp jab into her neck, then I could take the ring, find Rigo, and—

Something crashed into me from the side, and I went sprawling, the tongs clattering across the floor. Before I could even process what had happened, unnaturally strong hands yanked me up to my knees, one arm curled around my neck, and another held a knife to my throat. Golden curls wavered at the edges of my vision.

Narissa.

The Prioress had managed to shove her bound spirit into a container of blessed water. Having now heard the commotion, she turned, setting the container aside. A slow smile stole across her face.

"Well done, my dear," she said to Narissa, who merely grunted like an animal. I writhed in her grasp, which only caused her grip to tighten, the blade of the knife biting into my skin. I felt a warm drop of blood roll down my throat. Prioress Rosalind's eyes shifted to me. "And Annette. It is so nice to finally meet you face to face."

I didn't think. Instead I gathered all the excess saliva in my mouth and spat it in her face.

Prioress Rosalind simply blinked, undeterred. She pulled out a handkerchief and wiped her face, much like cleaning a pair of glasses on a rainy day. "I'll admit, I deserved that. I'm sure you think the worst of me already." Her head tilted to the side. "But have you truly figured out the extent of your role in all of this?"

Frowning, I fixed her with my meanest glare. I didn't know what she was talking about, but I wasn't going to give her the satisfaction of asking.

She knelt before me anyway, calm and proper as if to give a benediction. It felt perverse—with the corpse that was Narissa holding a knife to my neck, and Mother Vanessa's bleeding and tortured frame on the prayer table mere feet away.

"I never meant for anyone else to be swept up in this. But you, Annette, somehow you planted yourself there right from the very beginning. I've been trying for years to find a way to get Vanessa back for all the wrongs she's wrought upon me. You would know, wouldn't you? Having read my diary? Julián told me all about your little adventure." She offered me a serene smile, which was much more eerie than outright anger would've been.

"You see, you need not have interfered. I had already set out all the pieces of my puzzle. I found a dead orphan girl in some backwater morgue and pieced her back together into something living, something reanimated. I sent her several months ahead of the recertification to look for weaknesses. I sent Vanessa a relic of my own to render her off balance. I wanted to find a reason that I could use on which to pin the abbey's failure—only, Narissa relayed something much more interesting." Now she reached out and touched my face—tenderly, the way a mother might. I recoiled. Another sting of the knife, another drop of blood. "Imagine my surprise to hear that you were Vanessa's pet project. And that, when I instructed her to mess with the awards to see what would happen, you rose above even my wildest expectations and went rogue."

I sagged in Narissa's grip. It had been the Prioress all along.

"*You* instructed the abbess to deny me my award?"

I'd known she was controlling the abbess, but I'd never dreamed she would go this far. It made me sick, thinking of all the strings being pulled behind my back, made me feel like a childish idiot for thinking myself so clever and bloodthirsty.

Prioress Rosalind nodded. "Later, Narissa told me that she'd sensed a powerful surge of magic—and I knew then that, by some stroke of luck, you'd stumbled upon my old friend Julián. That only made things all the easier."

I would've spat in her face again, but my mouth had gone dry. Each action I thought was my own had been prodded along by the Prioress first. I wanted to scream. I was shaking with rage, burning with it.

Now she stood. "So thank you, really, for your efforts. You've paved the way for me to reshape this abbey under my own control. For that, I am in your debt."

The Prioress cast an almost loving glance at Mother Vanessa. My mind worked frantically around a stab of fear. Rosalind hated

Vanessa, had wanted her dead for years. I wasn't the only one who'd sought to sabotage the recertification—Rosalind wanted the same, only in her revenge fantasy, Vanessa was dead, and the abbey belonged to her.

I'd been so stupid.

"Dispose of her," said the Prioress calmly. "It's time I find Julián for our next phase."

No sooner had she started walking than Narissa released me. A split second later, she shoved me from behind so hard I flew to the ground. My cheek smashed against the stone, and I tasted blood—I'd bitten my tongue. A glance back at Narissa revealed only a creature's blank stare. There would be no point in attempting to reason with her. She didn't exist—never had. So ears, ringing, I started crawling, searching for the tongs I'd dropped earlier.

A hand closed around my ankle and began yanking me back. I dug my hands into the floor with a cry—and a piece of stone came away as Narissa dragged me back into her clutches. I kicked out with all my might. I needed to get off the floor and away from her to have a chance at survival. She kept grabbing, relentless, spurred on by the Prioress's relic-bound demand. Shouldn't she have been weakened by the abbey's walls, like Rigo had been?

Rigo. His words from before suddenly crashed into my head. *Consecrated stone, remember?* My mind whirled. Narissa was a sophisticated reanimation. She'd lived within the abbey for months, so she clearly had a higher tolerance. Merely touching the stone wouldn't be enough, but maybe. . .

My eyes dropped to the stone I clutched in my hand, my bloodied fingernails curled protectively around it.

The next time Narissa grabbed for me, I pulled her close.

And I shoved the stone into her mouth.

It went roughly, with a clanking of broken teeth. I kept pushing, not caring as her remaining corpse teeth scratched at my fingers. Then I scrambled away.

A low, animalistic moan came from the creature that was Narissa. She began to convulse like Mother Vanessa had on the table. Then, like when she'd revealed her corpse skull to the Prioress before, her skin peeled apart from the top of her head and began to fall. The skull beneath dissolved slowly into bits of gray matter that fluttered, flowerlike, to the ground, leaving only a pile of empty robes.

I stood, shaken. I'd killed her. But had she ever really been alive?

"A–Annette?"

A weak voice rasped from the table. My heart leapt. I scrambled over to Mother Vanessa, who, miraculously, was alive and reaching for me.

"Abbess," I gasped. I clasped her hand—the only part of her uninjured—as hot tears filled my eyes. "How are—"

"No time," she murmured. It was the weakest I had ever heard her voice. "Go," she commanded. "We cannot let that demon reign free here."

"But—your wounds—"

"If the Mother wills it, I will live," Mother Vanessa said simply. She handed me the bracelet, the one in which her relic had been imprisoned. "Take this. Save us all."

I nodded. I took the bracelet. And then I ran.

Chapter Twenty-Nine

"Demonkind may enter and exit the human world through what is called a rift: a breach in the barrier between Above and Below. What creates a rift? That much is still uncertain. Common theories include dark magic rituals, blood sacrifice, or the most simple and rare of all—love, or any other strong emotional pull."

—Perspectives on the Below: A Scholarly Approach to the Demon Mirror World and Its Inhabitants

Where was Rigo?

Had he managed to get to Julián before the Prioress? If he'd found him, he'd need a way to corral him—

I skidded into the main hall from the chapel just as a clatter of footsteps rang on the steps overhead. Looking up, I saw Rigo—and behind him, Sister Colette.

"Did you find him?" I called.

Rigo looked stricken. "Yes, but he ran from me. He's—"

His next words were lost to a powerful explosion that rent the entrance hall apart. I curled up into a ball to protect myself, but still I went flying, my left shoulder and hip hitting a wall on my way to the floor. The impact knocked the air from my lungs and left me dizzy. The bracelet slipped from my grasp. Ears ringing, I gasped for breath.

A familiar laugh rang out through the rubble.

Julián.

"Well, wasn't that dramatic," he drawled.

As the dust cleared, a figure came strolling through the hole blown in the main hearth. Piles of stone were strewn about the hall. Sister Colette lay near what remained of the staircase, partially buried, unmoving. My heart lurched as my own bruises began to ache. I couldn't see Rigo anywhere.

Instead, I saw Julián. My first look at him in fully corporeal form was unnerving. He was an eerie mirror of Rigo, with the same skin tone, bone structure, and hair, though slightly taller, and infinitely more hostile. At his side stood Prioress Rosalind. I didn't miss the intimate way her hand was twined with his. She'd given him spare robes to wear, which were much too short in the arms and legs. Even with his wrists and ankles exposed, a sight that should've been silly, Julián still managed to ooze malice.

"Again," said Prioress Rosalind, and giggled like a young girl.

Julián flicked his hand and more stone went flying. I flinched. He could bury Sister Colette further. He could trap Rigo, wherever he lay. He raised his hand once more—

"Stop!" I screamed.

I had had enough. By drawing attention to myself, I could only hope that Rigo was still alive and nearby, and that he could find a way to subdue his brother.

"Annette," Julián intoned, and it was like hearing the voice of my nightmares come to life. Through clouds of dissipating dust, he began to advance on me, barefoot across the rubble. "My favorite little gnat. I was wondering when you'd resurface again." He left the Prioress to stroll toward me. "What is it? Come to stop me? I'd like to see you try. We've already opened a rift to my world. Soon, Rosalind will dispose of her enemies there, and we together will rule this place."

I fixed him with my ugliest glare. And though I hurt, and wanted nothing more than to cry in a corner, I pushed myself to my feet and faced him as an equal.

Julián knew me, but I knew him, too. He was self-centered. I knew if I could keep him talking, it would increase my chances of survival. It could give Rigo a chance to do something, if he wasn't already buried beneath too much stone.

I had to hope, to trust.

For a moment, I let my eyes slip shut in a quick, frantic prayer: *Mother, attend me, now in the hour of my greatest need.*

Then I returned to scowling at Julián. "You lied to me from the beginning," I snarled at him. "I owe it to you, and to myself, to thoroughly express my displeasure."

Julián shrugged. "What would you like me to say? I'm sorry? I am not. You were a convenient tool." He looked me up and down, once, twice, then narrowed his eyes. "One I'm pleased to see my lesser brother finally took advantage of. I was wondering when your attraction to him would win out over your piety."

That made me feel sick.

"That's private."

He scoffed. "Nothing about you is private. Not to me."

If he could tell that I'd been with Rigo from a mere glance, then I'd been an idiot before to think I could hide anything from him. He'd known everything about me right from the moment I put on his ring—and he'd never commented. I'd been so dirt-damned stupid.

But no more.

Behind him, the Prioress lingered, utterly unconcerned. She wasn't even looking at me. She didn't consider me a threat—not with Julián here. She must have felt that he could handle any challenges to her authority.

Which was something I could use to my advantage.

I lifted my chin. "Where is the ring?"

Prioress Rosalind displayed the back of her hand and waggled her fingers at me. Julián's relic ring glittered around her pointer finger. "This one? You must be quite stupid indeed if you think I'll just hand it over."

She and Julián dissolved into laughter, and I saw red. I'd had quite enough of being underestimated. Pushing past the despair of the impossible situation, I forced myself to think instead, though the last of my strengths was being quick on my feet. Then an answer bloomed up toward me as suddenly as yesterday's rainstorm.

I thought back to when I'd first found Julián's relic and granted it permission to remain in my body. To later, when Rigo had torn off the ring, and with it, Julián had been torn from me. I didn't know much about relics, but from what I'd gathered, they, like demon magic was purported to be, were highly rule-based.

Rules had long been everything to me. Following them had earned me a slap in the face. Breaking them had ripped a hole in the world.

If the Mother was feeling merciful, perhaps by some stroke of luck, I could bend this one final rule to my advantage.

"I don't need the ring anymore," I announced. Julián and Prioress Rosalind fell silent, smiles slipping from their faces. Speaking to Julián, I added, "Do you remember when we first met? And I granted you permission to remain in my body?"

Julián eyed me with wary irritation. "Yes? And what does that have to do with anything? I'm free now, nun. You hold no claim over me."

"That's true. But you're only free of the ring, Julián, not of me. The permission I granted you was contingent upon my choosing and consent. And if I recall correctly, I don't remember ever granting you consent to *leave*."

Shocked silence filled the hall. It was a gamble, one I thought might work. Julián began to laugh—a high, nervous peal that told me I just might be right.

But I had already grabbed his presence. And begun to *pull*.

His laughter came to an abrupt stop. He gave a violent flinch.

"What—what are you doing?"

"Putting you back where you belong," I answered through gritted teeth.

I pulled at him the way I had learned to tug on his presence to channel his invisibility—like pulling a blanket of cool water up toward my head. Despite no longer wearing the ring, it had been only about twenty-four hours since, and our bond had yet to dissolve. I could still sense him well enough to reach out and snag his presence like the stem of a weed. And he came like a particularly stubborn weed, clawing and fighting all the way.

My vision dimmed. My eardrums pulsed. Cold, clammy sweat bathed my skin with the effort. As I pulled and pulled, Julián faded from corporeal form with an enraged scream—until he snapped back into me with enough impact to nearly knock me off my feet.

YOU CONNIVING BITCH— he thundered inside me.

I stumbled, trying to stay upright.

Julián screeched obscenities inside my head. Like a child's tantrum, he punched and kicked out at the walls of my mind. His presence strained at the confines of my body. I was full of pressure, set to burst. Doubling over, my limbs began thrashing uncontrollably.

Without the ring to corral his demon spirit, I was at risk of losing myself to Julián's aims. I saw flashes of things that might have been memories or desires or something else entirely—Rigo's face smearing sideways beneath his fist; a wall collapsing into stone; a flash of deep brown skin beneath silken sheets; a blood-red rip in the fabric of the world.

His rage became mine. His panic, my panic. And I understood, in that moment, why I'd been so drawn to his relic in the first place.

We were alike, Julián and I. Broken and wanting and messy, and so so committed to revenge.

Hands smacked into my shoulders. Prioress Rosalind had rushed me and now hauled me upright by the front of my robes.

"Give him back!" she screamed, smacking me in the chest. As if she could dislodge Julián. Tears made tracks down her beautiful face. "Give him *back!*"

I shoved her away. My vision wavered, pulsating black and gray. My stomach began to roil. The effort of both keeping Julián contained and preventing him from commandeering my body entirely was draining me of everything I had. I wasn't sure how much longer I could last.

The Prioress's face appeared before me again. On her finger, a familiar bit of silver glinted, glittering against the dusty dark.

"Don't you dare take him from me! Give me back my Julián!" Bits of spittle pelted my face as she yelled. "Give him *back*!"

So I did.

I grabbed the Prioress's hand in mine, touching Julián's ring, and *shoved*.

Neither of us were prepared.

As Julián was forced from my body and into the ring, I stumbled back and fell to my rear, while the Prioress, now bearing the full force of him, swayed. I watched as his ring glowed lightning-white on her hand. She scrabbled at the ring in an attempt to remove it, but it seemed fused to her skin.

That was when she began to scream.

Bones cracked, skin bulged. Beams of deep, blood-red light shot from the Prioress's eyes, nose and mouth—Julián, lashing out with his power in an attempt to escape another imprisonment in the ring. The Prioress held to her faith, letting loose an unending stream of prayers. She might've trusted Julián, loved him, but she didn't want his unfettered power loose in her body any more than he wanted to be in the ring.

Julián's efforts at escape, combined with Rosalind's attempts to subdue him and cast him out of her body, began to consume them both.

And it was the sweetest, most twisted sort of pleasure to watch.

The two of them warred with each other within her body. The Prioress's back bent. She let out a shrill unholy scream as they became each other's undoing.

Her scream crackled up my spine, raising all the hairs all over my body. It grew and grew into an unbearable crescendo. And finally, it clambered up along the stained glass windows in the entrance hall, and tucked in.

Glass shattered in a tinkling explosion of knife-edged glitter. I had only the slightest sense to close my eyes and cover my face.

When I opened them again, it was to the sight of the Prioress melting within her skin. Her body pooled into a skin-colored mass of liquid flesh within her robes. Julián's ring, and the others she wore, oozed out to the side like pebbles along the shore. Julián's ring emitted a tinny, unrelenting barrage of screams.

"Mother have mercy," I said, and collapsed.

The effort had taken everything from me. Each time I blinked, I doubted I could open my eyes again. I rolled to my elbow, then to my side.

"Annette!"

Out of the staircase rubble came Rigo, roaring my name, along with a very wobbly-looking Sister Colette.

Weakly, I asked, "Where were you?"

"Looking for the stupid bracelet—I thought—I didn't know—" Rigo broke off into a stream of curses in Old Demonic as he inspected me for injury. I didn't know how to tell him I hurt *everywhere*.

Suddenly, the abbey itself gave a huge jolt. It shook everything sideways and sent more rubble crashing to the ground.

"The rift," Rigo said, eyes wide. "It's closing. I can feel it."

Through the hole Julián had made in the entrance hall, I glimpsed the red tinge to the sky beginning to recede. It went like milk seeping into tea—red blending to white, receding, fading fast.

"The ring." I pointed.

He grabbed it, looked back at me. Julián was still screaming from inside. Rigo slid the ring onto one of his fingers and grimaced as Julián's screams only increased in volume.

"I can't leave you like this," he said, forlorn. "What if you don't survive?"

I wondered what I looked like to him. I knew I was bruised, and bleeding, but was my skin peeling like the Prioress's? Was I, too, set to dissolve from within? How much had my battle with Julián taken from me?

"If the Mother wills it, I will live," I said, repeating Mother Vanessa's words from earlier.

Sister Colette reached us then, dropping untidily to the floor. Her face was caked with dust, and she favored her right leg, but she was mobile.

"I've got her."

She took my head into her lap. Cradled me like a child. She and Rigo exchanged a look. I wasn't sure what she saw, then, or what Sister Colette had divined about our connection, but in that moment, it didn't matter.

I lifted my eyes to Rigo. If I was selfish, I would've asked him to stay. But he'd gotten what he needed to clear his name. And we couldn't risk Julián escaping again.

"You have to go," I said, even though inside I was screaming, *please stay.*

The rift's fading tinge was now almost entirely white.

Rigo grasped my hand, touched it briefly to his lips. "I'm coming back. I promise you that."

I nodded. "I trust you."

After all of this, he had been the one to help me save the day. He had proven himself trustworthy. His presence alone had been enough to convince me that not everyone left, not always. But now he *did* have to leave, and there was nothing either of us could do about that.

The edges of the rift squeezed around the entrance hall. I could feel it like the eye of a storm closing in. Pressure popped my ears, made a thin trail of blood ooze from my nose. Behind Rigo's beautiful silhouette, my hand still in his, the sky's red tinge quickly receded toward a single point.

Still, he hesitated, gripping my hand. He had to go, now, or he'd never unmake the mess Julián had created for him all those years ago.

I gathered all my strength and shoved him. "*Go!*"

Finally, Rigo listened. He stood and dove through the rapidly closing rift, disappearing as the opening closed with a decisive snap. One more soul-shaking jolt from the abbey, and everything swung, with a sickening speed, right side up.

My eyelids fluttered closed.

Around me, I heard signs of life—shouting, doors closing, sobbing. Prayer and shifting stone and cries for help. Sounds that told me the abbey lived on. That I hadn't ruined it all.

The last thing I thought of before tumbling into the dark was Rigo's face, uncertain, my hand with its bloodied fingernails pressed to his lips.

Mother, if I live, return him to me. That's all I ask.

Chapter Thirty

"Order acolytes conceive of the afterlife as an endless, sweet-smelling garden. Upon death, they are buried and given unto the earth, where their souls are absorbed and transported to the Mother's eternal garden. If the acolyte's life has pleased the Mother, they are free to eat as they wish from that garden. If they've done something to draw the Mother's ire, eating from this fragrant garden will result in permanent soul death."

—Excerpt from: An Exploration of the Order of the Revenant Mother and Other Island Religions

The days that followed passed with a slow, sleepy, creeping sort of continuity.

My body needed time to recover from challenging Julián, so I slept and rested more often than not. Construction crews were called in to repair the damage his demon magic had done. Finally, one week to the date after the Prioress's arrival, we returned to our regular proceedings—though it was in the form of a funerary service.

Inside the chapel, the atmosphere felt muted, like a secret held close. Days after the fact, I'd found out that the combined efforts of Julián and Prioress Rosalind had not only spelled out their own downfall—three acolytes had been killed. They'd been found in the hours afterward, buried deep in the rubble.

Three innocent lives whose faces I recognized but whose names I did not know. Now their bodies lay cleaned and dressed along the tables at the front of the chapel, in a similar spot to where Prioress Rosalind had tortured Mother Vanessa. We filed in to respectfully lay them to rest.

As I took my seat, a ripple of surprise stirred the crowd. We'd all been expecting Sister Colette, who had stepped in to oversee the aftermath and keep things running while Mother Vanessa recovered in the infirmary. And while Sister Colette was indeed present, another familiar figure followed behind her to the lectern, then to the seats below, with the slow, stilted steps of someone who had very nearly died.

Mother Vanessa.

I closed my eyes against a sudden wave of relief. This was the first time the abbess had been seen out of the infirmary, and each acolyte among us took it to heart. Countless whispered prayers of thanks formed a gentle susurration as the rows of the chapel filled.

Sister Colette brought us to order with a call to prayer. "From earth we are born, and to earth we return," she intoned.

In the typical way, our standard morning prayers unfolded. I found a certain comfort in the ritual of the familiar words, especially after such a long period of tumult.

"And at last we pray for joy, for devotion, and steadiness in our task," said Sister Colette near the end of the sequence. She lifted her head expectantly.

Each of us in the chapel chorused, "To heal the sick, and sicken the wicked."

Then we Grounded ourselves. Shoes off, toes dipped into the dirt-filled troughs that lined the ground along the pews. This sacred soil had never felt more welcoming. My mind calmed, all of my frenzied restlessness settling into a deep sort of content.

With the Grounding completed, Sister Colette shifted smoothly along into the memorial. She stood behind the three cloth-draped bodies as she addressed us.

"Each of these acolytes served our holy Order in exemplary fashion. Though it pains me to acknowledge their untimely passing, and the difficult circumstances surrounding their deaths, it also brings me great joy to know they will soon be received into the Mother's embrace." She walked between each body, and with a gloved hand, placed a fresh cutting of foxglove atop each funeral shroud. "May the Mother receive them warmly into Her eternal garden."

"May the Mother receive them warmly into Her eternal garden," repeated the crowd.

Now, Sister Colette returned to the lectern. "To close our proceedings, I'd like to invite Sister Annette to the front to grace us all with her rendition of the Mother's Aria."

Shock speared through me, a little flutter of nervousness in my chest.

They wanted *me* to sing? When I'd been the one to nearly destroy everything?

I locked eyes with Sister Colette from across the chapel. She offered me a reassuring nod in return. So she meant it—they truly wanted me to sing.

I stood, gathered my robes, and made my way to the front.

Since Narissa's unexpectedly requested performance of the Aria over a month ago, I had not sung at all. It hurt too much, a bruising reminder that I'd been usurped in one of the few things that felt truly mine. Singing even another song besides the Aria felt like sating myself on mere droplets of water instead of full glasses—it would do in a pinch, but it wasn't enough, wasn't what I really wanted. So I'd stopped entirely. Now, as I looked out over the sea of acolytes, faces turned up to me expectantly, I wondered if I could still do the Aria justice. If I was still worthy.

A flicker went through the prayer candles lining the stage, then, followed by all the flames standing momentarily, briefly still. It sent a thrill up my spine. The Mother was with me, with *us*, and with Her strength behind me, I could not let Her down.

I opened my mouth and sang.

This was the Mother's story: a healer, driven toward good, always seeking to better herself. When She befriended a demon and sought its help to advance Her medical research, She'd unfortunately been betrayed and killed, then reborn, from dirt and from weeds. When Narissa had sung this song, stolen it from me, all those weeks ago, I'd felt an eerie parallel to the Mother's origins in that betrayal. Now, the similarities were starker.

Like the Mother, I had befriended a demon—two, to be precise. One, in fact, I'd done more than befriend, all in the name of keeping the abbey safe. And though the other had betrayed me, *I* was the one who'd emerged victorious. In my case, though a demon's betrayal had not led to my death, I still felt myself reborn. The Aria coursed through me, its notes clear and sweet and crisp, and I poured into my performance every prickly thought and emotion I'd kept to myself for far too long.

It was a cleansing of sorts. One badly overdue. The song was bittersweet and heartbreaking, but it suited me, and it was mine.

My eyes were watering by the time I'd finished. I felt that I'd shown too much of myself to the others and wanted to hide.

But Sister Colette did not release me as I expected. "Thank you, Sister Annette." She exchanged a glance with Mother Vanessa. "We would also like to thank Sister Annette for her special efforts to expose Prioress Rosalind's crimes."

Chills swept up and down my skin, my arms turning to goose-flesh. By now, the entire abbey knew what had happened and knew of my role in the proceedings. I'd been shown a strange deference since that I had simply attributed to the other acolytes remaining afraid and wary of me.

It had never occurred to me that I might be heralded as a hero for my efforts.

Sister Colette continued, "Sister Annette demonstrated impec-cable courage, determination, and strength against intimidating odds. She alone exposed the true threat that Prioress Rosalind posed to this abbey and to our sacred Order. It is because of her that more of you did not lose your lives. Because of her, this abbey still stands." Her words rang out over the pews like a bell, commanding attention. "Please rise and share with her your blessing."

My knees wobbled as the entire chapel full of acolytes rose as a wave. They each gathered a pinch of dirt from the troughs at their feet, clutched their fists around it, and raised that fist first to their lips, then their forehead. It was such a simple gesture—the Mother's highest blessing, a symbol of goodwill, gratitude, and appreciation. I'd seen it many times, though never en masse like this, and never directed at me. I had never even *imagined* myself worthy of it.

Once more, my eyes watered, a lump forming in my throat.

Fifteen years I'd been at this abbey, and not once, until now, had I ever felt like I belonged.

The weight of so much attention was deeply uncomfortable, had me sweating beneath my robes. I was unaccustomed to the scrutiny, wanted to look away. But this was a gift—albeit a strange one—that I'd earned by following my own fleeting, churning heart, giving in to my thirst for justice. It was mine to claim. I would not refuse it, no matter how much the appreciative regard made me want to squirm.

So I inclined my head politely to receive the blessing.

At the conclusion of the service, the chapel began to slowly empty. A few of the instructing Sisters who were tasked with performing death rites and burials for the community would now transport the acolytes' bodies to the graveyard and supervise their burial. Meanwhile, the others would proceed into the refectory for a special funerary repast.

I remained at the front of the chapel for a long moment. Behind me was the table where Mother Vanessa had been tortured, and next to that, the square of stone where Narissa had held a knife to my throat. Just outside in the front entrance hall, evidenced by the broken stained glass windows, were the spots where the Prioress and Julián had met their defeat. I felt at once very close and very far away from it all, like a dream I couldn't quite touch.

"Annette?" I turned toward the hesitant voice. Behind me stood Mother Vanessa, leaning heavily on a cane. "Could I speak with you, please?"

"Yes, Abbess, of course."

Mother Vanessa's resulting smile was weak, but she proceeded along the path to her office with stubborn determination. She'd been tortured so cruelly that even the demonic spirit placed inside her had given up and fled. How badly did she hurt? How was she even *standing*? Truthfully, I was surprised she was already mobile. I was still so exhausted from the whole ordeal that I'd been tempted to skip the memorial service entirely.

Inside, we both paused. There was much history in this office between us. All of it seemed to flash before me in the moments before she spoke: her screaming at me for daring to wonder why I did not receive my promised award, slapping me, caning me, pressing hot poisoned wax into my bare skin. I wanted to rage at her and make her hurt the same way she'd done to me. I wanted to scream at her and revel in the terror on her face.

And I wanted none of those things all at the same time. None of that had been her, not truly. She deserved none of my ire.

"My dear—" Mother Vanessa began, and then I crushed myself to her.

Her arms folded gently around me, frailer than ever, but it left the embrace no less sweet. Holding her now, I felt how fragile she truly was, how much strength it must have taken to remain upright and attend the memorial ceremony. The relic the Prioress had inflicted upon her had done its damage.

"I am so terribly sorry," she cried, and then we were both weeping, clutching each other tight. "I cannot believe I—" She broke off, shuddering, her head pressed to my shoulder. "I saw everything that Rosalind's horrible relic made me do to you. Experienced its glee through it all. It made me sick. And now, in my nightmares, I keep seeing the look of hurt on your face—"

"Shhh." I patted her back like one might a child, comforting both her and myself. "It's over now."

I had not admitted to myself until now that a part of me had always believed myself deserving of her recent outbursts, even as I knew, simultaneously, that something was very wrong. I had simply resigned myself to accepting and enduring the abuse. With the abbess's apology thick in the air between us now, I knew how wrong I had been. I knew I deserved better. I should've known that all along.

Mother Vanessa's embrace felt now like what I imagined my mother's might. After so many years of feeling unloved and unwanted, feeling stuck stubbornly on the outside looking in, I began to sense the shape of a reality that included rather than excluded me.

At last, we pulled away, each swiping at our tear-stained faces. Mother Vanessa went to her desk and sat heavily.

"I didn't just ask you here for this," she said. Without fanfare, she announced, "I've been asked to take Prioress Rosalind's place. I've been given a few days to finish out my work here—primarily documenting this botched recertification. Soon, I'll be leaving Moriah Abbey, leaving my duties as abbess to Sister Colette instead."

I couldn't help but smile. "Abbess, that's wonderful news!"

And I genuinely meant it. If anyone would make a solid Prioress, it was Mother Vanessa. Even if it meant our abbey would lose her.

And I could not ignore the precious, juvenile irony of it all—Mother Vanessa taking Rosalind's spot after all that had transpired.

Perhaps now would be a good time to broach the subject of my award. I'd been waiting for the right moment since I'd woken after surviving Julián.

"And as Prioress," Mother Vanessa continued, "I'll have the freedom of appointing my own staff. This includes, among other roles, my own personal Chief Poisoness." My head snapped up. "You would be working directly with me for the first few months as we both learn our new roles together. Then, we'll likely split for our separate travels in service of the Order."

I could hardly believe it. All I could do was stare at her as the reality of the only thing I'd ever really wanted became a true possibility once more.

"I believe this is yours." She handed me a deep brown folder, which I opened with trembling hands to reveal my award, *the* award, written in script on cream paper. "This was meant to be yours all along, Annette. Rosalind's relic had seized control of my body just before the awards were meant to be finalized. I was trapped inside the entire time and I knew—I *knew*—how difficult it would be for you, the award going to another. I'm so, so sorry you had to endure that." She paused. "Yet, at the same time, I fear for what may have happened had you not sought to seek revenge afterward. It's very possible that without your efforts, Rosalind would've succeeded, and not a one of us would still be here at all."

Then I was crying again. I quickly shut the top of the folder so my tears would not sully the paper.

"I'm sure you know this, but do keep in mind that you're under no obligation to accept my offer. The award, and the title, remain yours regardless of whether or not you choose to work with me or go into business for yourself."

I truly had no words—I could not remember the last time life had felt so vibrant for me. By all accounts, I'd earned my freedom. I now commanded a Chief Poisoness title. The world was mine to do with as I wished.

That realization very nearly brought me to my knees.

"Thank you," I croaked out. I was meant to give an answer, but I had none yet.

"I know this is a lot to take in, so please, take a few days to consider my offer. There's no rush." I nodded. "Now, if you'll excuse me, I need to lie down."

I left Mother Vanessa to her rest and stumbled back out into the hallway, reeling, with the folder clutched tightly to my chest like the holy thing it was. I'd been in the abbess's office long enough that some other acolytes were now filtering out of the refectory, having finished breakfast. It was my first time walking the halls in days, having spent so long in the infirmary and then my room recuperating, and only now did I realize that the nature of the usual stares I attracted had changed.

Instead of hastily averted gazes and nasty things whispered beneath cupped hands, I saw nods of respect and quick smiles.

Apparently, I now commanded a new respect. I wasn't sure what to make of that.

I found myself in the refectory with food before me. Eating and staring at the folder that represented the rest of my life, a small pinprick of doubt crept into my bright, shiny mood. This award was all I'd ever wanted. Only now, it was bittersweet.

I hadn't yet heard from or seen Rigo. For days, I'd both been yearning for a glimpse of him and forcing myself away from the thought of him. When I wasn't strong enough to resist, my mind conjured up all sorts of horrifying possibilities, each worse than the last. Maybe he hadn't made it back to his world or his family. Maybe Julián had overpowered and killed him on the way, or he'd entered the rapidly closing rift too late and been scattered among the space in-between worlds. Maybe, if he had made it back successfully, he was unable to clear his name, unable to leave once more. Did he need the opportunity of another rift between worlds to return? Or was it as simple as snapping his fingers?

There was still so much about him I didn't know, and wanted to, badly.

I had no way of communicating with him. All that remained was his promise to me that one tender morning before we'd walked into an abbey ripped upside down: *I promise you that I will always come back.*

I'd believed him then, and I still did. But I also knew just how flimsy a promise could be. I had one shot at the rest of my life—and as much as it pained me, I could not forfeit it to wait around and hope he would return.

Taking Mother Vanessa's advice to heart, I mulled over the offer for several days. Each morning, I woke with an uncertain hope along my collarbones, thinking that maybe this would be the day I'd wake to Rigo crouched, grinning, at the side of my bed. I gave him every opportunity I could.

When he still hadn't returned to me by the eve of Mother Vanessa's deadline, I folded my disappointment quietly away. I told myself that if he wanted to, he would find me when he could. And I informed the abbess that I would be accepting her offer.

Chapter Thirty-One

"Annette,
I don't know what to say to you—nothing, or everything.
I'm stuck here for this infernal trial and I'm on the verge of
losing my mind. I should be happier. After twenty years, I'm
back in my homeworld. There are good things about it, of
course—the food is better here than in your abbey, for one.
But none of that really seems to matter. I grew so used to
having you around that your absence is like missing a limb.
I should be focusing on the outcomes of this trial. But all I
can think about is when I might see you again.
Yours,
Rigo"
   -An unsent letter from the desk of the Acosta family

T he sights and sounds of the harbor were a pleasant assault on
my senses.

The Codrington Sea, in all its vibrant aqua glory, spilled out below the docks, stretching west before me as far as the eye could see. To my left, if I faced south, the northern shores of Manzanilla glittered like a row of colorful teeth. Though I'd been raised on an island where it was difficult to ever be too far from the ocean, this was the most intimate the sea had ever felt to me. And this was only the beginning.

"Quite loud here, isn't it?" I turned to find Mother Vanessa behind me. Cane in hand, wearing her traveling robes, she squinted at me beneath the sun's bright glare.

"Yes," I agreed, nodding. "It is a bit noisy. But I don't mind."

And I didn't. Beneath the minor irritation of squawking seagulls and the shouts of the dock workers, I felt calm and hopeful.

She offered me a smile. "I expect you're simply thrilled to be traveling."

I was. I'd never been to the harbor. I had never left my home island. The very day itself seemed to buzz with possibility, right down to each molecule of my skin. Clear blue skies and pleasant, though not oppressive, warmth suggested positive prospects and a rare good mood. I tilted my face to the sun and sighed, content.

We were set to sail northwest to Winthorpe & Colette, a few days' journey that would deliver us to an Order outpost. There, Mother Vanessa would undertake her training period as the new Prioress, and I would commence my first set of duties as Chief Poisoness—finding an antidote to a new and mysterious spate of poisonings among the area's middle-class politicians. The former abbess was not quite fully recovered, but given that the previous Prioress had died so suddenly, her replacement was urgently needed. Mother Vanessa had rested for as long as she was able before the demands from the Order's most highly ranked grew too challenging.

I was glad I had chosen to accompany her. I'd be able to keep an eye on her and offer any assistance she needed. Today, though, seemed to be one of her better days.

With both of us in good spirits, we passed the time until our ferry's departure sitting on a bench along the harbor and enjoying the breeze. She sorted through official correspondence and I perused a prayer book. As the hour ticked along toward early afternoon, Mother Vanessa stood.

"I'll go and find us some snacks to hold us over until dinner, hmm?"

We'd be receiving meals on the ferry, but likely not until much later tonight. I appreciated the offer. But I could do it myself.

"No, let me. You should rest your leg—"

"Nonsense," she said, dismissing my concern with a wave. "It's a beautiful day, I feel good for once, and I intend to take advantage of it."

She hobbled off with a surprising spring in her step before I could protest further. I watched for a moment as she angled herself across the boardwalk, toward the assembly of street vendors that lined the other side. Once I felt certain she wasn't going to fall, I stood and looked out once more across the sea. For years, the sea had served to only further reinforce my lack of options. It had been a sparkling jailer boxing me into the confines of the abbey, of my home island.

Now that I knew it was mine to explore? I could not stop looking.

I was drinking in the sea air, eyes closed, when my senses prickled toward something behind me. I fought down a scoff of irritation.

To my dismay, I'd discovered that Mother Vanessa and I together attracted a great deal of attention when we were out in public. It was as if no one had ever seen a nun before. Mostly, they just gawked, but a few bolder types had made lewd comments. That was what I expected now, and readied myself to offer this person my meanest glare—

But when I whirled around, it was not a stranger I found.

Instead, it was Rigo.

Inside my chest, my heart leapt, a sudden and wild thing. His hair had grown ever so slightly longer. He'd gotten himself proper clothing—deep gray trousers and a white shirt of lightweight fabric. His expression, however, hadn't changed. Still those same deeply piercing eyes, no pupils. Still that same intensity in his gaze.

So thoroughly had I already resigned myself to the idea of never seeing him again that I struggled to accept the reality of him standing before me. I was rattled to the bone, though I quickly determined I would not show it.

"Rigo," I breathed, keeping my voice neutral.

My demon smiled, showing all of his teeth. He looked to be in much better health—more flesh on his bones, more color illuminating his skin. No longer nearly ghostlike. This new and beautiful strength suited him.

"I told you I'd come back, didn't I?" he said.

"You did."

I wanted to throw myself at him, crush him to me. I wanted to shove him off the docks. I was a fragile and tender miasma of longing and hurting, and I couldn't sort out what I was meant to feel. During his absence, I'd grown so used to veering my thoughts away from the open wound of him in my mind. Now all of that pain swirled up in me, roiling between us until I thought I might burst. He'd hurt me deeply with that absence.

But he'd also returned, as he promised.

"It's good to see you," he said. "You look well."

Just the sound of his voice brought me a comfort I couldn't put into words.

I nodded. "So do you."

I turned back to the sea, resting my elbows on the railing, to keep from falling apart. In the corner of my eye, I saw him reach a hand out for me, then drop his hand, reconsidering. Tears pricked my eyes, so I squeezed them shut tight for a moment to grasp control.

"I'm sorry," he said, without any fanfare. "Things. . .took a lot longer than expected."

"That they did."

When I didn't offer anything else, he went on. "I managed to bring Julián back without incident, but afterward—" He paused, rubbed a hand over his face as if remembering something unpleasant. "—It got messy. Everyone wanted to know where we'd been, what had truly happened. It took time, but we finally untangled truth from fiction. There was a trial. Julián was sentenced for his crimes. Eternity in a demon prison. You won't be seeing him again."

I absorbed this all. "And you? What of your alleged crimes?"

Now he offered me another brilliant grin. The parts of me that cared for him, knew him intimately, went warm and malleable at the sight.

"Cleared of all charges, thanks to your help. I have my freedom back. I can do whatever I like."

Complicated though my feelings were toward him, I couldn't fight my resulting smile.

He was silent for a moment before sobering. "Because of the trial, we weren't permitted to leave, or contact anyone outside our world. So that's why. . ."

"Oh."

Relief poured through me, though it didn't erase the lingering sting. So he had truly had a genuine obstacle to returning to me as he'd promised—he hadn't, as I so desperately feared, abandoned me. But I had already rearranged my whole mental landscape to tolerate the idea of his absence. Was there any space left for a further rearranging? What sort of twisted luck did I have that he would show up now, when I was on the cusp of starting a new adventure? Was this return of his too late?

Letting him in, truly welcoming him back, meant trusting him again. And I wasn't sure I was ready to do that.

"I understand," I responded. A pause, then I added, "I've been given back my award. I'm heading off to Winthorpe & Colette to train with Mother Vanessa. She's replaced Prioress Rosalind."

"I know. I stopped by the abbey first and asked about you there."

Now I looked at him head-on once again. He'd asked about me? I couldn't deny how good it made me feel to hear that.

Where did this leave us?

The clatter of a cane on wood broke into my spiraling thoughts.

Mother Vanessa gave a little gasp. "Ah, Mr. Acosta!" She reached over and clasped his hands in one of her own. "What a pleasant surprise," she said, and seemed to actually mean it.

I looked between them in confused shock.

"I was hoping to have the opportunity to thank you in person for your efforts," she said. "Because of you and Annette, my former abbey still stands. Sister Colette spoke so highly of you and your efforts to save the abbey at Annette's side. Truly, it is an act of inter-world collaboration for the history books."

Rigo demurred. "Thank you, Mother."

"And congratulations on your appointment. Might I presume that's why you're here? Official business as Liaison for Church–Demon Relations?"

He hadn't mentioned that to me, yet. My shock compounded, my mouth falling open.

Rigo inclined his head. "Yes, that's right," he said, but his gaze stuck on me as he spoke. "That's the reason I'm here."

Mother Vanessa glanced between us. It might have been the sun, but I could've sworn I saw a twinkle come into her eye. She'd honed her observational abilities as abbess and had not, apparently, left them behind. The woman missed nothing. But I certainly wasn't going to make it easy for her. I kept my gaze averted, though every cell of mine yearned toward Rigo, and I was sure she could sense it.

"Well," she said pleasantly, "we have much work to do, and as Chief Poisoness, Annette here may be in need of an assistant. One with knowledge that can aid hers." She tilted her head to the side, considering. "And one with diplomatic ties to the demon world can't hurt."

I lifted my head to look at her in disbelief. This was as good a signal of approval as she would offer. Hope stuttered, fragile and fleeting, within me. Could I truly have it all?

A loud horn sounded then from the direction of the boat: the signal that passengers could begin to embark. Suddenly, the board-walk came to life. All the others who'd been lounging on benches, reading newspapers and wrangling unruly children roused them-selves in a shuffle of voices and clattering luggage. In a slow jumble, they gathered toward the platform that granted access to the ship.

Mother Vanessa looked between us once more.

"I'll go ahead and get on. See that there's nothing wrong with our seats, and that our bags were brought to the right place. I'll see you on board, Annette."

She left with the staccato clatter of her cane a stark backdrop to the hustle and bustle of the crowd.

I couldn't look at Rigo. I yearned for him so badly, I could hardly stand it. And try as I might to deny it, I'd missed him terribly. I wanted him almost as much as I wanted this adventure. No matter how much I tried to convince myself I didn't.

Rigo said nothing, just stood quietly, while I warred internally with myself. I couldn't put this off forever. The boat's departure had given us a deadline I couldn't ignore.

Finally, I said, the words trembling in their vulnerability, "It makes sense that I would be in need of an assistant."

I kept my tone casual, but didn't miss his sudden intake of breath. I was still trying to wrap my mind around the fact that this could work.

"Does it?" he murmured.

"Yes." Now I looked up at him, met that piercing gaze. His expression had grown tender and tentative, and I loved that about him. He would do whatever I asked, would *wait* for me to ask, knowing the asking made me beyond uncomfortable. "Do you have any particular candidates in mind?

Rigo only smiled. I tamped back my own and turned toward the boat.

"I suppose, if that assistant were willing, they could accompany me on board. They'll have to purchase a ticket, though."

"I don't think that should present too much of an issue."

A shared look, and I knew we were both thinking of him magicking money into existence not long ago during our rain-soaked escape from the abbey.

"Well, then." I squared my shoulders, grabbed my prayer book off the bench, and slipped it into the pocket of my robes. "Shall we?"

Come with me. Stay with me.

I'd started shaking again, paranoid and half convinced he would leave after all. I wasn't sure I'd ever get used to the idea of someone choosing to stay. So I guarded myself against it, pretending until the last moment that perhaps this was all just a ruse, leaving an invitation open for him to follow if he chose.

I turned briskly away from him, toward the gangway.

But when his hand slipped into my own a moment later, I did not pull away.

Acknowledgements

This book means so much to me, and I really hope you liked it.

I wrote this during the fall of 2023. I was still reeling from trying to get one of my other books traditionally published, and absolutely crashing out at that complete and utter failure. I wanted to write something angry and wild and unhinged that was even more purely *me*. I think, in the back of my mind, I intended for this to be my revenge query book – my next shot that I'd toss into the tradpub gauntlet and hope it might work out. Instead, I fell even more deeply in love with this book than I was with the other one, and realized this was something I needed to keep for myself.

Annette is the first character I've written where I was explicit about giving her autistic experiences similar to mine. As I was writing this, I was coming to terms with my own autistic identity, and it's no surprise it seeped onto the pages here. Her feelings and reactions to things and the way she sees and experiences the world are very, very similar to how I do, and I was surprised by the relief I felt writing this. If she resonates with you, awesome.

If not, I hope the depiction of her neurodivergence has taught you something, or encouraged you to be a bit more open-minded toward the neurodivergent folks in your life.

I didn't realize just how much this book would come to mean to me until now, when I'm writing these acknowledgements, and preparing to yeet this sucker out into the world. In a way, I suppose this book is a message to all the other late-bloomer autistics out there. You are worthy, and valid, and I hope you find someone who sees and appreciates you for who you are.

Okay, that's enough emotions! Gross, lol. Moving on.

Thank you to my husband, Josh, for your encouragement and support. And also for knowing me well enough to ask, when I first showed you the blurb for this story, "Is she going to bang the demon?"

Thank you to my beta readers: Elayna R. Gallea, Chrissy Hopewell and Rhianne Williams. Your feedback on the early draft of this book was invaluable in making it stronger.

Thank you to Lillian, for proofreading.

Thank you to several Discord communities that have kept me sane throughout my writing adventures over the past few years: the Inteleon Den, the FaRo writers Discord, and the Pitch Wars 2021 Mentee Discord. You guys are all great!

And finally, thank you anyone who gave this book a chance and enjoyed it. Stick around! There's so much more to come.

The Official Poisoner's Vengeance Playlist

1. Omen – Bullet for My Valentine

2. Holy Roller – Spiritbox

3. Seven Devils – Florence + The Machine

4. Drumming Song – Florence + The Machine

5. Heavy In Your Arms – Florence + The Machine

6. Unholy – Sam Smith, Kim Petras

7. Unholy Confessions – Avenged Sevenfold

8. The Curse – Agnes Obel

9. The In-Between – In This Moment

10. Take Me There – As Everything Unfolds

11. Dead, Again – Jadu Heart

12. Savages – MARINA

13. Ghost – Sir Sly

14. All Went Black – The Haunt

15. Hypnotic – Zella Day

16. Running Up That Hill – Placebo

17. Breath of Life – Florence + The Machine

18. Blood Sport – Sleep Token

19. Taunt Me – Dream State

20. Chain Reactions – Dream State

21. Just Pretend – Bad Omens

22. Comfort in Chaos – Dream State

23. FEEL NOTHING – The Plot In You

24. be very afraid – Architects

25. spit the bone – Architects

26. God Hates Us – Avenged Sevenfold

27. My Demon – Stitched Up Heart

28. Grayscale – As Everything Unfolds

29. Another Life – Motionless In White

30. Shivering – ILLENIUM, Spiritbox

31. Coming Undone – Korn

32. Sound Effects and Overdramatics – The Used

33. Circle With Me – Spiritbox

34. Blessed Be – Spiritbox

35. New Waves – Dream State

36. Disease – Beartooth

37. Big Bad Wolf – In This Moment

38. Saturn – Sleeping At Last

39. White Flag – Dido

40. Can You Feel My Heart – MOTHICA

41. I Feel It Too – Dream State

42. Show Me Your God – The Amity Affliction

43. As Above, So Below – In This Moment

44. Bad Guy – Conquer Divide

45. Rule of Nines – Spiritbox

46. THE DEATH OF PEACE OF MIND – Bad Omens

47. Sun Killer – Spiritbox

48. Alkaline – Sleep Token

49. Like A Villain – Bad Omens

50. Rotoscope – Spiritbox

51. CASUALTY – MOTHICA

52. Chokehold – Sleep Token

53. Atonement – Conquer Divide

54. The Offering – Sleep Token

55. Paralyzed – Conquer Divide

56. The Kill – Thirty Seconds To Mars

57. Vigilante Shit – Taylor Swift

58. Little Girl Gone – CHINCHILLA

59. Stand In The Rain – Superchick

60. Fall For Me – Sleep Token

61. Heaven Is Here – Florence + The Machine

62. Cosmic Love – Florence + The Machine

63. Blinding – Florence + The Machine

64. Rabbit Heart (Raise It Up) – Florence + The Machine

65. Blinding – Florence + The Machine

66. Never Let Me Go – Florence + The Machine

67. GODMODE – In This Moment

68. Temptation – Imminence

69. Thistle & Weeds – Mumford & Sons

70. Devil Devil – MILCK

71. Sleepwalking – Bring Me The Horizon

72. Final Girl – CHVRCHES

73. Let's Have A Satanic Orgy – Twin Temple

74. Glass Houses – Bad Omens

75. Dethrone – Bad Omens

About the Author

Talia lives in the mountains with her husband, two chaotic cat children, and a stubborn corgi. When she's not writing, she's drinking iced coffee or watching truly terrible horror movies.

WANT TO STAY IN TOUCH?
JOIN MY NEWSLETTER: HTTPS://WWW.TALIAGREERBOOKS.COM/NEWSLETTER
VISIT MY WEBSITE: HTTPS://WWW.TALIAGREERBOOKS.COM/
FOLLOW ME ON SOCIALS: @taliagreerbooks or TaliaGreerBooks on the following platforms.

instagram.com/taliagreerbooks/

tiktok.com/@taliagreerbooks

amazon.com/stores/author/B0C5467N5V

bookbub.com/authors/talia-greer

goodreads.com/author/show/35989564.Talia_Greer

Also By

Also by Talia Greer

Wild Wanderings
Sasquatch Summer
Alder King Spring
Book Three (2025)

The Wild Wanderings collection is a series of standalone, small-town monster romances. These books fall under the genre of fantasy romance or paranormal romance and have high heat levels. They are romance-first, fantasy second.

***

The Ardor Magic Cycle
A Cure for Magic
Book Two (2025)

The Ardor Magic Cycle is a secondary-world fantasy trilogy. These books fall under the genre of romantic fantasy or dark fantasy and have medium heat levels. They are fantasy-first, romance second.

★★★

Standalones
Poisoner's Vengeance

Poisoner's Vengeance is a secondary-world fantasy standalone. It falls under the genre of romantic fantasy or dark fantasy and has a low to medium heat level. It is fantasy-first, romance second.